Terminus Shift

Chris Reher

Chris Reher

Quantum Tangle

Terminus Shift

Entropy's End

Also by Chris Reher

Sky Hunter

The Catalyst

Only Human

Rebel Alliances

Delphi Promised

ACKNOWLEDGMENTS

Thank you to Dee Solberg, Susan Kaye Quinn,
Jim Kolter and the S3G

Chris Reher

ONE

"How dare you delay me! I am a representative of the Imperial Majestic Over-Vizier of the Third Royal Family of Gramor on an urgent mission to Pelion. Move aside at once or face the wrath of our Lord Olas."

"Gramor has no royal family. How about you send some ID before you face *my* wrath, pilot?"

Sethran Kada slipped into his pilot bench, a little surprised to find Air Command hailing him out here. He scanned for more unwelcome escorts and found another military cruiser between him and the jumpsite. Of course they had collapsed the gate as soon they emerged, making a quick exit impossible.

"Did I say Gramor? I meant Callas." He shifted his attention to the markers for two more ships approaching rapidly from the planet behind him, armed, fully shielded and definitely not belonging to Air Command. Those he did expect. Since eluding them on the Aikhor airfield he had kept well ahead of them but this encounter with the patrol was whittling away his head start by the second.

"Sethran Kada, it says here," the officer said. "Quite the sheet you have. Visual, please. What are you doing out here?"

An audible signal alerted Seth to the Union ship's scanners taking a closer look at the *Dutchman*, easily poking through the cruising shields to look at the interesting bits. He kept his eyes on the few compartments liberally doused with sensor-scattering filaments. Their content remained invisible on the screens.

"That shouldn't be a mystery." Seth activated a camera to let the officer make a visual confirmation of his identity: Centauri, black haired and long-limbed like all of them, violet eyes that reflected nearby light, and a friendly grin that often charmed even the most bad-tempered of cops. The Human taking a snap of his irises didn't seem charmed. "Since I'm currently traveling on a mathematically correct trajectory *away* from the only two habitable planets in this sector and the only other point of interest here is this jumpsite, the astute observer would conclude that I am about to enter subspace."

He heard a sigh, followed by a dead silence suggesting some unheard conversation between the two military ships. Seth kept busy. The *Dutchman* confirmed the switch from auto-pilot to Seth's neural interface, giving him both mental and tactile control of all systems. He drifted toward the jumpsite aptly named Pelion Gate. It appeared on his monitors as an empty bit of space ringed by a set of Union-owned beacons waiting for him to align and activate.

Sites like these channeled commercial and military traffic among populated sectors of this small, crowded piece of their galaxy along easily monitored shipping lanes with great efficiency. The beacons enabled even the most untried of navigators to find a way through the dead nothing of subspace and emerge unscathed at the intended destination. Stable and accessible, allowing no deviation between entry and exit, these conduits provided safety as well as close surveillance of all those who passed through the ring of beacons. Seth usually had the means to counter their soulless intrusion, but not the Union patrol intent on waylaying him today.

"You're not actually supposed to be on Pelion, are you, Kada?"

"That's still before the ministry," Seth said, wondering

when his contacts would get around to expunging that particular misdemeanor. "Besides, I'm not going to Pelion. Just passing through."

"To Callas."

"Maybe." Seth's scanners picked up the patrol cruiser's request for identification of the two other ships. It now broadcasted on a variety of channels; clearly their initial hail had gone unanswered. "What's going on? Never seen this gate manned before."

"Just the usual chatter among rebels."

"If it were usual you wouldn't be out here harassing tourists."

"Is that what you are? A tourist? You might as well wait for that incoming traffic and share the load."

"I'm expected. No time to waste." The two approaching ships were not the sort looking to hook up for the subspace leap. Entering a gate in a convoy significantly reduced the strain on each ship's processors as they worked together with the beacons but these two would have other priorities. For the most part, he supposed, blowing the *Dutchman* to bits was at the top of their list. Two bored Air Command patrol crews would not discourage them today. Perhaps it was better to just get out of everyone's way. "So I'll just get jumping, then."

"You're vacationing on Callas, another three days away, and you can't wait a few more minutes to get there?" The voice of the officer aboard the patrol ship took on a less genial tone. Perhaps the continued silence from the heavily armed new arrivals was a little more worrisome than a minor felon entering Pelion Gate. "You'll want to stop at the station, *Dutchman*. That's not negotiable."

Seth cursed silently. The massive Union station on the Pelion side of this breach was, indeed, his destination but he had hoped to get there unannounced. Now his presence in the sector would no doubt be reported to the management of Pelion Gate as soon as he opened the jumpsite. The patrol's message packet sent through with him would arrive at the ring before he did. "Need service anyway," he said blithely. "You folks have yourself a lovely day."

"It's night."

"Whatever." Seth sent a mental signal to the ship's chronometer to adjust the time to Pelion's rotation. The Union cruisers moved away and turned their attention to the incoming private vessels. Relieved, Seth began to feed the jumpsite, using the beacons to conserve energy. Instead of taxing his own systems, he let the site's processors work with the *Dutchman*'s to calculate the traverse through the Big Empty. A slight tremor moved through the ship in preparation for launch.

And then a forceful and all too familiar blow struck the ship. His hands gripped the armrests of his bench when the *Dutchman* switched into a defensive configuration without warning. The shields were already at full service for the jump but now the weapons systems came online as well. Power routed from the gravity spinners and all components signaled combat readiness.

"Damn." Seth dove out of the way of another volley emitting from the cruisers streaking toward them, his mental reflex faster than a physical interface could react. The Union ships, too, took up a defensive posture.

"Stand down, Air Command," a female voice cut into their sound systems. They heard excited voices of others in the background. "This is not your fight."

"Identify," the officer replied. "Identify and stand down."

"Those are Shri-Lan rebels," Seth supplied, naming the Union's greatest foe and the primary reason for Air Command's presence in this sector.

No time to question, no time to explain. The two rebel ships bore down upon the cruisers near the jumpsite, now targeting the forward shields of the Air Command patrols, more as warning than to cause damage. The shots impacting the *Dutchman*'s shields hit home with far greater accuracy.

"We just want the Centauri," the woman said. "Move aside or we'll destroy you, too."

"Get out of here, Kada!" the Union officer ordered.

"Yessir!" Seth signaled the beacons surrounding the site and accelerated toward the slowly forming aperture. He relaxed into his headset, using only his mind to direct the *Dutchman* into the breach.

But would those rebels give up if he left? The patrol would have alerted the Union base back on Aikhor who would have scrambled by now. This was not rebel-held territory and an attack on a military ship was not only an act of war but also damn cheeky. The only way to escape now was through the jumpsite to the Pelion sector. And the only way to the site led past the undoubtedly very irate military patrol.

"Bitch took out my fucking aft shield!" The Union pilot's exclamation was edged in panic, betraying his lack of experience with Shri-Lan rebels bent on retribution.

Seth switched to the real vid display showing the field behind him. The rebel ships had fully engaged, no longer interested in avoiding a fight with Air Command to get at the *Dutchman*.

Seth allowed the newly formed field to collapse and whipped the *Dutchman* around to return to the Union ships, his hands flying over the tactical controls as he returned fire. He dove below the cruiser to his left and came up in time to blast one of the rebel ship's shield seams, using his neural interface to place the charge with precision. Wounded, the Shri-Lan ship spun away to present another side to the melee only to take another hit.

The *Dutchman* shuddered when a projectile rammed into its undercarriage. He reached up to slap a few internal shields into place when a containment warning appeared on the holo representation of his ship beside him. He moved back to let the Air Command cruiser take a shot at their enemy and grinned when it disintegrated over their heads. A few solid chunks of hull slammed into his shields, barely raising a note of concern from his monitors. He came around and lobbed a missile at the remaining rebels' left crossdrive, watching it crumble with a burst of quickly-extinguished sparks.

"Pretty!" he said.

"Remaining bogey's disabled," one of the officers transmitted. "I'm lame, too."

"Backup coming in from Aikhor," his colleague reported. "Should be here in a few hours. No other unidentifieds in the vicinity."

"Tourist, eh, Kada? What are you packing on that boat? You cut through that shield like *churry* lard."

"Lucky hit," Seth said and turned the *Dutchman* back to the jumpsite.

"I'd thank you for saving my ass but I think we have to thank you for starting all this to begin with."

"I have to go."

"Negative, Kada. You're staying here till we know what's so important about you."

"No, really. I'm expected." Seth moved into position. "I had fun, though. Thanks."

"Kada…"

"Let Pelion deal with him," the officer on the undamaged ship said. "We'll know soon enough what had this Shri-Lan scum so excited."

"Unlikely," Seth said to himself after shutting down their com link. Unfortunately, whatever story the surviving rebels had to offer Air Command investigators was surely worse than the truth. They'd not pass up an opportunity to create more trouble.

He returned his attention to the jumpsite. A pleasant tone rang through the ship to announce the imminent jump. The *Dutchman* accelerated correctly, steadily, while ramping up all shields for the assault about to be unleashed upon it. The shields would form a small bubble of safety for pilot and cargo, allowing him to pass from one sector to the other in mere moments. He breathed deeply, steeling himself, before placing his hand on the control panel, confirming what his mind had already conveyed to the processor.

The ship slipped into the breach, immediately out of

sight, immediately just simply erased from Seth's senses. Only a growing dread remained when all light and sound disappeared, gravity did not exist; engines and neurons ceased their work. They would never know the many other worlds that existed in real-space between this point and the site's terminus at Pelion. Mere notations on astronomical charts, they were without interest until someone discovered the correct, microscopic rupture in space to span the way there. Seth often thought that many of those worlds should consider themselves fortunate to remain unexplored by Union interests.

Then he was out. He gasped for air, as always, even though he had been deprived of it for mere seconds. He groped for his mental control of the ship to decelerate and adjust its course, aided by the matching beacons that greeted him here. A quick systems check assured him that, despite the tremendous strain of the traverse, the *Dutchman* had once again delivered him safely.

"Someday I'll get used to this," he told his ship. Then again, as uncomfortable as these jaunts felt, they were nothing compared to those made by the true subspace navigators. Those rare talents, the Level Three spanners, needed no pre-defined charts or Union-controlled beacons to guide them through raw *keyholes*, tiny fissures in space, to feel their way to a distant destination. Highly valued and highly paid, they worked for Air Command and the larger shipping companies. The more enterprising among them also made deep space exploration possible and led the way to new destinations. Alive, if at all possible. Their work turned simple keyholes into jumpsites, providing the maps for chartjumpers like Seth.

He sometimes considered going into business with such a navigator to help him get around more easily, if not more cheaply. But the one he knew comfortably enough to want to share his small ship preferred to hear about Seth's adventures from a safe distance. Given that last time he served as navigator he had lost a hand, it was probably just as well. For the most part, Seth was quite content to avail himself to the charted jumpsites, even if that meant being harassed by patrols with tedious regularity.

An automated guide signal arrived from the station and he responded without demur this time. Pelion Gate, just ahead of him now, formed a traffic hub linking the busy Targon sub-sector with the more remote Magra-Aikhor corridor. The massive station, ring-shaped like many of its generation, hosted a town's worth of residents, traders, service depots and, of course, a full complement of Air Command personnel.

"Welcome to Pelion, Mister Kada," he was eventually greeted.

"Thank you," Seth said, his attention on the approach to the station. Without the jumpsite in its active state, the ring seemed to float purposelessly in the inky nothing of space, too far removed from the Pelion system to seem to belong anywhere. Still, it was lit dramatically on one side by the system's single star and illuminated by hundreds of windows on the other. An impressive sight, as always swarmed by vessels of all sizes and configurations, surrounded by satellites and solar collectors, and protectively patrolled by Air Command fighter planes.

"Approach denied. Drop your shields and prepare for boarding."

"I'm starting to think people don't trust me," Seth grumbled, but what had he expected after his run-in with the patrol back near Aikhor? As he'd assumed, their message packet had come through the gate in his wake and found receptive ears aboard the station. After a moment's hesitation, he returned a coded message, as always reluctant to use his key unless he absolutely had to. Sometimes it was better to be thought of as a tourist.

Minutes passed during which one or two of the agile Air Command Kites swooped around him as if a closer look somehow told them anything about the plain, tired-looking cruiser with the plain and unoriginal name. His was a ship like thousands of others that came through here and even their careful scans showed little of what the *Dutchman* really had to offer.

Then a different voice: "Boarding pass accepted. You're cleared for docking, small craft ring, bay nineteen."

"Aren't you going to wish me a nice day?"

"Don't push it, Kada. Whatever you're doing here, do it quietly."

Seth decided to forego further response and brought the *Dutchman* around to the assigned dock. He nudged the ship gently into its berth and felt the docking rings slide over the entrance to his small cargo bay which also served as air lock. The gently pulsing indicator beside him reminded him that his ship needed attention after the hit he'd taken from the Shri-Lan cruiser. A minor thorium leak in the area he had shielded off. Hoping for a reasonably priced repair, he chatted with the station's service department before powering the ship down.

He left the cockpit to enter the cluttered main cabin, the only place he called his home. This also needed attention. A cleaning company could probably restore some order in here although he'd wait until he returned to Magra to hire crews he trusted with his ship's secrets. He slipped into his boots and faded flight jacket and ran his fingers through his hair. Before he reached the pressure door to the cargo bay, he stopped by the tiny crew quarters to place a hand onto its key plate and then used his foot to push the door open.

"On your feet," he said.

The Caspian female curled up on the lower of the two bunks peered out at him with unblinking yellow eyes. "They caught us," she said, using her native tongue. "The Shri-Lan."

"They tried. Come on, get up. I don't want to spend any more time here than I have to." He took a step into the cramped space, careful to stay out of her reach. Unclothed, as was their custom, she had no weapon other than the fierce talons on her three-toed feet. Seth had been on the receiving end of a vicious kick from her only this morning and had learned to stay clear. Still, he did not draw his gun to move her from her bed.

She unfolded herself slowly, without expression on her narrow face. Her gleaming hide bore the pale spots of Caspia's coastal plains where Shri-Lan rebels recruited most successfully from among her people. "You got away."

"Don't sound so disappointed. We're at Pelion Gate." He snatched one of his shirts from the tangled pile on the upper bunk and handed it to her. Although she was barely distinguishable from the males of her species, custom aboard most Union stations decreed some sort of attire. "Put this on."

"It smells of Centauri."

"Yeah, but we smell good. Are you going to behave or are you planning to slice my other leg open?"

She lifted a thin upper lip to snarl at him with sharpened teeth.

"This was your choice," he reminded her. "Take one step out of line and I'll hand you to Air Command instead. I don't care who takes over from here. Are we clear on that?"

"Your bounty is greater if you don't."

He shrugged. "Let's go. Keep your mouth shut and stay close."

She shuffled ahead of him through the cargo bay and then outside for the mandatory decon process. A scan of his violet iris confirmed the access code he sent earlier. The burly guards at the entrance to the concourse didn't seem to care when the Caspian in Seth's care ignored the scanner altogether.

This ring contained docks and flight services crowded with workers and travelers and echoing with a noise level to match the bustle. The ring above this one offered just about any amenity a weary traveler could want and Seth resolved to head up that way in search of a long, hot bath, even as he nudged his passenger into a lift leading to the lower tier. He wondered if the friend he had made last time he passed through here still worked at the transfer station. He smiled at the memory of a few nights they had shared. But first he'd get rid of the rebel.

The brilliant sunshine flooding the bottom ring caused both Seth and the Caspian to squint and hesitate before stepping out of the elevator. He gripped her arm as they accustomed themselves, not having seen daylight for a while. Even Aikhor's sun rarely made it through the dense shroud of fog that forever obscured the skies there.

The gravity spinners resided in the central spool of the station and so they walked with their feet pointed that way. The high ceiling bowed outward, almost entirely transparent and now facing Pelion's sun, allowing natural light to turn this segment of the station into a verdant space of multi-level gardens and pleasant little parks.

Seth admired the pretty sights created here even as he scanned the area for signs that not all was as charmingly bucolic as it appeared. No one seemed to be in a hurry here, vendors were not allowed, neither were vehicles nor, apparently, anything above a whisper. They passed a small pool of liquid home to a swarm of round, spinning sea creatures. He felt oddly out of place here, armed and decidedly scruffier-looking than the other visitors to this place.

The Caspian stopped. She tilted her head in puzzlement as she gazed out of the panoramic ceiling to see a dozen or so individuals drifting about in pressure suits out there. Thin scaffolding held nearly invisible carbon fiber netting in place, offering the illusion of floating in space. "What are they doing?"

Seth watched some of the figures bounce a large ring around in some contest. "Playing," he said. She just stared at him until he shrugged. "Good exercise, too."

He felt the tension in her arm when they finally approached a group of Caspians waiting by the numbered column designated as their meeting spot. They stood silently, their yellow eyes on the woman. The hides on all of them bore the same pattern as hers. He tightened his grip when she looked around, perhaps for one more chance to escape.

A tall female raised a hand in greeting but her face remained immobile. Within moments, the others with her had surrounded his captive, quick to remove the wrinkled shirt from her to replace it with an elaborately embroidered kilt. Someone handed the shirt back to him with a slight nod of dismissal.

The tight knot of Caspians move away. No one had spoken. "What will happen to her?" Seth asked the elder male who remained behind, using their language. It was probably far too late to ask this now. Although fiercely loyal to their complex clans, the coastal tribes of Caspia were not known for their empathy toward anyone. Perhaps it would have been kinder to turn her over to Air Command after all.

"She'll live," the Caspian replied, using Union mainvoice. The rippling tones that accompanied their language were not easily mastered by other species and Seth was glad for the switch. "We cannot continue to allow our people to join the Shri-Lan. She is fortunate that her clan wants to see her returned. Others have paid a heavier price for their treason."

Seth's eyes shifted to the elder. "She's young, Ton Kedi. She's lost." He didn't mention that he had found her in the bed of a Caspian Shri-Lan rebel. She had enough trouble.

"She embarrassed her family by joining that rabble of thieves. She'll not leave Caspia again. Perhaps she'll come to see the wisdom of that."

"She won't be hurt?"

Ton Kedi began to stroll along the cobbled path and Seth fell into step. "I think not. Her clan's pride is not irreparable and she is a minor, if treasured, daughter. But she has forfeit some freedoms, I'm sure of it."

"The Shri-Lan weren't happy about her leaving. They're worried about what she knows." Seth had doubts, given the rebels' vicious attack on him and the patrol, that the girl's paramour was still among the living. Whatever secrets he had whispered to his young lover now rested with her. Seth's own, non-invasive attempts to pry those secrets from her had netted him a claw in the shin.

The elder Caspian nodded. "And in time she will reveal that to us, have no doubt. I will share if it matters."

"You mentioned you had something for me now?"

"Indeed. The girl in exchange for information." Ton Kedi lowered his ancient frame onto a curved bench and stretched his clawed feet out in front of him with a grateful sigh. "The body gets tired after all these years, even with gravity as light as it is here. I sometimes wish I could move my clan to a place such as this."

Seth nodded and waited politely. He didn't really need the fee paid for the girl's return, nor was her capture of much consequence to anyone but her family. But Ton Kedi had promised greater value in exchange for her. Seth hoped it was worth nearly getting an Air Command cruiser destroyed.

The Caspian turned his raptor-like eyes to Seth. "Arawaj spanners," he said. "Four of them, fleeing Tadonna before the Union takes over there. You'll find them on Tayako."

"Did you say Arawaj?" Seth had expected some bit of news about a Shri-Lan base, perhaps, or yet another tedious plot against the Union's governors, but what was this about spanners?

"I did."

The Arawaj rebel faction, a smaller but far more ideological organization than the profit-driven Shri-Lan, infiltrated every segment of Commonwealth society. Their opposition to the Union's expansion here in Trans-Targon often approached religious zeal. While Shri-Lan robbed, extorted and smuggled, the Arawaj assassinated, spread malcontent, and sabotaged. It was fortunate, Seth thought, that their ideals didn't attract a greater following.

A large number of Caspians, including this girl's family, belonged to the faction, but Ton Kedi was not one of them. "What are they doing all the way out on Tayako?"

"They're working for a smuggler. A Centauri named Velen Phar. Tayako is as far as he can go without getting arrested. Or so he says. The Union is taking over his home planet so he's decided to give up his gunrunning operation. He's not the only Arawaj leaving the planet. They're all being driven away by the locals before Air Command even lands there to do it for them. I told him you'd come and pick them up. You have a talent for slipping past Air Command eyes."

"It's a gift," Seth agreed, not quite comfortable under the Caspian's unwavering stare.

Ton Kedi glanced around the sun-dappled arbor before leaning closer to Seth. "Meet the captain of the *Othani* on Tayako. You know where. He'll have the spanners with him and he will hand them over to you. He won't want uniforms around. Not if he still wants to live among his own."

"I'm starting to feel like a shuttle pilot," Seth sighed. Four spanners! The single greatest advantage the Union had over any of the rebel factions was their team of spanners who travelled where chartjumpers like him could not, coming and going as needed. Most of them were Delphian, an aloof species whose mental abilities set them apart from other navigators. Their matchless talents and utter disinterest in wealth allowed them to choose assignments that fed their interest in space exploration, whether for civilian or military aims. Siding with the Commonwealth only out of loathing for the rebels, no Delphian stooped to working with either Shri-Lan or Arawaj. Without them, the rebels were left with inferior navigators who often needed pharmaceutical support to achieve the Delphians' legendary abilities.

But any spanners working for the rebels, even the lesser talents, were of the highest priority to Air Command. Much effort was expended to locate and appropriate, by force if necessary, these navigators. They were known to Air Command intelligence and their moves carefully tracked until they could be seized.

"Air Command doesn't know about them?" Seth asked.

"Not only that, but from what I learned, these spanners are of a special breed."

"How so?"

"Big talents. Maybe even greater talents than Delphians. Velen Phar has a way of crossing subspace that others haven't even begun to figure out. Always works two spanners at once but that still doesn't account for how fast he gets around."

"Better than Delphians? You're talking GenMods."

Ton Kedi shrugged. "Possible. You don't do that kind of work without some sort of brain adjustment. But what do I know about such things."

What, indeed, Seth thought. He suspected that the old spy knew a whole lot more about a great many things.

"He's been keeping his team busy and his flight plans to himself," the Caspian continued. "Stays out of everyone's sight. But it won't be long before our friends the Shri-Lan take notice. See if you can get there before they do and you stand to make a large sum upon delivery."

Seth nodded. If these four were not yet identified and if they were even remotely as talented as Ton Kedi believed, their value to any interstellar operation, military or civilian, was incalculable. It was definitely worth taking a closer look. Bringing these four in for some decompression and attitude adjustment would gloss over the little incident with the patrol at the gate. And even if they could not be rehabilitated, keeping them out of rebel hands was paramount.

"Give him this." Ton Kedi removed a broad leather band from his wrist. "It'll let him know who you are. He'll hand his crew over to you."

Seth peered at the thin datasheet on the inside of the bracelet. "How do the spanners feel about that?"

The Caspian tilted his head as if not understanding the question; his expression looked quite like the Caspian girl's had when seeing people at play outside. "They are Arawaj. Who cares?"

TWO

She woke when her head bumped softly against the edge of the upper bunk. This time she only sighed in resignation and made sure that she still floated above her mattress. In some nether region of the ship, Dom's mood usually dictated whether or not they received warning before gravity was shifted. She turned and reached for the blanket that had floated free. The cabin was chilly, as always.

Ciela listened for sounds in the corridor. The ancient *Othani*'s unstable gravity generators really only balked like this when the shields came down. Given that there was just about nothing worth dropping shields for several centuries in any direction, this could only mean that another ship had requested docking. Another ship out here sounded interesting.

She slid out of her bunk and bounced upward to catch Miko's arm to pull him back to his bed. It would take more than this to wake him. He mumbled something when she fastened the wide restraint over his chest to keep him in place on the upper bunk. Luanie, in the opposite bed, was already tied down. She had made the last jump and it would be hours yet before she'd have any reason or energy to crawl out of her blankets. Deely's bed was empty; likely he was already on the bridge, preparing for the next jump.

Ciela drifted to the door and out into the hallway, bouncing lightly on her toes as she pulled herself along a handrail. She amused herself by spinning around a bit, deftly hooking her feet under the pipes running along the wall and ceiling.

"What's going on?" she said when Zev Erron, a portly and habitually irritable Human crew member, rounded a corner. She turned over again to wait for him upside down.

He frowned up at her as she walked across the ceiling. "Those are air lines," he informed her. "Don't be kicking those."

She flipped back again, making a point of poking him with her bare foot. "If my toes can break one of those we're in a whole lot of trouble. Who docked?"

"Scout ship. Vichal and his dogs."

Ciela wrinkled her nose. So much for interesting. A scout ship in this remote sub-sector usually meant a crew of ruffians looking for Union patrols to harass and traders to loot. The Arawaj faction made up only a small segment of the rebels fighting against Union dominance but that didn't keep their troopers from acting like thugs when given the chance. "How did they get out here?"

"Why don't you ask them? The big Caspian looks particularly friendly."

She shrugged. It didn't matter to her. More important to their smuggling operation than any other crew member, she and her team had little to worry about, no matter how foul-mannered these new passengers were. Spanners like her made it possible to avoid the very public, Air Command-riddled jumpsites and instead slip through uncharted breaches from one sector to another. It allowed them privileges not granted lesser talents.

"We're at the keyhole," Zev said. "Deely's ready to jump. Boss is going to want another one of you on the bridge."

"Guess that's me," she said. "The others are sleeping. Never a good idea to wake a sleeping spanner."

A shudder went through the ship, lights flickered, and

both of them grasped the handrail while the generators labored to restore first the shields and then the missing gravity. Ciela waggled her fingers at Zev and returned to her cabin.

There she slipped out of the loose pants and shirt in which she had slept and stepped into their little bathing chamber for a quick decon. It took only a few seconds but she finished with a blast of cold air, feeling her skin prickle with a delicious shiver. She completed the task by frosting the tips of her thick black hair with a glorious shade of pink.

Miko was awake when she returned to the cabin. He had freed himself of his restraints and propped his head on his hand, apparently not inclined to get out of bed just yet. "Are we there?" he asked, watching her dig through a cabinet. Usually, she and Miko had the cabin to themselves and sometimes she worked alone, but the captain wanted to pick up two leased ships at Tayako Station before heading out again. It was nice to have them all together again for a while, but it made for cramped quarters.

"Apparently," she said as she dressed in a snug body shirt covered by a looser blouse, a comfortable pair of tights and soft boots. Their life aboard this interstellar transport rarely required anything sturdier than that. If Deely had been here in place of Miko she would have dressed out of sight but the slender youth lounging on the upper bunk had little interest in females. "Took on some scouts," she said.

"Out here?" He yawned and stretched. "I'll come up with some food, if you want. Unless you're stopping in the galley."

"I want to see what's up with our guests. I'll just have some biscuits, thanks."

"Are you jumping?"

"No. It's Deely's turn. You better not be keeping him up when he gets in."

"The old grouch," Miko agreed. Even a relatively short jump through an uncharted site took a tremendous toll on spanners as well as the machines supporting them. Most of them required a long period of rest and silence to recuperate from the mental strain, making multiple jumps nearly impossible for one person. Few ships were lucky enough to work more than one spanner. The *Othani* often carried two, allowing them to move rapidly through available breaches in space without needing to rest a lone navigator between jumps. Only the time needed to travel through real-space between keyholes slowed them during their frequent runs between the habitable worlds of Trans-Targon.

Angry voices met her before she had even reached the door to the bridge. People were always shouting and arguing aboard the *Othani* but this did not sound like the frequent but short-lived brawls between crew members. Ciela hesitated before placing her hand over the door's sensors and then quickly slipped to the back, near the com station, to observe the mood on the bridge.

Velen Phar, their Centauri captain and employer, stood at the center, facing four armed rebels. Two were Caspian, one Centauri and the woman with them appeared to be Human. Typical of rebel 'scouts', they were brawny and dressed for combat as if to display their readiness to engage at any moment. Their expressions were equally threatening. She remembered their leader, Vichal, as particularly unpleasant.

"You're not changing course, are you?" Vichal asked. He gestured toward Deely reclining in the navigator's couch.

"What, of course not," Velen Phar, replied. "We're going to Tayako Station to take on two more ships. As planned."

The rebel drew a long-barreled pistol from his belt. The technician beside Ciela covered a startled cry with her hand. "Someone told me your plans changed," Vichal said. "Told me that maybe you heard Sebasta was coming to meet you at Tayako. So you decided you'd rather be elsewhere." He tilted his head toward his Caspian cohort who was busy at the helm. When the rebel looked up and nodded, Vichal grinned, showing teeth blackened by too much *voril* gum. "I think you lied to me, Captain. That's not charted to Tayako, is it? Or maybe you've got your maps upside down."

"What's going on?" Ciela whispered. "We changed course?" She turned when the door opened and another of the troopers entered, pushing the *Othani*'s engineer ahead of him.

The tech shook her head, looking very confused. "I have no idea. They think we're smuggling you out of the sector."

"What? Why?"

"I'll tell you why," the Centauri said. His violet eyes found them at the back of the room. He nudged the captain with his gun until Velen Phar dropped into his chair with a grunt. "Seems like someone's trying to make a deal with the Union." He tilted his head and then raised his hand to gesture to her.

Ciela stepped forward, past another crewman and into the brighter light of center bridge. She glanced at Deely who shrugged, as bewildered as she was.

Vichal looked her over and found the small metal implant embedded in her temple. "You're one of the spanners?"

"Yes. What's going on? What deal?"

"Stay quiet, Ciela," her captain said under his breath. He moved to get out of his chair but the rebel's gun convinced him to stay there. "Look," he said to the Centauri. "We're all on the same team. Where did you get the idea that I'm dealing with the Union? Why would I?"

"I don't give a damn why you'd do anything, Phar. But you're not handing them over." He waved his gun in Deely's direction.

"What are you talking about?" Ciela asked.

Deely removed his headset and turned toward their captain, a question on his pale face.

"There are Union agents meeting you on Tayako," Vichal said. "Isn't that right, Phar? Vanguard, probably. You're going to let them have your crew."

"What?" Ciela gasped.

The captain scowled at the armed rebels before looking up at Ciela's astonished face. "It's not what that sounds like."

"Talk to me, Velen!" Ciela said, feeling more anxious by

the moment. "Why is he saying that?" She had been a member of his company ever since her training had ended on Tadonna, their home planet, five years ago. A rough-tempered boss with little regard for his crew's personal comfort, Velen Phar demanded much of his team. Their trips were far-ranging and exhausting, taking them through sectors the Union had not even heard of. The ever-increasing Air Command forays into this sub-sector meant that they were constantly on the move to supply the Arawaj posts with what goods could be smuggled past the patrols. The much-abused *Othani* had carried rebel troops, small batches of fighter planes, weaponry, contraband and the occasional high-ranking rebel, relying on the spanners' expertise to elude capture on many occasions.

But he had always treated them fairly, generous with shore leave and pay, and had made sure the entire crew functioned with at least a measure of respect for each other.

Vichal's lowered brow rose as a slow grin spread over his features. "They don't know?" he said to the captain.

"Know what?" Ciela said. "Velen! What's going on?"

The ship's second in command finally found his voice. He nudged Ciela aside to stand by the captain's chair. "Nothing's going on," he said to Vichal. He pointed to Deely. "The chart isn't finished yet, that's all. We're going to pick up the new ships and then head out on a long run. We need all four spanners for that. Why would we give them up to the Union? Without them we might as well scrap the *Othani* for all she'd be worth."

"Well, then let Mr. Deely finish his work and then we'll all jump to Tayako together," Vichal said. "We'll come along to make sure you don't get lost on the way. Surely you don't mind an armed escort to look after you?"

"We get by precisely because we don't carry more armament than we need to," Ciela said. "You'll only be waving flags in the air. I don't know what's going on but we're not jumping until someone explains all this." Her words were directed at the captain.

Vichal used his gun to scratch the side of his shaved head. "You see, Ciela - is that your name? What your boss didn't mention is that he's thinking of retirement. Isn't that so, Phar?" He did not wait for the captain to reply. "As I heard it, someone on Tadonna – let's call her the Esteemed Consul - had a chat with Air Command. And then Air Command had a chat with the Union Factors. And now everyone thinks it's a good idea to hand Tadonna over to the Commonwealth Union of Planets."

"What?" Ciela said. "The whole planet?"

"Did I get that right, Phar?" Vichal smiled at the captain. "The good folks of Tadonna don't want Arawaj rebels cluttering up the place anymore? Rather join the Commonwealth, would they?" He turned back to Ciela without the smile. "They'll come in and remove our bases, including your home. You know what happens to rebels when those soldiers land."

Ciela gaped at the Centauri, feeling an unpleasant tingle of fear shiver up along her spine. She knew about the atrocities at which he hinted. She had heard of the unspeakable terror unleashed upon those who cooperated with any rebel group. There was no mercy for her or her kind as long as they opposed the expansion of the Commonwealth in this sector. "Did someone warn them? Do they have time to get out?" She turned to the captain. "Forget about Tayako. We can make it back to Tadonna in one jump."

He shook his head. "It's too late. There's nothing we can do. Air Command's already landed in the islands to cover the port. They'll hunt us down like Rhuwacs if we go back." He raised his hands in a tired gesture. "I don't have the fight for that anymore."

Her tingle of fear turned into overwhelming dread. "So you're just going to hand us over to *them*? To the Union? Don't we get a choice? We can work anywhere."

"Let's not forget about the money," Vichal said with an unpleasant smirk. "Tell them about the pile of currency you're getting for them, along with whatever pardon they've promised you, Smuggler. Good thing we arrived just in time to express our concerns."

"That's a lie," Velen Phar said to his crew. "I'm asking for nothing." He looked from one to the other. "I just didn't want you to end up..." he looked up at the Centauri "...like them. You deserve better than that."

"And you think being thrown in prison by Air Command is better?" Ciela said, glaring at the captain. He dropped his eyes to the scuffed floor of the bridge. She had trusted him for years to keep them safe while they did their small part for the rebel cause. Certainly there were profits to be made but they risked their lives and freedom with every smuggling run through the sector. Nothing mattered more than to fight the escalating Commonwealth occupation. Without resistance, soon every planet accessible via sub-space leaps would be theirs to be exploited. And now Tadonna was lost to their persuasion and coercion. She thought about the people still on Tadonna, her teachers and friends. Would they have warning before their hiding places were raided, pointed out to the Union soldiers by the traitorous locals? She turned to Vichal. "So then what do you want with us?"

"We've made a much better deal for you," Vichal said.

She frowned. "Deal? What sort of deal? You mean another smuggler?"

"Not precisely. We're just here to make sure your good captain doesn't veer off course. Sebasta's ship will be waiting for you at Tayako." He smirked at the Human woman standing behind him. She returned his leer with one of her own. "You'll be quite safe, don't worry. No one wants to harm a spanner. You're just too damn valuable."

"I don't like where this is going," Deely said.

"You don't have to like it," Vichal said. "Just do your job and you'll be well taken care of. Doesn't matter who you work for. We found a buyer for you."

"What?" Ciela exclaimed. "This is outrageous! You can't do that."

"We *are* doing that."

"You are worse than scum, Vichal," Velen Phar said. "You're talking Shri-Lan, aren't you?"

"I am. Sebasta is waiting for you at Tayako to take you to the new bosses."

Ciela felt her knees buckling and fought to remain upright. The Shri-Lan faction, far larger and more established than the Arawaj, presented the only real challenge to Air Command's complete military control of the Trans-Targon sector. They had wealth and guns to achieve their goals more effectively and brutally than the Arawaj. But those goals consisted mostly of amassing more capital and no longer had anything in common with Arawaj ideals.

Attempts had been made, even just recently, to combine Arawaj with the Shri-Lan faction but ideology and power struggles had caused all but a few joint ventures to fail. Arawaj sought to slow the Union's expansion; Shri-Lan strove to take its place as the governors of the Trans-Targon sector. Ivor Sebasta, commander of a small, heavily armed Arawaj combat unit, was one in favor of joining forces.

"We will not join Shri-Lan," Deely said, every bit as frightened and livid as Ciela. "We are Arawaj. You're mad if you think we'd cooperate with that."

"We're wasting time," the Human who had arrived with Vichal said. She moved to the console in front of Deely and worked with the system for a moment. Almost as an afterthought, she struck him hard enough to slam his head against the backrest of his bench. "Get busy with that keyhole, Spanner."

Ciela stepped forward before realizing that the rebel was easily twice as wide as she and most of that was made up of muscle. "Stop that. You'll only damage his interface."

The woman sneered. "I'd kick his ass if he wasn't sitting on it. I don't suppose that is attached to his implant." She grasped Ciela's arm and shoved her into the other navigator couch.

Ciela glared at her but said nothing. She glanced over to Deely who was dabbing sullenly at his bleeding lip. His hand shook. Unlike her, he had served on other, less well-managed, Arawaj ships. If he chose to keep his head down among these ruffians, it was probably something to emulate. She had never known Arawaj troopers to show much respect for those they thought of as civilians.

"I can't do this," he said, more to Ciela than the others.

"I'll help you," the Human said. She stood behind Ciela and jammed her gun into her nape. Ciela froze when she heard the weapon reset. "How's this? Open that keyhole and chart us to Tayako. And if we come out anywhere *but* Tayako, your little girlfriend here is going to be in pain for about a week. Deal?"

He glowered at her but finally nodded. With a long gaze at Ciela, he turned to his console and fastened the headset to the neural interface at his temples. She did the same, shrugging her shoulders angrily as if to dislodge the gun at her neck.

"There," Vichal said, pleased. "Now we're all ready to go."

Deely took a deep breath and closed his eyes. The display in front of him came alive as the ship's processors recognized his mental interface. The overhead lights dimmed when all resources focused on the tremendous energy needed to calculate the keyhole's trajectory.

Unlike the stable and charted jumpsites elsewhere in the sector, these miniscule breaches had to be manually plotted for each passage. The ship's processors took care of the calculations but it required a sentient, highly trained mind to find the correct exit. It was this sensory aptitude that set spanners apart from other navigators and made them a rare commodity in Trans-Targon.

"This is suicide," the helmsman, who had so far only watched in silence, spoke. "They can't jump like this. We'll end up stuck in sub-space if he's off."

Velan Phar nodded. "He's right," he said to Vichal. "I've been through hundreds of uncharted sites. You can't go in there unless you've got your brain working properly. A nervous spanner is dangerous."

"What about her?" Vichal's companion gestured to Ciela. "She doesn't look nervous."

"Makes no difference," Phar said. "We're taking a chance."

"You're stalling, Phar," Vichal decided. "Hoping to run us into whatever Union agents are meeting you over there. I'd like to get to Tayako before they do." He waved his gun at the helmsman. "Get going or my pilot's doing your job. Unlike these two, you are expendable."

"All right, Vichal," the captain said. "There's no need for anyone getting killed here." He nodded to the helmsman.

"Suicide," the pilot grumbled but began to feed the keyhole to open the aperture. "Going negative."

The captain signaled the intent to jump although most of the ship's passengers were currently here on the bridge. Some moved into the available seats and jump couches, others grasped the handrails provided for the leap into nothing.

The ship moved into position in front of the breach and began to accelerate toward it when Ciela signaled the pilot. The *Othani*'s energy emissions widened the breach to allow them to enter and her shields would keep them from being crushed once inside. But only Deely's mental control of the ship's processors would allow them to exit again.

Ciela reached for his hand when her own connection to the ship alerted her to several failed algorithms. "I got it," he said but he sounded far from certain.

The *Othani* had reached maximum velocity and streaked toward the open gateway into sub-space, soon beyond any point of return. Ciela probed the ship's systems, hoping to support Deely's efforts. The calculations were coming together but she felt nothing resembling the exit to Tayako. "I don't see it."

"It's not there," he said, panic rising in his voice. "It's not there!"

"Calm down," she implored him. "You'll find it. You've

been there. Just grab it."

"I can't! It's scattering."

"Ciela..." Velen Phar began.

"Back loop. He's looping!"

"Told you," the pilot said, his voice too shrill in their ears. "I can't abort."

"Dammit, Ciela!"

She reached up and knocked Deely's headset away before the ship's processors found their way into his brain. She took over where he left off, grasping for the exit, any exit, before they plunged into the vast nothing of sub-space. A searing pain drove into her skull when the processors swapped his patterns to her interface.

The communications tech's sudden scream was cut off when the *Othani* plunged into the breach. There was nothing here now. Each of them existed as some insignificant entity traversing some unimaginable distance without seeing or feeling any of it. No sound or sensation intruded upon the brief and absolute moment of terror that sub-space travel induced in all living creatures. The absence of everything, perhaps a glimpse of death without afterlife, perhaps a promise of the end of time. And with the great fear of the unknown came the reminder that countless others had gone into the breach and had not emerged.

"We're out. We're out! We're back, we're out."

Ciela groaned when the hysterical repetition of that discovery drilled into her eardrums. She kept her eyes shut, dizzy and exhausted beyond all measure.

"She got us back."

"Where are we?"

"Ciela, are you all right?"

"Bearings, Helm!"

"Ciela!"

Ciela ignored them. None of this had anything to do with her. She felt someone lift her from her couch. The captain, she thought. That didn't matter, either. She let herself drift away from all of this.

THREE

Tayako, a rare, habitable gem of a planet lost in what most referred to as the Badlands of Trans-Targon, was not a bad place to settle. The moon orbiting it and serving as a low-grav transfer station, on the other hand, was a disappointing sight for those arriving here for the first time. Without the funds to build one of the impressive orbital stations common in busier ports, the moon was studded with dusty, domed service installations looking like some weird fungus on the planet-side of the satellite.

Seth circled around a long pier jutting out from an elevated central hub above the moon, taking a quick look for possible Air Command cruisers before tucking into his berth. For the most part, all he saw were the lumbering freighters and inter-stellar transports too awkward and heavy to actually touch down on the planet's surface. Instead, they stopped here for service and transferred their goods and passengers to smaller vessels.

Tayako itself traded agricultural products, mainly rice and other grains, with the Commonwealth but offered little strategic value. Air Command patrolled this area only sporadically or when called upon by the local governments. That rebels also frequented this remote colony was no secret to anyone. The nearest charted jumpsite was so far removed that any visitor to Tayako appeared on long-range sensors long before arriving out here. The only other way in or out was a single keyhole, accessible only to Level Three spanners, nearly a day's travel away. Planets in other parts of Trans-Targon were colonized because their convenient proximity to a jumpsite meant less real-space travel time and costs. For Tayako, the distances created a cozy place for smugglers and fugitives, aware of visits by Air Command or anyone else well in advance.

Once docked, Seth bounced lightly from the cockpit to the cargo hold to pull a pair of heavy boots from a compartment. Bit by bit, he added weight until the sensors agreed on the best mass to allow him to move comfortably in the reduced gravity. After tying his hair into a short queue to keep it from drifting around his head, he exited the ship to walk through the short umbilical for the mandatory scan looking for foreign pathogens. The station owners seemed unconcerned about his identity and no one insisted upon a security check.

The air outside carried the sort of funk he'd become accustomed to after years of loitering around the less reputable ports of Trans-Targon. Moist, over-used, infused with the waste and refuse left behind by travelers from a dozen points of origin and not quite bad enough to require a respirator. He walked along a broken conveyor, a little unsteady as he got used to the moon's gravity. By the time he turned into an intersecting tunnel things were starting to feel normal, including the stale air.

The *Othani* freighter awaited him at the far end of the loading platforms. The battered and patched hull dwarfed some of the smaller vessels nearby, looking like she'd seen one too many meteor showers. No transfer shuttles lined up here to move cargo but even from a distance, he noted a crowd of people and vehicles near the umbilical that tethered her here. He ambled closer to join a few spectators.

"What happened here?" he said to a Centauri woman wearing something made to look like snake skin and worn just as tightly. She seemed fascinated by the number of bodies lined up on the platform. As they watched, another stretcher emerged from the access tube to the *Othani*.

"Rebels, the lot of them."

"Arawaj rebels?" Seth scanned the crowd and the bodies on the ground. Although they had been weighed down a little, no one had bothered to cover the Caspians, Centauri, and two Humans. All combat-sized and dressed for work. A few official-looking individuals seemed occupied with removing the bodies but it didn't look like anyone was investigating a crime here. As always in places like these, if this didn't involve civilians, no one cared or dared enough to meddle in rebel affairs.

She shrugged her overly perfumed shoulders. "I didn't ask. I don't hold much with rebels. It's always good to mind one's own business." She cast a professional glance over Seth to gauge the depth of his pockets and his willingness to part with their content. "It was done very quickly. Just some shouting, really, and then a whole gang of no-goods took off in a couple of skimmers. By the time we got out here, it was all over."

"None of them locals?"

"None I recognized." She shifted herself into an inviting pose now that she had his attention. "Not that I know all the locals that hang around here, of course. Just passing through myself."

"Of course," he said diplomatically and moved away before she got around to her offer. One of the Humans near the entrance drew back when Seth approached him. Seth did not have to draw deeply upon his lifelong study of xenos to recognize when a Human was nervous. "You the captain?" he said in lieu of a greeting, keeping his voice low.

"What? No." The man's eyes were fixed upon the dead rebels on the ground. "He's inside. They got him, too."

"Shri-Lan did?"

"Arawaj!" the Human cried. "Damn Arawaj!"

"Your own?" Seth said and turned his wrist out as he slipped the data sheet from the armlet he had been given.

The rebel looked down at it with a puzzled frown. Then his brows lifted. "You're Ton Kedi's contact," he exclaimed and then immediately lowered his voice to a theatrical whisper. "Kada, is it? You're too late, Kada."

"I can see that."

The rebel pulled a frayed, too-small jacket tighter around his ample frame. "Velen Phar is inside. He can explain this mess. I'm done with this. I guess we're all done with this now."

Seth stepped around him and slipped through the ship's umbilical. The *Othani* was no more attractive inside than out. Too many jumps through sub-space, too many times loaded and unloaded, no coin spent on the comforts he took for granted even on his own small cruiser. The deck plates clanged against each other as he walked the otherwise silent corridor, peering into cabins as he went. A medic of some sort emerged from a door up ahead and he followed the sound of voices into what appeared to be the ship's galley, made for a crew of about a dozen, unadorned and without luxury.

A Centauri sat shirtless on one of the benches, scowling at another medic who was patching up his badly burned chest and shoulder. He looked up when Seth entered. "Who, by Cazun's arse, are you, now?" he growled.

"Your disgruntled customer," Seth replied. He stepped around a smear of blood on the floor and dropped Ton Kedi's data sheet onto the table.

Velen Phar waved the medic away. She shrugged and packed up her tools. He caught her arm and waited until she handed him another packet of painkillers before leaving the room. "Nothing left here for you, Kada."

"My cargo?"

"Gone. Damn Sebasta got here first."

"Ivor Sebasta?" Seth knew Sebasta by reputation, which wasn't a good one. He was the sort of Arawaj rebel who gave the entire faction their reputation for resorting to reprehensible methods when outgunned, which was often.

"Yeah, I heard he was coming for us and meant to head into the Mrak sector. But he set his dogs on us to make sure I didn't give him the slip." Velen Phar winced as he shrugged a shirt over his bandaged shoulder. "Then it all goes to piss when Vichal decides he wants payment for delivering us here. Got the end of a pistol instead. I lost two of my crew, too."

"We had a deal," Seth reminded him. "It took me ten days to get all the way out here. Targon time."

The captain snarled at him. "Do I look happy about this? I'm stuck here now with this mess to clean up. I'm being charged for the body dump."

Seth went to the galley counter and helped himself to a cup of tea. At least the supplies here included a decent selection of flavors that appealed to Centauri and not the fruity stuff preferred by other species. "Any idea where your spanners are now?"

"Forget it, Kada. Nasty bunch. Takes more than the likes of you to get the better of Ivor Sebasta."

Seth shrugged. "Just want to talk to him."

"You won't get near the spanners. They've got them locked up by now."

"Locked up? Why?"

"Those spanners aren't coddled little princesses like the Union navigators. We made sure they can look after themselves if need be. Should have seen Ciela put up a fight." The captain stared off into the middle distance for a moment. "They were so scared. This wasn't supposed to happen like this." He leaned forward with a pained grunt to pick up a discarded wrap, the sort of pretty thing a woman might like. Seth watched in silent amazement as he held it to his nose. "None of them know anything but Arawaj. They don't know anything but what they've been told." He folded the scarf carefully and placed it on the table. The floor here was littered with scattered dishes and evidence of medical intervention but that didn't seem to bother him as much as the small wrinkle on the cloth.

"Where are they being taken?"

Phar lifted his bloodshot eyes to watch Seth sit on one of the tables, his feet on a bench. "To be sold, Kada. Sold like slaves to the damnable Shri-Lan."

Seth's cup paused halfway to his lips. "What?"

The captain nodded. "We're coming apart. I can feel it. There are many among the Arawaj who want to align with the Shri-Lan, Sebasta most of all. Fucking traitors. And the price of that is a handful of spanners who know nothing more than working on an old smuggler's barge."

"Such an alliance was once nearly achieved," Seth reminded him.

"And we've worked hard to make certain it never comes to pass. We won't bow to the Shri-Lan. Nothing but wealth and power matters to them. They're no better than the Commonwealth spreading like a tumor through this region."

"So you tried to get your spanners out of the way."

"Aye, and failed. When those traitors heard I was leaving Tadonna before the Union soldiers close the noose around our necks out there, they tracked me here." He laughed without humor at the blood on the floor. "And look how I got paid for my effort."

"Where is this trade happening?"

"Do you think they'd tell me that?" Phar roared and slammed his fist onto the table. His other hand immediately went to his injured shoulder and he lowered his head, reminded of his defeat. "They're gone, Kada. And it's my fault for choosing this dump to hand them over to you. I don't know how they'll cope. They loathe Shri-Lan as much as they hate the Commonwealth. We saw to that."

Seth nodded, aware of his complete lack of sympathy for the captain's regrets. These spanners he just lost to the Shri-Lan would have been brainwashed by Arawaj doctrine until there was nothing but distrust of all that the Commonwealth brought to the sector. It would take Union experts a long time to bring them around, using decompression and therapy methods that often succeed and sometimes failed. Rebel or not, a spanner capable of cracking a keyhole was worth any expense to ensure they did so for the Union. But now the prospect of adding four more spanners to Air Command's fleet suddenly seemed like a very remote possibility.

"Do you have any names? The ship they're using? Anything?"

Velen Phar heaved himself to his feet and went to the door. "Erron!"

It took a few minutes before the Human rebel who had spoken to Seth earlier came into the room. He stared at the blood on the floor, looking like he had seen more than his share of the stuff today. "Air Command just came through the jumpsite," he reported. "Battlecruiser, even. We better get on our way."

Phar jerked his thumb at the man. "Zev Erron. He talked to Vichal's posse some before things got ugly."

"I'm looking for the spanners," Seth told him.

"They're gone."

Seth glanced at the captain. "Where do you find these geniuses?" He nodded toward a video screen on the wall. "Can I see them?"

Phar nodded to Erron who worked with the display to bring up video profiles of the four spanners. The information listed for them was thin. Names, physical description, nothing more. And images. Seth cocked his head and squinted at the greasy screen. "GenMods?"

"Some minor alterations," the captain admitted.

Seth stood up and walked closer to the display. A pale, white-haired woman with a woeful expression. An unsmiling male without hair on his head or brow, wearing a long caftan over baggy trousers. A dark-haired youth with a devilish smile that begged to be echoed. And, finally, another woman with a thick mop of hair as black as a Centauri's. Only one eye was visible behind the hair falling into her face but it was also black, lacking the deep violet common among Centauri. All of them seemed related; tall, long-limbed like Centauri or their Delphian cousins, with sharply defined features. There was something unsettling about them. Seth spent many of the solitary hours aboard the *Dutchman* immersed in the study of Trans-Targon and the creatures that inhabited it, but he had never seen sentients like these. He wasn't even sure exactly what seemed so odd about them. "Didn't think Arawaj meddled with genetics."

Phar shrugged. "They're damn prodigies. Uncanny spatial memories. That one there, Ciela, can tap an exit like she's got one foot in subspace already. Damn brilliant."

"And working for a gunrunner," Seth scoffed. The woman gazed back at him from the screen with an expression suggesting that something amused her even though not a hint of a smile showed on her face. She wore boots, faded black trousers and a snug shirt along with a holster. The capable-looking image of a warrior was ruined by thin green streaks in her hair and a mass of pink beads wrapped around her neck.

"They're working for the cause," the captain corrected. "In whatever way they can." He turned to Zev Erron. "Did you get anything from Vichal's group? Any talk between them?"

Erron scowled at Seth, possibly for having been called a gunrunner. Or a genius. "Vichal was going to meet up with Sebasta's group coming in on a Titan class freighter. Retrofitted. Legit transport. Grains. Pretty safe from searches 'cause you can scan for that without boarding. Slow, though."

"Half of the scows here at Titans," Seth said.

"That's all he said. No one mentioned where they were going but it won't be the jumpsite, that's for sure. They wouldn't risk getting hassled outside Tayako air space by that Union ship."

Seth nodded, mostly to himself. Even if Air Command left them unmolested, the jumpsite led to Zera, a sector heavily patrolled these days. Sebasta was sure to head for the keyhole instead. Seth's onboard navigator had reported just two known exits from there, one leading to the Mrak system, the other to Feron.

"Feron," Seth said thoughtfully. "Must be heading to Feron. Nothing happening in the Mrak sector these days."

"Seems likely," Phar said. "But there's only one more keyhole in that sub-sector. At least only one *they* know of."

Seth looked up. "What do you mean? Are there more?"

The captain shrugged. "I'm a smuggler. We know where to hide."

"Mind sharing the co-ords?"

"You're a spanner now?"

"I just like to collect information."

"Forget it. I doubt your ship would even recognize that second one if you flew into it." His eyes narrowed. "And that's final. I think I've bled enough for one day."

* * *

"*Dutchman* to Tower," Seth said after opening a local com channel once back aboard his ship. A report on his screens showed that an Air Command transport had indeed spanned the jumpsite and headed this way. No doubt someone had sent a message about Arawaj brawling amongst their own. Few rules governed the faction but they weren't given to murdering each other on a public and largely neutral port. It would be enough to pique Air Command's curiosity. If nothing else, a visit by an Air Command patrol would ensure the more law abiding folks that Tayako Station wasn't about to become another rebel lair.

"Tower," came the lazy reply. Seth recognized a fellow Centauri by the drawl.

"Tower, I'm looking to hitch a ride out of here. Got anyone ready to depart that can pog onto? Save me some coolant."

"You and everybody else. Every time Air Command breezes in we lose business. Where to?"

"Not Zera," Seth said evasively, meaning their only jumpsite, the one decent folks used. The one that just spewed a military ship into the sector. All of the interesting ships would be heading toward the keyhole. At least those who had a spanner capable of using it.

"And you think anyone *not* going there is going to tell us where they're going?"

"Yeah."

There was a pause. "If they did, it might be *Tambda Vi*, possibly *399-CE*. Just guessing."

"Just those two?"

"They might take on a guest or two. For a fee. On the other hand I guarantee both *Nge-2* and the *Hajsa* would just take your plane and space you as soon as they clear Tayako. Don't let the grain bins fool you."

Seth made a note of those names. *Nge-2* sounded like a Noth ship unlikely to carry oxygen but the *Hajsa* seemed familiar. "Thanks. I'll try to avoid them."

"Seems wise. The *Hajsa*'s not leaving until 39-7 anyway. Being scrubbed for bugs."

"The live sort?" Seth asked, thinking it might be time for his own ship to be inspected for listening and tracking devices. Fortunately, many ports of call offered the service if you knew whom to ask.

"Yeah. *Hajsa* picked up something nasty on Phi Seven. We had to delouse the entire crew before letting them into the station. This is why I like you all just fine on the other side of the decon screen."

"Can't blame you," Seth said amicably and signed off. He tapped through his archive until he found the ship's name, indeed a Titan class, and several anecdotes linking her to Arawaj owners. There was nothing about the other transports.

He placed his hand onto a sensor on the com console. Taking his time, he encoded a message packet to Targon, the seat of the Union's military in the sector. Specifically, the packet tracked to Colonel Tal Carras, now deeply entrenched in covert operations despite his official retirement.

"Code One, Staff B message direct, closed band." Seth waited for the coding process to begin and composed a message without video, addressing no one. "I've located the spanners where expected, but it seems that other eyes were on them, too. Ivor Sebasta took ownership and is heading for a date with the Shri-Lan, possibly aboard Titan *Hajsa*. The spanners seem to be payment for something. I'm assuming he'll jump to either Feron or Mrak very shortly so you might want to catch the show there. He's still in port - I'll send another message if I find them. If not I'll head to Feron. Send directives, advice and those little biscuits your mom makes. Love, Margaret."

He dispatched the missive to the jumpsite's Union relays and from there onwards to its destination. His work as black ops proxy for one of the Commonwealth governors had suited him well until that disaster over Shaddallam a year ago. Since then, Colonel Carras had been his single point of contact with Air Command, taking advantage of Seth's training and deep cover among rebel entities. Over time, he had come to trust the colonel's instincts for this kind of work and, in turn, the colonel allowed him free reign to determine his methods. Also, he suspected, their collaboration gave the good colonel a way to keep an eye on someone who was once trained to Air Command's highest standards before deciding to go his own way.

His message to Carras would ensure that an Air Command battlecruiser stood ready at the keyhole terminus in each sector by the time Sebasta arrived. Then it was just a matter of ducking out of the way when the shooting started. Seth loved his life and the freedom it gave him to choose his work, but being frequently taken for a rebel came with the job.

Seth once again left his ship, this time heading down the gravity-defying lift from the docking platforms down to the surface of the moon. He emerged inside one of the domed facilities housing the permanent services offered to travelers. For the most part, that included ways and means to get off this rock and get elsewhere. He looked around the gray, echoing hall, hoping it was more air tight than the hangar it resembled.

Apparently, ships and their passengers were shuttled in and out of here with efficiency; only a few bands of travelers made use of this place. Some sort of near-violent argument was going on around a billet station involving what looked like the entire extended clan of a Nebdanese *rhong* and Seth made a wide detour around that one. They were known to spit when angered. A couple of passengers had elected to sleep in the hall; perhaps the accommodations here were too expensive. He didn't want to know why there was a naked Aramese walking about. It was common to see Caspians unclothed, maybe the folks in charge of this place extended the same courtesy to all furred species.

A few careful questions and some coin in the correct hand led him to an access lift to the loading platform where the *Hajsa* moored. Unlike the activity on the other dock, here everything seemed in motion. Bins of standard sizes and shapes moved along magnetized rails at dizzying speeds, apparently unconcerned about pedestrians getting in the way. Cargo bays yawned open to admit the containers as Tayako's trade goods were transferred from merchant shuttles arriving from the surface to the freighters heading into other parts of Trans-Targon. Scanners at the entrances looked for destination information, contaminants and contraband. Some dock hands moved among all that, supervising whatever here might need supervision.

Seth ducked out of the way of a trolley loaded with someone's crew heading somewhere and stepped up to an open window from which food was served to passersby.

He settled on a packet of *daijo* bean curds and declined the offer of the thick, syrupy liqueur favored on Tayako. The curds weren't bad but he wondered when he last had a real meal. "You wouldn't have seen a couple of Centauri uglies walking around, would you?" he said conversationally to the woman serving him. He pointed his skewer toward the entrance to the *Hajsa*. "Looking for the chief or first mate."

The Human looked at him as though he lacked the

fundamentals of common sense. "What? After what went on before you think I'd be pointing them out?"

He smiled his best and let his eyes linger on her pretty, if tired, face, wondering what had brought someone of this relatively rare species to serve snacks in the Badlands. At another time, he would have asked her to share her story, another piece for the vast puzzle he had worked on for years in trying to understand the people of Trans-Targon. "Yes, I do." He pushed another bit of currency across the steam table.

She blushed under his scrutiny but quickly took his money. "Most of them are back aboard. Cleaning crew's gone now. They been keeping to themselves, anyway. Not even sent for food. Other than you, no one's come looking for them."

Seth nodded. No doubt they'd want to keep anyone from noticing four reluctant spanners in their midst. "Did you catch any names?"

"No." She glanced across the traffic between them and the docks to find a group of people clustered around a Caspian in bright yellow coveralls. "That's the boss over there. Shouting at the controller. What'd you want with him? He's not friendly."

Seth reached up to loosen a few strands of hair to let them obscure the small metal implants at his temples. In these parts, only navigators and those who operated heavy machinery would be using a direct neural interface. "Going to get a job," he said.

FOUR

"This board is totally sub-standard. I don't know how you expect me to work with this." Ciela stood before the manual control panel managing all functions of the *Hajsa*, hands on hips and an appalled look on her face. The helmsman paused his preparations for departure from Tayako Station to frown at her impertinence.

The hulking Centauri leader standing far too close behind her cursed. "You just got off a tinbucket heap of a freighter. This is what you're used to."

"Pfft," she said, testing his patience a little further. "Your interface mods look like someone dropped them randomly. If that display is correct, you don't even have your coolant gauges calibrated for this sector. And look at that bench! If you expect me to jump I'll want that cleaned up."

Ivor Sebasta growled but did not snap at her the way she had heard him snap at his crew members. She had gambled that he would indulge her as Velen Phar had and so far that was working. They had nothing to gain by being treated like prisoners. She looked past him at the others huddled in confusion by the door to the bridge, guarded by several oversized Humans. Miko's brow furrowed as he tried to decide what she was up to. Deely glowered at her, buying her act as much as Sebasta was. Luanie was still crying.

"You don't have to jump at all," Sebasta said. "My spanner can get us through that keyhole just fine."

"That might be best. I need to sleep anyway. Want to be in top shape to meet the new bosses." She avoided Deely's angry expression, already too intent on hiding the fear that threatened to paralyze her. "That last jump just about did me in and I've only had a few hours to rest up."

"As you wish, Princess," Sebasta said. He gestured to his guards who began to herd their charges from the bridge.

"You are traitor and a disgrace to the Arawaj cause!" Deely shouted at Sebasta. "We will not stand by while you make pact with the Shri-Lan. Murderers and criminals, all of them."

"Yes, yes," the Centauri said. "Are you done? You don't really have a say in this."

"I will not work for them! And I won't work for you. You are no better than the Union overlords." He shook off Luanie's hand when she grasped his arm. "I can't believe you're doing this, Ciela! Did they get to you, too?"

Ciela walked a few steps toward him, pleased when no one stopped her. "This won't help us, Deely. He's right, we don't have a choice. And maybe it's time we admitted that we need the Shri-Lan to get ahead. Alone, we'll never make a difference to anything the Commonwealth does to these worlds."

"How can you say that? Look at all we've already done. It's because of us that Caspia is free of Union interference."

She shook her head. "You know that's not so. I've thought about this for a long time now. I'm sorry I didn't come to you with this, first. I didn't want Velen to know. But I made my choice. Please, be sensible."

"Listen to the girl," Sebasta advised, a cruel grin on his face. "She's got a good head on her. Not like some of you."

Ciela glanced at Miko and had to look away again. He knew her better than the others and she hoped he could keep the small grin from his lips a little while longer. She turned back to Sebasta. "Just give them time. I can get them to understand."

"You better. I'll not have us embarrassed in front of Shri-Lan leadership. The folks coming to meet you are highly placed. This is our chance to show them that we are sincere. That's not going to happen with a bunch of fanatics happy to keep fighting with sticks and suicide missions."

"Ciela," Deely pleaded. "Don't do this."

She did not look at him. For all his stand-offish, cantankerous ways, she loved him dearly and had done so for as long as she could remember. It hurt to see him doubt her like this. "It's for the best. He's right. With just a little of Shri-Lan resources, we wouldn't have to creep around the Badlands in junk farm vehicles."

"Watch it," Sebasta said. He waved his arm. "Take them away. The girl can have Jula's cabin." He glared at Deely. "Lock the other three up. Separately. They can have a proper bed when they've come to their senses."

Miko winced at Ciela as they were led away and then glanced at Deely. If he understood her plan, he would not now have a chance to explain it to the others.

Not that she had a plan. All that could save them now was to find a way to get off this freighter and seek refuge with the administration of this station. Would they stand against a crew of Arawaj traitors? Would they fear reprisal, after what happened on the *Othani*? In many ports, locals who had nothing to gain from rebel activities but much to lose if they stood against them simply turned away when they could. The rebels were Air Command's problem. In places where Air Command had no jurisdiction, that problem landed on the local government. And for many of those, avoidance, if not outright collusion, was the best way to stay healthy and, if done right, very wealthy.

She, too, went to the door. "Please don't hurt them," she said when Sebasta followed her into the narrow corridor. The remnants of ozone and disinfectant stung her nose as they walked to the crew quarters. "They are my friends. They... they just don't understand. Things are changing. The

Arawaj must change, too."

He peered at her through narrowed eyes. "Who would hurt a spanner? The worst they'll find is an empty stomach and a cold floor to sleep on. I don't intend to coddle them. They're spanners, not imbeciles. If they don't find their way, they'll end up working in servitude. You and I both know that our Shri-Lan leaders will have more confidence in us if your friends didn't fight us over every jump they make."

"They won't," she promised. "Let me talk to them. I'll make them see. They can't work well if they're frightened or angry. None of us can. We almost lost Deely on the way here because of that pirate."

"You'll talk to them once we clear Tayako," Sebasta said. Apparently his trust in her as a newfound ally didn't prevent him from making hostages of her friends. When she started to object he raised a hand and quickly scanned up and down the hall. "We are both clear that our Shri-Lan partners expect more than just four new spanners, am I right?"

Her steps faltered when he said that but the odd stumble was to be expected in this gravity. "Of course," she said lightly, recovering. How much did he know? "We must pool all of our resources if we want to defeat our oppressors."

* * *

Ciela waited only long enough for the corridor to clear before slipping out of her assigned room again. She walked purposefully back to the lift, her finely honed navigator's mind studying and remembering the ship's design and measuring distances as she worked her way to the main processor of the *Hajsa*.

All of this would have been far easier if someone hadn't taken her data sleeve, she thought moodily as she tried to decipher signage written in something that didn't even look like writing. But she had spent most of her life on ancient wrecks like the *Hajsa* and the basic configuration felt familiar.

An access panel she had noticed earlier beckoned her with a tantalizing array of apparently active controls, but there were people in the hall. Sebasta had decided not to make a prisoner of her but surely a stranger poking around the com system was going to get noticed. She leaned against the wall by the lift, watching, waiting for her chance. A direct link to the central processor was what she wanted, the com system would do if that's all there was.

A young Caspian hurried past, or as fast as his clawed and oversized feet would allow him to hurry, with barely a glance in her direction. She knew little about Caspians but something had this one in a bit of a lather. Another rebel caught up to him and she heard their loud whispers from a distance. She hoped that whatever was going on didn't mean trouble for her and the other spanners.

She worried about them. Luanie would be frightened. As would Miko but he'd look after her. Deely had likely withdrawn into that crusty shell that none of them could get through when he was in a mood. He'd be furious with her. Would he really think her a traitor? These people just murdered Vichal's gang for no reason other than to avoid paying for the spanners. Did he really think she'd cooperate with people who would do such a thing? Sometimes she wanted to shake the man to get him to look past his endless calculations.

Ciela stepped into the lift and dropped to the lower floor, hoping to find a less conspicuous way to access the ship's database. With luck, it would show the location of the prisoners. The passage now before her lay empty and she smiled when she saw far more extensive access ports at the far end of the corridor. Other than a low thrumming note in the air, silence prevailed.

She hurried to a wall display beside a sliding door marked with more of those indecipherable symbols. Her nervous breathing seemed to echo in this space and she paused a moment in search for some semblance of calmness. Her people managed their resources far more efficiently than most species and she was able to quiet herself as she placed her hands on the panel. Shutting out her surroundings, she linked her neural interface to the ship's system and carefully interacted with the database, avoiding command functions, using the com system to find her way into the processors. The talents that made her a superior navigator also allowed her a near perfect interface between mind and machine. Her Arawaj training ensured that her contact circumvented security failsafes.

The ship's schematics were easy to decipher now. Within just moments she knew the design, its modifications, its weaknesses and its secrets as well as if she had worked here for years.

"Aren't you a beauty," she murmured when the larger of the two cargo holds revealed only a single row of grain bales around its perimeter, leaving plenty of space for a Fleetfoot cruiser, completely powered down and hard to detect within this apparently ill-used hulk of a long-range hauler. It left doubt whether the dorms and cabins were occupied by deck hands or Arawaj troops.

She shifted her attention to the surveillance system which also included locator scanners. One by one, the most likely locations of the other spanners became apparent. She knew them well enough to recognize their life signs, size, gestures even through the impersonal mechanical sensors.

Ciela whirled around and nearly stumbled over her own feet when the door beside her slid open. She grimaced when her interface with the computer severed abruptly.

"What are you doing down here?" A Centauri woman dressed in engineer's coveralls stepped into the corridor.

"Hungry," Ciela said. "Ivor said I could have some food. I'm looking for the galley."

The engineer regarded her coolly for a too-long moment. That wasn't unusual; most people had trouble deciding to which Prime species Ciela belonged. While most assumed her to be Centauri, another Centauri was not so easily fooled and often pegged her as Human. "Down here?" the woman said finally. "Get back topside and head aft. It's not hard to miss. Good luck finding anything edible now. Third shift is kind of thin."

"That's okay. I could eat *churry* curry right about now."

The Centauri smiled and began to say something when her wrist array warbled a notice. She unspooled the data sheet from its housing and slipped its tab over her finger. Then she flipped her hand over to show Ciela the image of the ship's first mate now in her palm, rolling her eyes as she did so.

"Krinn, we're taking off now," he said. "Get your crew together."

"Now?" Ciela said. "I thought they were still irradiating the... the holds."

The woman looked up from rapidly entering some commands into her palm. "Air Command's on its way, so I guess we're done with the scrubbing. You better get back to your cabin. Stay out of the way. Things can get crazy when we have to bug out so fast." She turned and left without another word.

Now a voice from unseen speakers in the ceiling also announced the imminent departure. Ciela raced to the end of the hall and used a service access tube to climb up to the main level of the ship. The crew quarters were clustered in the aft section and she headed that way, having been informed by the ship that Miko was locked up in a storage room down there. She met only two crew members who glanced at her curiously but continued to their stations. The door of the storage room was unguarded and the lock unsecured.

"Ciela!" Miko exclaimed and then covered his mouth when she hushed him. He had been busy with removing a wall panel, hoping to get at the key plate from inside the room.

She looked up at the warped edge of the sheet. "I know where the others are. Quick. We're about to leave the station. If we don't get off this ship we've had it."

He smiled broadly, flashing brilliant teeth and deep blue eyes. "I *knew* you didn't go bad on us! You had me going for a while, though. And you totally convinced Deely. Poor guy."

"Serves him right." Ciela peered out into the hall. "He's down that way, near my cabin."

"How are we going to get off this ship?"

She blinked. "Um, I have no idea."

"You think maybe there's a door open somewhere?"

She grinned. "Yeah. Or a window. Come on."

They scurried along the passage, stopping to listen to the sound of voices and the tread of weighted boots on the deck plates. The vibrations rumbling through the ship were clearly those of the pogs slowly releasing from the docking clamps.

Ciela held her arm out to stop Miko from rounding a corner. "Centauri up ahead."

They edged forward to see a tall man standing by what used to be Ciela's cabin, apparently having just knocked. He carried a covered bowl, possibly food for her. He wore his hair fairly long in contrast to the bald pate favored by many Arawaj grunts but his clothes and weapons suggested guard duty or combat. Heavy boots, scuffed trousers, a well-worn flight jacket no doubt stolen from a Union officer. He opened the cabin door and peered inside. After a moment he closed it again and strode away.

Ciela nudged Miko to continue their quest to reach Deely's prison. "That one," she whispered just as someone's arm snapped out from an open door to wrap an iron fist around her neck. Miko cried out in surprise and fear when the Centauri stepped into the passage and shoved her against the wall.

"Shut up," the stranger snapped. He checked her for weapons with a few practiced pats but it took only a glance at Miko's snug clothing to see that the man was unarmed.

Ciela dug her nails into the Centauri's wrist, encountering only the thin layer of graphene cloth that held his data array. She tried to kick at him but he stretched a leg out in front of hers. "Stop it," he hissed. "I'm here to help you. Velen Phar sent me."

She gave up her struggle at the mention of the name. The

stranger overpowered her easily anyway. He released her carefully, as if not quite trusting her to stay where she was.

"You didn't have to choke me," she said angrily, rubbing her neck. "Who are you?"

"Don't worry about it. We have to get off this ship."

"Really. What do you think we're trying to do?"

He jerked his chin into the direction from which they had come. "Exits are that way."

"We're not leaving without the others."

Miko nodded emphatically. "Deely's in that cabin there."

Seth stood aside when Ciela brushed past him to access the key panel. He watched as she manipulated the display until a soft buzz indicated success. Light from the hall fell into the small space when the door drew aside. "Deely, are you in here?"

Something moved in the corner and, slowly, the spanner came to his feet. "Ciela?"

"Yes, come on. Hurry."

He stepped into the hall, blinking. The long tunic he always kept spotless and free of wrinkles looked like something dragged around the floor for a while. "What... what's going on? What are you doing?"

"Later. Just come along. We have to get Luanie."

Miko grasped his arm to propel him along. "Does this teach you to trust our Ciela?" he said to Deely, ignoring the man's scowl.

"Shh, down this way." She steered them around a corner until they stopped near the ship's small mess hall. "There's a locked storage room in there," she said.

Seth glanced at his wrist. "Two other people in there, moving around. Cooks, probably." He drew his gun. As an afterthought, he drew another which he handed to her. He raised an eyebrow in question.

She nodded and hefted the gun. "Go."

He released the door and, keeping his gun out of sight, stepped into the galley. "Are we in time for dinner?" he asked the Human facing him across a conveyor stacked with bins. He gestured for Ciela to find the storage room.

"What kind of a question is that? We're getting ready to leave," the cook said, looking from Ciela to the two men standing in the doorway. Miko was anxiously scanning the hallway. "What do you want in there," he added when she rattled the handle on the food locker.

Seth raised his gun. "Over there," he directed, and then looked to the second crewman. "You, too. Move."

Ciela aimed her pistol and shot at the mechanical lock. It twisted under the assault and she stepped back to kick it away. Luanie emerged almost at once and Ciela wrapped a protective arm around the woman's shoulder. "It's all right," she whispered. "We're here."

"So dark in there," Luanie said. "I was so scared."

Seth looked around as if counting heads and then quickly shot both of the staffers.

"What are you doing!" Deely exclaimed.

"They're just out for a while," Seth said. He leaned against a cart on the conveyor to shove it aside and then looked down into the shaft used to supply ships and take away refuse. There would be people down there, and perhaps safety. "We're going this way."

"Are you crazy?" Miko said. "That goes straight down to the surface."

"Hush," Ciela said. "Pull your inserts." She sat on the edge of the conveyor and unclasped the pockets on her boots holding the thin counterweight sheets. The others followed suit, not without extreme misgivings about leaping down an open tunnel to whatever awaited them below, even at reduced gravity.

A strident alarm brayed once in the hall and Seth whirled around when the access port to the delivery shaft slammed shut and the airlock pressurized.

"What? Are we leaving?" Luanie said.

"Seems like it," Seth said. He checked his proximity scanner. "We'll try to make it to the escape pods. If we drop as soon as we leave the station we should be able to get back to the moon."

"Should!" Deely muttered and reinserted the weight he had just removed from his boot.

Miko nudged Ciela and then cast a quick glance at Seth, a theatrical leer on his face.

She frowned and looked over to where the Centauri crouched to help Luanie with her weights. As usual, Miko had found a way to ignore all things dark and dire and turned his attention to more amusing things. Ciela watched the stranger's long-fingered hands re-fasten Luanie's boot and smooth her skirt back down over her knees before rising to pull her to her feet. It wasn't easy to ignore the lean grace of his body and the assuring smile he gave to the woman. The smile extended to the warm glow of his eyes and Luanie returned it tentatively.

Ciela sighed and punched Miko with her elbow, as she had done a thousand times before. Would he ever grow up?

"Out," Seth said and went to the door, again checking for people in the corridor. "To the left. There should be a service passage." He hooked his hand around Ciela's arm when the others filed past him into the hall.

"What?" she said.

"Let's see how smart you are." He pointed at a com panel by the door. "Get in there and block all access to the portside escape pods except the one from here. You should be able to go through maintenance for that, not security." He turned to the others. "Go! That way!"

"Ciela!" Miko whispered urgently, unwilling to leave her.

She tucked her gun into the back of her trousers and her hair behind her ears. "Go, I'll catch up," she said without looking at him, already tapping her way into the system. Her neural interface kept the security measures at bay while she coded an emergency lock on some of the compartments, making it look like a pressurization problem. It would also put the escape vehicles into standby mode. She hoped. "If they're not onto us by now, they soon will be."

"Wait," Seth said and placed his hand over hers to stop

her rapid commands. He waved to the others waiting down the hall. "Get in there. Weights off now."

He steadied Ciela with his arm when a shudder went through the ship. Both swayed on their feet when the *Hajsa*'s thrusters came online and the gravity spinners wound up in preparation for lift off. The maneuver, for an instant, engaged every system in one more maintenance check for any last minute faults. Indicators flashed on all components of the panel. "Now."

Ciela entered the final sequence to activate the internal pressure doors at the aft section of the ship. A notice appeared on the panel, easily dismissed as yet another task on the engineers' list of things to do.

"Nice work," he said, flashing a broad grin. She noticed a faded scar above his eye and then saw the neural node embedded in his temple.

"You're a pilot?"

"Yeah." He bent to wrestle with his counterweights again.

"So where's your ship?"

Luanie's scream reached their ears from the service passage, followed by angry shouts warning them to stay on the ground.

"Crap!" Seth grasped her arm. "Run."

"I can't!" She stumbled forward, nearly glued to the spot by the weights on her feet.

He lurched to the cabin door opposite the galley and shoved her inside. They scrambled to unload their boots, aware of more shouts in the hall. Clearly, they heard Deely yelling at the rebels who seemed to have caught up with them now.

Seth looked around. "Come on." He pulled her up and through a shared decon chamber into a second crew cabin.

"Stop. We can't just leave them!"

The door beside them slid open to admit two Arawaj, weapons drawn. Seth swept the leg out from under the first so quickly that his partner stumbled over him, taking Seth's elbow to the side of his head. Ciela darted forward and pressed her gun to the downed man's head, silencing him. Seth grappled with the other until something snapped audibly, followed by a silence that made clear that it wasn't just a bone that had snapped. She froze until she saw that it was the rebel who fell to the floor.

"Gods," she huffed, watching Seth wipe blood from a split lip. "You're fast."

He moved to the door, not even winded from the effort of this brief but intense bout. "It's all in the wrist," he said and motioned her to follow.

"The others? They don't know how to fight. We have to help them."

"That's not working so well for us right now. We're just a little outnumbered." He pulled her along the hall until they found another route into the service passage. Someone shouted behind them and both ducked through the opening. "See if you can seal that door."

Ciela glared at him, knowing there was nothing they could do now for the others. But having him point that fact out to her was a little irritating. She drew her pistol and shot the key panel. "There. Sealed."

He exhaled sharply and pushed her further down the hall into the port cluster of escape vehicles, already open and waiting for them. The *Hajsa* held four of these, designed to facilitate a quick exit from the ship, equipped with enough air for a few days for six people. Given the glimpses she had so far of the ship's general upkeep, her faith in their capabilities was limited. "Get in there."

The interior of the pod consisted of a circle of benches, two of them with access to a control panel. She dropped into one of them and snapped into the crash restraints. He sealed the door and took the other seat.

"The *Hajsa*'s already pulled away from the station," she reported after a few moments of checking the pod's displays. "And they got through the compartment doors now. Coming this way."

"So let's go." It took only a few taps on the controls to

catapult the vessel away from the *Hajsa*. Anyone trying to flee a ship in peril was able to execute this maneuver and they were away within seconds. She ground her teeth against the sudden acceleration away from the ship's gravity well and the moon's weaker pull until they finally floated free.

"They're firing!" she yelled.

"What the hell?" He switched on the overhead video display. "Are they insane?"

Not only had the rebel ship opened fire well within the airspace belonging to Tayako Station, they were now clearly intent on destroying the very spanner they had promised to the Shri-Lan. And, of course, the *Hajsa* itself squatted like a bloated beetle between them and the moon now.

He punched up shields that were never meant to stand up to a firefight. "We're going to have to go down."

"Down? What do you mean: 'go down'. You can't be serious!"

A scattered volley of projectiles peppered the shields. The image on their screens rotated as the pod spun away. "I am. I think they're angry."

"Are you sure about that?" she snapped. "You better be one hell of a pilot, whatever your name is." They took another hit. "Those are just warning shots. They could have toasted us by now."

"Did you want to go back?"

She just squinted at him.

He let the pod spin until it pointed generally toward the planet and engaged its bare-bones boosters, doing what he could to keep them dodging in a loose evasive pattern.

"Someone's giving them grief from the station," Ciela reported with her ear to the emergency com system. "Lots of shouting now. Sebasta is accusing us of being Shri-Lan infiltrators."

"Inventive."

"Think they'll send someone after us? *Hajsa* won't be able to enter the atmosphere."

"Depends on how persuasive Sebasta gets. Or how much

coin he's willing to spend." Seth gave her a curious glance. "How much are you worth to him?" She started to answer when another broadside slammed into their shield. "Dammit." Something whined at them about a malfunction. "Hang on, we're going in."

Ciela gripped her armrests, putting all of her faith into this stranger as they barreled into Tayako's outer atmosphere. She might have been screaming.

FIVE

"Waiter! A bottle of wine for my table, please."

The woman bent over an illuminated tabletop map looked up to see who had broken the studious silence of the research room. Her stern face softened to smile at Tal Carras outlined against the light from the corridor.

"Your kind can't afford our selection," she said and left her work to meet the colonel at a more brightly-lit workspace along the wall.

He slid into a chair with an audible grunt and waited for her to take the opposite seat. "I don't know how you can huddle here in the dark all day, Daphine. That's just bad for mind and body."

"So is the wine and sweets you like so much," Major Daphine Verick replied, hinting at the sizeable girth, uncommon for a Centauri, that he had squeezed behind the table.

He nodded when she raised an eyebrow in question and so she activated the nearly invisible partition to create a soundwave-scattering baffle between them and the handful of other agents working here today. None of them had even looked up from their charts and holograms and monitors; down here rank was observed only when the general decided to visit, which wasn't often. Daily briefings kept him abreast of Intelligence developments and his staff came by for more thorough updates. Colonel Carras, operating a team of field agents whose names appeared on no one's roster, was a more frequent fixture.

"What brings you to these hallowed halls?" She watched him access his data sleeve.

"Just trying to put some threads together," he replied. "Probably nothing terribly important but I like things tidy. Probably just gossip."

She nodded. "And you know how much I love gossip."

He chuckled over this, knowing quite well that the woman would rather leap naked into one of the fuming mud cauldrons that clustered near the base here on Targon than disclose anything she didn't have to. Her team ensured that the correct information reached the appropriate ear and nothing leaked unless it was meant to. "Your boys still sorting through the Precia interviews?"

"Endlessly. Ever try to pry information out of a Highland Bellac? They talk for hours without ever saying a thing."

"There's probably an algorithm for that." Carras ran his hand over the dense stubble on his head, forgetting again that he had resumed shaving when he came out of retirement to take over Targon's covert ops. "While on the subject of babbling, I think what I'm looking for is anything you might have in terms of chatter lately. Specifically about some deal between Shri-Lan and Arawaj. Fairly high level, not the usual small-time collusion we see now and again."

She pursed her lips. "Hell, yes. What do you have, Tal? Out with it, I'm taking notes."

He tapped his com screen and played Seth's message for her, recorded only a few hours ago on Tayako station. Verick listened in silence, eyebrows raised.

"Ivor Sebasta," she said when the short message ended. "That name just keeps coming up everywhere. Do we know which spanners he's got his hands on?"

"No. I don't like that at all. We thought all Arawaj spanners are accounted for. But giving up four of them to the Shri-Lan is what interests me."

"And not voluntarily. This isn't the first I've heard about some very serious dissention inside Arawaj. A rising number want to join Shri-Lan. Not just cooperate, but plain out leave the faction. We're not sure if it's a strategic move to strengthen their number against us or just a matter of economics. Arawaj is barely managing to keep their fleet in the air these days."

"So these four spanners are probably a peace offering."

"Seems like it. We know that there is a conference of sorts on Taancerum in a few days. Both Shri-Lan and Arawaj ships are mobilizing but the meeting will be limited to few observers. The more intelligence we pick up the more we think that it's bigger than it looks."

"Taancerum? That is a problem. We can't even get close to the place with our hardware."

"Indeed not. But we've managed to land some Vanguard agents among the Shri-Lan."

"What did they find?"

Verick tapped the table top to activate a hologram. After a brief search she pulled up the most recent files smuggled out of the sub-sector by Air Command agents. The rocky terrain scrolled before them, apparently recorded from orbit, showing a network of canals and rivers crisscrossing the surface. The Union once had an outpost there, a very efficient and self-sustaining, fully enclosed habitat that easily withstood the planet's atmosphere. Taancerum had rich resources of fresh water but the air was unbreathable for most Prime species.

Too remote and of little commercial value other than a few mineral mines, the installation went understaffed and neglected for years until the Shri-Lan, in search for safe havens, took notice. Instead of taking the habitat by force and risking damage, they simply bribed the native population to expel the Union from their planet. Which they did. And so this remote and very secure location fell to the rebels.

"Not keeping up with the landscaping, I see," Carras said

when the image shifted into a broad valley among the mountain ranges and focused on the habitat. A five-sided pyramid, massive compared to its barren surroundings, reached for the sky in a glittering display of solar panels covering all sides. Evidently, in the fifty years since the Shri-Lan took over much of the site had fallen into disrepair. Some of the panels were gone or broken but by the tilt of some of them, the system was still very much in use. The panels provided the electricity needed to separate oxygen from the ground water, sustaining a maximum population of nearly a thousand. A covered concourse led from the pyramid to some low buildings to which cruiser-class ships docked. Anything larger would have to remain in orbit. The image showed several Fleetfoot ships, favored by the Shri-Lan, as well as an astonishing number of Shrills, the small, agile fighter plane used almost exclusively by them. Air Command relied on the more powerful Kites in their fleet.

"They've added a hangar for the Shrills but other than that, nothing much has changed there. Our agents have not been able to access the upper levels of the pyramid, which seems to be a sort of command center for them. We even had hopes that this might actually serve as the current Shri-Lan headquarters but it does not appear that way. They're using most of the lower levels for storing contraband and fuel. We estimate perhaps three hundred rebels there at a time, some with families."

"Cozy. Those are new, though?" Carras' hand moved through a cluster of smaller, rectangular buildings with sloping sides near the foot of the pyramid.

"Yes, looks like a bit of an industry's sprung up there. The locals have gone to work for the Shri-Lan, extracting belene crystal and shipping it out to Pelion. It's worth a fair bit there. Of course, the Shri-Lan collect the largest share of that. In exchange, they provide sugar and *mince*. They seem to be hooked on both now."

Carras grunted in disgust. "I guess we can't expect them to trade anything actually useful with those people." His attention turned back to the pyramid. "As safe a place for their summit as any other. Any approach from above will be spotted and the underground levels are bunkers of solid rock if needed."

"Not to mention that we're not welcome there. The Union Factors won't ever allow us to deploy on Taancerum if the locals don't wish it, no matter who's hiding out there."

Carras looked up. "So who is?"

"One rumor we've heard is that both of Tharron's sons are going to be there for the meeting."

"That's big." Carras tapped a thick finger against his lip, pondering this. The rift between the Shri-Lan and the Arawaj had been steadily widening since the rebel leader died, leaving sons in place whose competence was still in question. The division, of course, was most welcome by Air Command. Any new alliances brought nothing but headache to an already chaotic situation. "If those two attend the chance of a formal alliance is far more likely."

"I'm afraid so. The Brothers wouldn't step out their front door for four spanners, although that's a nice present. For them to show up personally is making this a whole lot more significant. Got any of your people in the area?"

"Not so far. I wanted to hear what you have."

She pointed at his com band. "Who's Margaret?"

Carras winced. "Sethran Kada."

"Kada." Verick actually sighed and rolled her eyes skyward. "Tal, the man is a liability. A freelancer if not outright rebel sympathizer."

"He's not failed me yet," Carras said, feeling oddly defensive. "Probably one of my most effective agents."

"When he's not delivering hostages to the wrong team or destroying evidence when we need it."

Carras smiled grimly. "Fortunately, his specialty is black ops and I no longer have to worry about Vanguard rules. The end justifies the means, Daphine. Mercenaries are always best kept at the end of a long stick and paid in gold."

"Well, he seems to have lost the spanners," she said,

dismissing the agent from her mind. "But I think we can upgrade this event. Sounds like more than just a few disgruntled Arawaj are getting ready to jump ship. Not the sort of expansion we need right now."

"Indeed. Can you get some more ears on the ground? We need to know how many are deserting, which groups are involved, and what they're bringing to the table, other than these four people. This could cause problems in any number of sectors, not to mention Caspia itself."

The major looked across the room to the consoles and map tables that took up most of the darkened space, projecting maps and plans upward. A specialist was walking through the subsector containing Caspia, a vital planet in the Commonwealth expansion plans. Regrettably, it was also the birthplace of the Arawaj movement and still home to many of them. Only a single jump distanced it from Magra where a significant Shri-Lan presence was tolerated by the government of one of the planet's continents. If Caspia slipped through their fingers, so would what remained of Magra. "How are those talks going?"

"They're not. We were hoping to scatter the Caspian group as we did when we liberated Bellac. But if they ally themselves with the Shri-Lan I doubt that Caspia will join the Commonwealth. There isn't a chief on Caspia that doesn't fear Shri-Lan reprisal." He leaned back comfortably and crossed his arms. "I wonder if the less traitorous Arawaj are prepared to do something about this. It's not something they'd just watch from the sidelines."

Verick regarded him through narrowed eyes. "What do you have in mind?"

"Mobilize the radicals. The last thing they want is to partner with the Shri-Lan. If they knew when and where this is happening, they'd want to stir up a little trouble. Shame if the Brothers got in the way of all that."

The major smirked. "Sure would be."

"Wouldn't be the first time Arawaj has done our work for us. Another reason we really don't want these two factions getting along too well."

She nodded thoughtfully. "I know just the man. Sco Cie Pacoby's been ingratiating himself with Ivor Sebasta who seems to be leading this exodus. He'd just as soon eat his own foot than work with Sebasta but it seems to be working. I've got an agent in his house."

Carras winced. "Pacoby's a nasty piece of work."

"But reliably fanatical. We'd assumed he was planning an assassination but now we think he's looking for something bigger to undermine Sebasta and his posse. This is exactly what he's been waiting for. If anyone can get into this pyramid, it's him."

"All right. Have your agents convey the date and location of this meeting. Then leave the playpen to the Arawaj."

"Could get ugly."

"I have no doubt. Be prepared to pull the Vanguard agents out when it does. They're damn expensive to replace."

The major's eyes shifted to the civilian buildings next to the pyramid. "Not just Shri-Lan on site," she said.

Carras nodded. "Mitigate what you can. We cannot allow an alliance."

SIX

"Seth," Seth said.

"Huh?"

He closed his eyes, not quite believing his own senses that the escape pod had finally come to a halt. His fingers searched along the raised tabs along the arm rest of his bench and, one by one, released the restraints that bound his body to the chair. Nothing seemed to be hurting in any extraordinary way. Nothing leaking, also a plus.

"My name is Seth," he said. "Are you all right?"

"Mostly."

He reset the external cameras to scan the vicinity. Although he had never been down here on Tayako before, the terrain around them looked much like the material stored in his archives aboard the *Dutchman*. Flat, marshy, covered in dense ground fog, some rolling hills in the distance. Here and there, stunted growth rose above the mist like motionless creatures observing the alien visitor. The hazy greenish light did not vary from one horizon to the other. Gravity slightly unpleasant, air relatively breathable, population reasonably friendly.

Seth looked over to the girl who was slowly testing her limbs as she sat up on her crash couch. She looked all right, he thought, although both of them should probably run a quick med scan. He allowed himself a quick peek along her nicely shaped torso and was rewarded with an icy glare.

"Not too shaken up? That was quite a ride." The pod entered safely into Tayako's atmosphere but the trip had strained their bodies and protective gear to the extreme. He'd been able to use thrusters and chutes to avoid a hard landing and the wetlands had helped to cushion the blow. No doubt someone had seen them drop, but he was less certain if he wanted to be found here.

"I'm fine." She looked at him more closely, apparently at greater liberty to drop her eyes down to his toes and up again. Her expression suggested a rather unfavorable judgment. "Why did you come here? You said Velen Phar sent you?"

"He did."

"Is it true you're a Union agent paid to collect us?"

"Is that what he told you?"

"I was expecting uniforms."

"It's being cleaned." Seth activated the external scanners to get their bearings and an environmental report. "We need to get away from the pod," he said. "Sebasta might send someone after us. Or someone from town might send a drone to take a look and then report back topside."

"Town? What town?"

He gestured at the screen. "West. Has an airfield. I'd like to get back to my ship."

"I'd like to get back to finding my people."

He stood up and started to open the overhead compartments. "That ship has sailed, lady. Sebasta will be long gone by the time we get up there. Air Command's on its way and he's got an appointment to keep elsewhere."

Her pale forehead furrowed as that realization seemed to sink in. "They're gone," she said. "Gods, how am I going to find them?"

He sniffed a ration packet that someone had opened and left in here. "Well, you're not. One spanner is better than none. I'm taking you out of here."

She continued to stare at nothing for a while before looking up at him. "What? Where?"

"Targon. They'll want to meet you, Spanner."

"You're out of your mind." She moved out of her seat and to the exit hatch of the pod. "You, some hired hand, some Air Command lackey, show up here, lose the others, almost get us killed crash landing down here and now you think I'm going to go anywhere with you?"

"I do."

She yanked the hatch release to flip the door aside. "Which way is the town?"

He leaned past her and pointed west. "That way."

She jumped to the ground, landing with a splash and sinking deep. Thick mist swirled around her legs up to the knees.

"Ciela?"

"What?" She pulled her feet from the muck, struggling with viscosity and high gravity.

He opened a hatch in the floor to retrieve a small backpack containing oxygen. "Supplemental, but you'll need it."

She snatched it from his hand and shrugged it over her shoulder before turning away. He waved and retreated into the pod to resume his inventory of the bins. The emergency food packets and water bags seemed to be relatively recent vintage. A med-kit, shelter and other necessities were also tightly packed in the compartments. He started to load up two backpacks with supplies, whistling.

Ciela returned only minutes later, out of breath and in a hurry to climb back into the hatch. She slammed the door shut and dropped into a bench, soaked to the knees.

"Back so soon?" He gave her a sensor array embedded in a flexible sleeve. "Shouldn't leave home without one of these, you know."

"You could have warned me," she snapped and slipped the band over her hand.

He sat down and once again ran the pod's scanners as

well as the one on his forearm. No ships approached, nothing moved out there except for the local wildlife. "This is much more fun." He nodded toward her feet. "Are those waterproof?"

"Yes."

"All right. How about you pay a little attention to where you are instead of stomping off on your quest to rescue your fellow rebels? Those things that almost chewed your feet off out there will actually take a leg if you let enough of them get close. Not to mention that you decided to march off to a town that's almost six hours' walk away from here without even taking a bag of water. You can't drink that stuff out there. Is this how they train Arawaj where you come from?"

"I'm a navigator. We don't camp out much."

"Taking a gun is also helpful. You don't know who's in that town." He stooped to pick up the weapon she had dropped during their cast off from the *Hajsa*. He snatched it away when she reached for it. "You'll just end up shooting me with it. I'm against that."

"I'm not going to shoot you."

"You're a rebel. That's your job." He pushed one of the backpacks toward her. "Are you ready to do this properly? If you follow my lead, we might get out of this bog in one piece."

She scowled at him. "You hope. How do you know so much about the place?"

"I like to read." He studied her sullen face. Even more so than the image he had been shown aboard the *Othani*, the unsettling *otherness* of her features continued to puzzle him. A Prime species, obviously, one of the people from a dozen different worlds that, for reasons much speculated upon but never proven, shared almost all of their DNA. Small differences set Centauri, Human, Delphian and Feydan apart only slightly; larger differences, like those found among the Caspians and Aramese, were the result of evolution in isolation. Interbreeding was rarely successful.

Ciela appeared Human, but not like any of the Human

sub-sets he had studied. Her voice sounded vaguely Magran but the sentient species of Trans-Targon in possession of a suitable larynx used hundreds, perhaps thousands of dialects. Her skin carried a pallor more common to Delphians or Bellacs, but the dark eyes and hair resembled neither. All that, combined with a lithe body, made up a rather attractive package. "You're a GenMod, then?" he said.

"You disapprove?"

"I disapprove of you being an Arawaj, but I have that in common with a lot of people."

She shrugged. "But you think being a headhunter is a noble way to spend your time?"

He almost voiced a retort to that when it occurred to him that she was probably right. He thought of the Caspian runaway he had delivered to Ton Kedi's group and now here he was, stealing Arawaj spanners for use by the Union. Hunting rebels seemed to have become a way of life lately.

He looked into those strange eyes that now watched at him questioningly when he remained silent. If he met her in battle, he'd shoot her without a thought. She was worth something to the Union and so he'd deliver her to her fate. Perhaps they could turn her into a useful navigator, perhaps not. It wasn't his problem.

"Let's go," he said, no longer interested in baiting her. Arawaj or not, she was in a bad spot, alone and probably frightened despite her belligerent facade. No need to make things worse for her. "This pod's a magnet for looters."

"What about those things out there? Big worms in the fog."

"Walk fast," he suggested.

The bleary, shadowless light outside had not changed when they left the vehicle; Seth's data sleeve informed him that they still had about twenty hours of sunlight but, at this latitude, a very short twilight before dark. His scan also told of higher ground ahead, slightly to the south of the town. He adjusted Ciela's backpack, pleased and a little surprised when she did not complain about its weight. He hoped they would not have to use the supplies he had assembled. The thought of spending any amount of time down here lacked significant appeal. Each of them now used an oxygen supply that enriched Tayako's gas mixture through thin tubes running beneath their noses.

"There! See that?"

He peered into the direction she pointed out and saw the snaking motion of the bog worm moving toward them. The drifting mist obscured its size but a quick blast from his gun stopped it immediately. "Scan the ground for more of these. Also look for deep spots as we go. We're heading up that way." He pulled her back when she went to take a closer look at the dead worm. Within moments, others arrived and only the splashing sound and agitated swirls of mist hinted at the savage feast they had served up.

"Cannibals," she said, wrinkling her nose in disgust. She activated her data sleeve to probe the terrain. After a moment she began to walk ahead of him, silent, only occasionally pointing out an undulating shape moving beneath the ground fog. She was quick to interpret the scanner's display and steered them around water-filled ditches and what turned out to be massive wads of egg clusters on the soggy ground. He began to worry less about her ability to keep up with the forced march.

They stopped for a rest and a quick bite only an hour into the hike, already feeling the strain of the planet's gravity as well as the swamp sucking on their boots with every step. The emergency rations felt a bit like chewing on damp socks and neither bothered to take a closer look at it.

"Hear that?" she said.

"What?" He looked up and then checked his scanner. "Four vehicles. Skimmers, I think. Coming from over there."

"Good! Maybe we can get a ride to town." She noticed his hand on the safety switch of his gun. "You're worried about them?"

"Aren't you? Stay close."

The noise of the machines drew closer, rapidly. Out of

the fog, four flat-bottomed scooters of some sort appeared, shaped otherwise like skimmers but held so low to the ground that their thrusters threw up tall plumes of water in their wake. Seth's hopes for a peaceful encounter diminished when the sleds circled them and they saw four armed men, waving guns over their heads and whooping like adolescents on their first solo trip on a skimmer.

He drew his own gun but the rider behind him approached closely and looped a rope around his arms and waist. The noose closed at once and he was thrown to the ground.

"Hey!" Ciela shouted. She rushed to Seth who was struggling to keep his head above the swamp water as he tried to get up on his knees.

One of the men pulled up beside her and gripped the back of her vest. He dragged her for a moment before pulling her into the footwell in front of his seat. His boot held her down while his gun stabbed her neck.

The others had come to a halt as well. Seth had risen onto his knees but when he tried to get up the man holding the rope heaved on it to force him down again. Tayako had no native sentient population and these thugs, under a crust of dirt, poorly-used clothes and tattoos, appeared to be Human or Feydan. Nothing about them suggested a rebel affiliation. None carried an oxygen supply; apparently they had been on the planet long enough to accustom themselves to the atmosphere. One of the men briefly left his skimmer to wrench Seth's gun from his grip.

"Let me go!" Ciela shouted and struggled against the boot pressing into her belly. In reply to that, the fist holding the gun to her head smashed into the side of her head.

"What do you want," Seth said, back on his feet now and furious over having been caught so easily out here.

"We got what we want," a Human whose entire head and face seemed to be covered in scraggly red hair answered. "They said there was a girl out here. A pretty girl worth a pretty coin. And a ship. Have you seen a ship out here?"

Seth did not reply. The rope around his arms seemed to tighten with every move he tried to make.

There was rough laughter and then the red man waved to two of his companions. "You take them back. We'll see what else we can find out here."

Ciela shrieked when the sleds set in motion again. Seth twisted desperately when he was thrown down again, now dragged behind one of the skimmers. Bitter swamp water rushed into this nose and mouth and he struggled to gulp for air as best as he could. The hose feeding a thin stream of additional oxygen into his lungs tore away when the tank on his back slipped off his shoulder. Something scraped along his forearm; it seemed that submerged rocks were going to make matters much worse for him.

Then it all stopped. The sound of the skimmers, the rush of muddy water, the lunatic whooping of the driver. The sled dragging him landed with a splash and Seth nearly collided with it before he also came to a halt. He scrambled to his knees and then up onto his feet to see Ciela struggling with her captor on the other vehicle. The man was doubled over and did not fight her when she grabbed for his gun and shot him.

The other thug had fallen off his sled and Seth lunged forward to ram head-first into his mid-riff when he ran toward Ciela. Both of them slammed back into the bog and Seth, heftier than his opponent, rolled over him to press his face into the mud. Ciela reached them within moments and dispatched this one, too.

Seth raised himself up, struggling for air. She tugged on the rope cutting into his arms. There was blood on the knife she used to cut it. He doubled over to put his hands on his knees, still breathing harshly. "Where the hell did you get the blade?" he coughed and straightened up again.

"You didn't say I couldn't have a knife. You're just timid about me having guns." She thrust the robber's gun at him and squared her shoulders defiantly. For all her bravado he saw the hand that still held the knife trembling before she put it behind her back. She kept her eyes averted from the dead man on the ground.

A distant buzzing sound drew their attention. "They're back," she cried, panicked by the sight of the other two locals returning.

He handed her the gun back and searched the dead man for another. Too late to veer away, the red-haired leader and his companion were already in range of Seth's well-placed fire. Ciela, at his side, shot wildly in their direction until both men and machines were on the ground.

Silence returned to the marsh, disturbed only by Seth's harsh breathing. Ciela untwisted the oxygen bottle from his shoulder and straightened the hose. He nodded when he felt air once again reach his lungs.

"You know," he rasped, "for an Arawaj, you are a terrible shot."

She looked as if she was about to snap something back at him but then suddenly her brow cleared and she grinned. "Yeah, I am." She gave him her gun and, after a short and silent stand-off, also the knife. "Are you all right? You're bleeding."

Seth raised his arm to see blood seeping through his torn sleeve. "Cazun..." he breathed. He staggered back to the inert skimmers where he paused to shoot into the roiling activity around the dead robber, grimacing when some of the bog worms surfaced, showing pink bellies. "Let's get out of here."

She climbed into the sled and started to work with its control panel.

"What happened?" Seth said. "Why did we stop?"

She raised her arm without looking up to show him her data sleeve. "I looped into the sled's control and cut the power link on both of them. Idiot wasn't watching." She tapped the console. "I hope I didn't ruin this permanently."

He smiled, surprised and a little confused. "You did this while bouncing around on that sled? With that guy's foot on you?" He went to check the other vehicle but it would not start up at his command. The driver sprawled over the seat and he saw the deep stab wound that had given her the chance to disarm and shoot him. He returned to watch her start up the other sled. "Tell me, though, why didn't you just take off? Leave me here?"

She shifted when he sat on the skimmer behind her, silent until they had returned to their backpacks. She watched him load the packs onto the back of the vehicle and climb back on before she spoke. "Those men are probably an example of what's going on in that town. I'm not a pilot. I can't get out of this place by myself."

He cocked his head and studied her guileless expression. "Is that so?"

"Well, yes." She looked up into his face, sitting close enough for him to feel the heat of her body against his chilled skin. "I need you," she said softly. "That's all."

He looked into her fathomless eyes, thinking how pretty she looked with the small smile she gave him. "Don't get cute, Arawaj," he said just as softly. "What you need is some decon for that scratch on your face. Swing around to that ridge. We'll dry out there before we check out the town."

She rolled her eyes and turned around to let the sled rise from the ground. "My name is Ciela."

It took an hour to reach the higher ground during which their scanners had not detected any life signs larger than the worms slithering through the mist below them. They stayed low to the ground, just high enough to avoid a plume of water in their wake. Seth was shivering by the time they stopped and his arm ached. But he had stowed a few pieces of clothing and insulating ponchos in their packs and, after Ciela's help with disinfecting his scrape, started to feel more like himself again. A few neutralizing tablets took care of the queasy feeling the swamp water had stirred up in his stomach. She, too, got some care for the growing bruise on her cheek but she refused to let him apply a medical scanner to check for greater damage. He did not press her; it was not unusual for GenMods to be cagey about their physiology.

Heating up some reconstituted soup almost made their little camp an acceptable way to rest for a while.

"Is this whole planet like this?" she asked, gazing out over the bleak landscape.

"No, just big parts of it, in the southern hemisphere. This is just the edge of the wetlands. North of here is probably the biggest rice-growing region in the sector. Sort of rice, anyway. Other grains grow in the dryer parts of the planet. It's a big industry but probably not a really fun place to live."

"Those men seem to have reason to be here. Didn't look like farmers to me."

He nodded, dispiritedly examining the tear in his favorite jacket. "It seems that some people are willing to live in the strangest places."

"Have you seen a lot of places? Not just weird ones?"

He smiled. "Yeah, although I think I have my fill of swamps now. You're a navigator. I'm sure you've seen some amazing sights."

She lifted one shoulder in slow shrug. "Not really. We just go from one station to another, or hook up with other freighters. Sometimes we get shore leave but I never really get to look around much. It gets boring sometimes."

"All for the cause?" he asked and immediately regretted that when she frowned at him.

"Yes, for the cause," she said. "We have no business interfering with these worlds. You have no business claiming them for your Commonwealth. We can't take two steps before stumbling over a Centauri and your people aren't even native to this part of the galaxy. You're colonists and invaders like the Humans you brought here with you." She stretched her arms out to encompass the horizon. "There is a difference between settling in a place where you don't displace anything but a bunch of slugs, and settling where you'll forever change a sentient population with your meddling."

He watched her animated features with interest, amazed as always by the fervor harbored by these rebels. She was right, of course, the Centauri did colonize this sector three hundred years ago and named it Trans-Targon. More of his people arrived regularly on massive immigrant ships to settle on these new worlds as soon as the Union deemed them suitable for habitation. But for most like him, Centauri, Humans, and more local races who had scattered on these few dozen habitable planets, this was home. "Some would say the slugs have rights, too. And a lot of those sentients you worry about are more than happy to join the Commonwealth. Our Union has changed many populations for the better."

"Like which?"

"Well, Feyd, for instance. Their people live comfortably just by trading their goods. Food, mostly, like this place. Wine, sugar. Aram now houses huge cryogenic industries. Bellac has oceans full of fish that others want. The Commonwealth is about trade, not conquest."

She seemed unimpressed. "And Targon's native people are now reduced to living in caves. Magra is perpetually at war. The Chaykos and Nebdans are routinely enslaved. Now your precious Union is taking over Tadonna. That's my home planet."

"And the Shri-Lan have done horrible things to the Rhuwac population. Turned them into fighting machines and shipped them off-world as cannon fodder."

"I am not Shri-Lan!"

"You will be if we don't get you out of here. Not that Arawaj are much better than Shri-Lan."

She gaped at him, astounded by his words. "How can you say that? The Shri-Lan only want power. They want to destroy the Union and take its place. Their territory is still growing, no matter what your Air Command does."

"Growing in places no one else wants," Seth reminded her. "You are well aware of how incredibly vast Trans-Targon is, and it gets bigger with every keyhole we turn into a jumpsite."

"That's exactly my point!" she said, more excited than

angry now. "You expand your territory and the Shri-Lan tries to take it away, especially if there's profit to be made from it. The Arawaj don't even want this expansion to happen. We want to stop you from invading peaceful, unaware worlds. Stop importing more transports filled with Centauri from Terra-Centauri. Leave this sector to those who belong here."

He started to gather up the remains of their meal. Like Shaddallam and K'lar, he thought. Or Naiyad, where ages ago, it seemed, he did his part to make sure that no one would ever find anything interesting to exploit there. The Arawaj were not wrong in their ambitions; in some ways he even shared their views, if not their means. "So you got something against Centauri?"

She frowned. "I didn't say that. You know we have plenty of Centauri among the Arawaj. We just don't need more of you here."

He shook his head. "What a strange bunch you are. But your methods are inefficient and unacceptable. Your actions have been as cruel as the Shri-Lan's. Sometimes more so. That isn't something the Union can tolerate."

"You can't compare us to the Shri-Lan!" she objected. "We fight against Air Command in battle. We sabotage their installations where we feel that'll slow the expansion. We teach locals to stand up to Commonwealth coercion and bribery."

"You actually believe that?" he said, incredulous.

"It's the truth."

"As you've been told."

She waved her hands in dismissal. "Don't hand me your Commonwealth propaganda. We know all about that."

"You've killed people," he guessed. "You had no qualms about those thugs back there. It looked pretty natural for you."

"No more than for you." She shrugged but did not look at him. "I've had to defend myself and my people. I've had training. But I'm just a navigator. On a smuggler's ship. I've never harmed anyone who wasn't an enemy. Who, um, who…"

"Who didn't deserve it?"

"Yes. We are defenders."

"Listen to yourself!" Seth said, drawn into the rhetoric in spite of himself. He had decided long ago to avoid these pointless debates that never found resolution. But she was so damn earnest about what she was saying that he could not stop the argument. "You defenders kept Bellac Tau in a state of insurrection for four years. Two thousand people died before things settled. It was Bellac's own government that called on Air Command to drive the Arawaj out. The dam your people blew on Magra Alaric destroyed a whole town. That's where they keep civilians in case you don't know. Not six months ago one of your more lunatic Arawaj pals nearly destroyed Delphi."

"It's Delphi's fault that Air Command is as powerful as it is," she returned but he saw the uncertainty in her eyes and heard it in her voice. She looked away. "What... what happened on Delphi?"

"Doesn't matter. Delphi is safe. For now."

"Because Air Command makes sure to guard their precious supply of spanners more than they protect any other place. Delphi isn't even part of the Commonwealth."

He stood up. "And that is their choice. Kind of messes up your theory about the Union forcing themselves upon unwilling populations, doesn't it?"

Ciela mumbled something faintly insulting to his heritage. She refused his help with her backpack and heaved it into the skimmer herself. "Can I have that knife back? I'd feel safer."

"I wouldn't."

"You can. I didn't shoot you when I had the chance, did I?"

"Probably would have missed, anyway."

SEVEN

The town finally came into view when they steered their skimmer over an even path used also for wheeled vehicles. Traffic here moved mostly in the form of long trains of rice bins, ready to be loaded into shuttles heading for the moon. A few times they moved out of the way of massive farm machinery used to take care of the efficiently automated planting and harvesting here.

Some homes and small farms appeared along the road, apparently making much use of rice fibers for construction along with imported shelter materials. Soon the isolated dwellings had turned into a busy hamlet on the fringe of the town and Seth stopped the sled near an open area bordered by shops. The place seemed to be a bit of a crossroads as goods were packed up for transport to the moon and shippers and farmers stopped here for entertainment and supplies.

Seth walked to where two elder Magrans worked on some sort of machinery that seemed to have no electronic parts at all. Ciela followed silently. She had not said much since their last rest stop but looked around herself with curiosity. The men ducked their heads in greeting when they approached. Another Prime species, Magrans resembled Feydans but did not approve of the narrative tattoos that covered most

Feydans' bodies. Even in this overcast climate, their skin was dark brown and tough as old leather.

Seth wrapped his right hand around the taller man's right hand. "Two lives, brother," he said in their language.

The man showed the gaps in his teeth. "For you as well," he replied.

Seth looked back to where the road left the village. "Travel is dangerous out there. Here in this place also?"

The men exchanged glances. "Only when strangers come looking for trouble. We value peace."

"Why are you holding that man's hand," Ciela asked, standing slightly behind Seth, a little unnerved by the throng of people pretending not to watch the exchange.

"They are from Magra Fell," he explained. "You can tell by those ripples along their necks. To touch while speaking is a sign of trust and honesty." His hand was now loosely clasped around the man's wrist. "Enemies don't touch, nor do people who don't like each other. By extension, that means liars and those with something to hide." He turned back to his conversation. "We need to find a way to the station. Do you know the way?"

The Magran chuckled. "Currency is always the way."

Seth nodded and gestured with his free hand to the skimmer. "All this can be yours."

They moved to the vehicle to let the Magrans examine it and the contents of the backpacks. Another man joined them and some of the items traded hands as they evaluated and judged. In the end, someone went into a nearby building and emerged again with a packet of flat rectangles embossed with strange designs and a holographic image. The trade also included a woven coat for Seth and a fringed scarf to cover Ciela's hair in the way of the local women.

Ciela fumbled with her wrap as they left the men to their new treasures and headed for the air field. "Why did you sell all that stuff?" She tapped his data sleeve. "Don't they pay you at Air Command?"

"They do, but something tells me that I don't want to be

flashing Union credit around here. The bald guy mentioned rebels on the air field."

"What? Here?"

"Yeah. Shri-Lan. Keep your head down when we get there." Seth nudged her into a narrow side street to avoid the main thoroughfare leading to the air field. "Why do I keep thinking you're worth more than I think?"

"What do I know what you think?"

The town's depot consisted of a vast tract of compound surface with weather-bleached markings to guide traffic toward the loading areas along the north side. From there, a steady stream of bullet-shaped shuttles lifted the grains to the orbital station. That the two private cruisers parked here were rebel-owned was probably not a secret to anyone. A few Shri-Lan, heavily armed and openly wearing their colors, loitered nearby, making the locals nervous with their scrutiny.

Seth pulled Ciela into a row of warehouses and they made their way through rows of storage racks and conveyors until they reached the other end of the air field. Sunlight streaming through transom windows below the ceiling painted thick beams through the dusty air. Ciela grimaced when her eyes followed them upward to see clusters of black insects crawl among the rafters, each as large as her splayed hand and moving far too quickly for comfort.

Seth looked up. "Silo spiders," he said. "They keep the bugs out of the grain."

"Do they bite?"

"Yes." He wiped cereal dust from a window set into a service door. The yard outside was busy with the loading of shuttles. He observed the activity for a while, seeing workers and overseers, identifying surveillance, counting rebels. "We should be able to get a lift to the moon on one of those. If we can get someone—" He looked around. "Ciela?"

She was no longer beside him. He sighed and raised his eyes to the ceiling as if the spiders had some explanation for this rebel's obstinacy. Some days it would just be easier to put on a uniform and slap his targets into irons to get them to where they were supposed to go. He set after her, easily following her footprints in the dust between tall pallets of grain bins to the other side of the building. They led outside and along the warehouse wall.

He made no sound when he moved to where she huddled, peering around the corner into the yard. She yelped when he gripped her arm to spin her around and slam her against the metal wall. "Help!" She cried out. "I'm being—"

He covered her mouth with his hand. "What do you think you're doing? Shut up!"

She glared at him, obviously not prepared to try to speak with his hand on her face. He pulled back by a fraction. "Let me go, dammit!"

"Go where?"

"I'm a navigator. Any of those shipping companies will take me on. I don't need you to get off this rock." She strained against him. "Are you done feeling me up?"

He pulled back but tightened his grip on her arm when she tried to squirm away. "Are you done acting like an idiot?"

"Don't talk to me like that!"

"How is this not idiotic? The place is crawling with Shri-Lan. Chances are they're looking for you up at the station, too. They'll have your picture. They may even have your DNA if they got to your boss. So you have a choice."

"Oh yeah?"

"Yeah. You've done your sworn Arawaj duty and had your escape attempt. So now you can behave and let me take you away quietly, or you can do something stupid and draw attention."

"That's kinda the point. You can't very well keep a gun pointed at me up there."

"Don't be so sure of that. Station admin won't help you if you're with me. Shri-Lan will try to take you by force and they will succeed, in case you actually believe any of these grain traders are going to help you. And you can be sure your Arawaj pals have cleared out by now."

"I can find my way. All I need is to get to Magra or Pelion. That won't be difficult for someone like me."

"Well, you're not, so quit arguing."

Her eyes widened at something behind him. "Look out!"

Taking no chances that this might be some ruse, he gripped both of her arms and swung her around and down, barely ducking the butt of a rifle swinging at his head. He pushed Ciela aside and drew his gun to fire at their assailant. The man went down, leaving two others to take his place. A bullet strafed past his head and hit the wall above Ciela. Seth launched himself at the Caspian woman with the pistol, taking her down into the dust. A few quick punches stunned her but something heavy struck his back and he rolled away to look up at a massive Human apparently made entirely of muscle. With more distance between them now, the rebel turned his rifle and aimed.

Seth stared in disbelief when Ciela launched herself at the man from behind, nimbly scaling his back to jam her fingers into whatever orifices his face presented. The Human howled in pain and surprise, staggering backwards, arms flailing to dislodge his attacker. She rolled out of the way when he crashed to the ground and quickly returned to heave her boot into his groin.

Seth found an opening and shot the Human, then turned to also take down the Caspian who had recovered enough to grope for her gun in the dust. He rolled onto his back, gasping, waiting for the dull pain across his back to recede. Ciela crouched beside him. "You all right?"

He looked up at her smudged face and coughed a helpless laugh. "Yeah." He let her pull him up and then leaned against the warehouse wall to catch his breath. He pulled off his blood-stained jacket and tossed it behind some empty pallets. "So you really want to put up with these bastards on your own?"

She looked at the bodies. "Be easier if I had a gun."

"You're too dangerous with a gun."

"Don't mock me! I can handle myself." But after a

moment the scornful look on her face faded and she slumped to sit on the edge of the pallets. She suddenly looked so lost and frightened that he almost felt sorry for her. Unlike her little act earlier this day, she now seemed genuinely helpless. "Can't you just let me go?" she said. "Can't I just go back to Velen Phar?"

"He doesn't want you, Ciela. That's pretty harsh but he is giving it all up. And he thinks the best place for you is with the Union. Doesn't that tell you anything?"

"He sold us," she said, trying to find some reason in this.

"He did not. He asked for nothing. He just wanted someone to come and get you so he can disappear. I'm sure he's put plenty aside for his retirement." He put his hand on her shoulder. "Look, Air Command wants you because you're a spanner. They need spanners. Turning yourself in can help us find your friends. You can't do that on your own."

She looked up. "You think they'll go after them?"

"They look for all spanners. And when they can, they pick them up, one way or another. It's the best way of slowing your rebel friends down for a while." Seth watched her ponder this for a moment, seeing a glimmer of hope lighten her expression. "No one will hurt you, I promise."

"I'm not worried about getting hurt. I worry about betraying my people."

He bent to grasp the lifeless hands of the Human rebel, preparing to drag him into the warehouse before someone else came around here. "Yes, well. Some of us live with that every day."

* * *

"That's your ship? It's so small." Ciela peered through the observation window set between each of the access tubes to the cruisers parked along the upper concourse. They had arrived, tired and disheveled, at Tayako station after Seth entrusted a warehouse driver with their currency to purchase seats for them aboard a shuttle. The gamble paid off although the price of the passage was apparently exactly the amount he handed over.

"Yeah, but it's home," Seth said, meaning it. Returning to the *Dutchman* after their unpleasant trip to the surface felt like he had arrived somewhere important. Like he had, in fact, returned home. He smiled happily, eager to get into the decon and into some clean clothes, and waved her into the airlock.

Once identified, the ship allowed him and his passenger aboard and through the cargo space into the main cabin. Ciela looked around, taking in the worn but comfortable seats and work table, the tiny galley separated from the central area by a high counter, and the lounger built into the wall, obviously serving as Seth's bed.

"I know," he said. "It's a mess. You can have the crew quarters. That's an even bigger mess."

She shrugged. "Looks comfortable."

Seth didn't mention that, when necessary, the cabin had outside locks that even she couldn't hack through. He poked into a cabinet and then held up a few shirts for her inspection, not surprised when she reached for the bright blue one. "We've got a little while before we can shove off. That door over there is the decon. The steam cycle is nice."

She nodded but looked around the cabin for a while longer, then peered down into the cockpit. "That's some pretty pricey Air Command gear you have. They must pay well." Her eyes lingered over the additional shield reverb he had bartered from an Ud Mraki salvager a while ago. "You got that to play nice with Union issue? Impressive."

"I have a good mechanic." He pulled his shirt over his head, wincing at the dull ache of his bruised back. "I think I've got a cracked rib."

"Where'd you get that scar?" Ciela squinted at a long scrape across his chest and arm.

He looked down. "Ex-girlfriend shot me."

"No, really."

"Really." He noticed a signal indicating a waiting message

and went to the com console. After a moment's consideration he decided that he wasn't expecting any super-secret messages and relayed the packet to one of the forward screens.

The image that appeared was of Colonel Carras on Targon, drawing a sneer from Ciela at the sight of his uniform. "We received your message," the Centauri elder began. "We've dispatched some yachts to meet your friends. We'll make sure they're looked after. It's not necessary for you to travel all the way here. We'll give your regards. Sorry, no biscuits." The colonel leaned forward to end the transmission but then looked up again. "Do try to find some explanation for that subspace scanner you picked up on Magra. It costs more than your ship."

"What did that mean?" Ciela wanted to know when the message ended.

"I am interested in subspace. It's a hobby."

"I mean all that other stuff."

"Oh. That. I told him earlier that you and your friends were here. He's going to see if he can head off Sebasta at either the Feron or Mrak terminus. See? I told you they'd be interested in finding them. We'll have you all together again in no time, I'm sure."

She watched him work with the ship's control console. "Are we leaving now?"

"Shortly." He glanced to where she lingered uncertainly in the entrance to the cockpit. "Are you worried?"

"Wouldn't you be?"

"Probably."

"How long before we get to Targon?"

"I'm not going to Targon. That Union ship that chased off Sebasta will be here very soon. I have no idea why they are here, but they may as well take you back. You heard the colonel. My services are no longer needed for this. Go get cleaned up."

Her face suddenly seemed very pale in the dim light of the cockpit. "You're just going to hand me over? To Air

Command? To *them*?"

"I told you: no one will hurt you. They'll have officers on board."

"Can't you take me?" she said in a small voice.

He shifted his eyes away from that troubled expression. Guarding a prisoner over what would be at least a ten-day trip ranked fairly low on his list of interesting things to do. He had seen her deal with the looters on the surface. She had swiped the knife without him noticing. There had been no hesitation in her attack upon the Shri-Lan at the warehouse. He did not doubt for a moment that escape was foremost on her mind. She claimed not to be a pilot but since when did he take any rebel's word as fact? He could easily imagine himself not waking up due to her knife lodged in some important body part.

"No," he said but for some reason he wasn't happy about it. There was something undeniably interesting about her. And oddly fascinating. Some mystery, perhaps. Carras had been quick to pull him off the scent here which just smacked of classified goings-on. Seth's interest in things other people didn't want him to know bordered on the obsessive and he itched to learn more. "We'll fly out to meet them. I have to get back to the jumpsite anyway. I'll make sure they treat you decently."

He turned away to start his preflight routines. The ground crew had delivered his coolant order; the supply bin was secured in the hold. He'd restock the galley once they were underway. He heard her sigh and a moment later close the door to the decon chamber.

The preflight checked out, as it usually did, and he barely glanced at the more routine housekeeping reports that popped up on the display. One of the items, however, caught his attention and he called up more information. The report was the result of the automatic scan that happened in the cargo hold. The *Dutchman*'s sensors analyzed anything that came aboard, looking for pathogens, allergens, disease, weapons and other things that shouldn't be allowed into the main part of the ship. Both he and Ciela had passed the initial scan and now the more routine results waited to be acknowledged and filed. He read about the scrapes and bruises they had sustained on the surface and there was a recommendation of additional meds for him to ingest after having taken a few mouthfuls of swamp water no doubt swarming with all sorts of creatures.

But what was this about Ciela? He queried the system again, frowning, but the information was undeniable.

"Ciela?" He left the cockpit when he heard her leave the decon. She gathered the small bath sheet tighter around herself when she saw him and slipped into the crew cabin.

"You could have told me you're not a GenMod," he said.

He waited through a short silence before she said, "Huh? What did you say?"

"You heard me."

She peered around the corner. "Why are you saying that, I meant."

"Passing yourself off as a Human GenMod. That joke didn't make it through my scanners."

She came into the main cabin, wearing her tights and his shirt. She gave him a tense smile. "I don't know why you're saying that. Your scanners aren't interpreting things properly. That's not uncommon with us."

"Don't bother. You know exactly what I'm talking about."

"I'm sure I have no idea—"

He grabbed her arm and spun her around to bend her over the galley counter. She tried to pull away when he yanked up the back of her shirt to expose her skin there. As he suspected, a line of fine dark hair grew along the gentle ridge of her spine. He pinched some of it between his fingers to give it a sharp tug.

"Hey!"

"You are one hundred percent pure Delphian," he said, both angry and a little embarrassed at having been fooled so easily. Few field agents had as much in-depth knowledge of

Trans-Targon's sentient species as he did. He spoke enough base languages to usually get along without a translator stuck in his ear. His onboard library rivaled that of most Union archives. And yet, this slip of a rebel had managed to dupe him for hours now. "There isn't a single tweaked gene in your body."

She twisted away from him and tugged her shirt back into place, once again hiding the telltale line of hair on her back. Now that he knew, other signs stood out quite well. Her narrow face and angular body were common among both Delphians and Centauri but the tilt of her eyes and cheeks was Delphian. Humans tended to be shorter and stocky. No doubt the natural blue color of her hair and eyes, along with subtle tinting of the skin creases had been changed chemically rather than genetically. She had lacquered her nails black to hide the blue beneath them and no doubt used lip stains to hide the cyan cast common there, as well.

What had fooled him most of all was her utter lack of mannerisms valued so very much by Delphians. Although capable of great warmth toward each other or those they knew well, Delphians practiced a social detachment that precluded even smiling in public. Emotions were private and shared only within their clan of friends and family. Their highly evolved minds achieved several level of consciousness that allowed them to appear composed even under great stress and hide their moods behind a veneer of indifference. So far, Ciela had displayed none of that behavior.

Of course, no one would suspect a Delphian among rebels, Seth reminded himself, perhaps to feel better about having failed to see through the charade. The methods used by any rebel faction ran so counter to Delphian sensibilities that any partnership was simply unthinkable.

"So what?" she said angrily. "I can't very well walk around looking like a Delphian, can I?" She turned her back to him as if she meant to stomp off somewhere but the *Dutchman* provided precious little stomping-off room. "No reason to rip my clothes off."

He raised his hands in an unfinished gesture. "What... I mean, how did you end up here?"

"You damn well know how I ended up here." She turned to face him. "You mean how did I end up with the Arawaj? I was raised by the Arawaj. They took us in when the good people of Delphi threw us out."

"What? That's not possible." Seth berated himself for his crude reaction to his discovery. Was he so used to treating rebels as they seemed to deserve that he could not be kinder to this woman? He gestured to the galley. "I'm sorry. It's been a rough day for both of us. How about we eat something and you tell me your story?"

She watched him walk around the counter and flip the lever on the tea press. "Berry, please," she said grudgingly. "What do you have to eat?"

"Sit down and be amazed by my ability to heat a tray of space slop by magically touching this panel with my finger."

Her lip twitched in what might have been a smile. "I don't have a story. My parents were rebels. Living on Delphi. When they were found out they were put on a ship and banished along with a bunch of others."

"Others? Other Delphians?"

"Yes. Seven or eight. And their children."

"And you ended up on Tadonna?"

She sipped from her cup and then stared into it. "Eventually. We... we were hunted down by Air Command. My parents were killed. The others, too. I don't even remember them. It was so long ago. The children survived the attack when the Air Command raid was defeated. We were taken to Tadonna. There were others there like me..." She ran a hand over her nearly black hair, likely without realizing it. "Seven of us. We lived there until we were old enough to make ourselves useful as navigators. Seems that Delphians have the knack for it."

"That's a modest way of putting it." Seth busied himself with his simple tasks. He could not fathom any group on Delphi even conceiving of banishing a family from the planet. They had rules of conduct among themselves but people were free to choose. Many of them had left Delphi to seek adventure within the Union as explorers, engineers, even pilots, and, although it was frowned upon by the elders, no one stopped them. Certainly, should any group decide to join the rebels, that too would be accepted simply with a sad shake of the head. But never expulsion. Delphi's population was shrinking at an alarming rate – any solution was better than to banish anyone, not to mention children, from the planet.

"How old are you," he asked finally.

"Twelve."

"Tadonna, you said?" He consulted his data sleeve for a conversion. "That makes you almost fifty on Delphi."

"So?"

"Delphi doesn't have a fleet of ships. But they have a massive interest in space exploration, especially astrobiology and physics. The Commonwealth is pretty keen on them sharing their discoveries and so they provide them with the ships to explore with. It's not likely that they'd use one of them to banish a bunch of dissidents."

She frowned. "How would you know?"

"I've been around them long enough." Seth tapped around on the screen he had pulled from his data unit over the back of his hand. "I thought I remembered this right. About fifty years ago a number of Delphian science expeditions disappeared. It was assumed they failed to navigate some keyhole. But there is also suspicion that they were taken by rebels, which is why all of their trips are protected by an armed escort now. They don't take children off-planet anymore."

"Taken by rebels? Why?"

"What do you do for a living? That's why. Delphians do not work for rebels. They don't care enough about the Union or rebels to get involved unless it suits them. We could all disappear into subspace forever and they wouldn't even notice. So the only way to get a Delphian to work as a rebel is to grow your own."

She ignored the tray of food he placed in front of her. "So what are you saying? That we were stolen from our parents? That they were killed so the Arawaj would have more spanners at some future time?"

"Pretty much."

She got up from her chair to pace across the cabin where she leaned against the bulkhead, arms crossed. "Ridiculous! The people who raised us were kind. They taught us everything we know. They protected us." Her voice shook as if on the edge of tears. "They would not lie to us!"

"I think they would," he said gently. "Your cause, to some of them, is more important than anything. Even if that means stealing children." A crime, he reminded himself, which had no equal among Delphians, whose birthrate had crashed long ago. "If your parents refused to cooperate they would not want to keep them around. So they raised you as their own and taught you what they thought you needed to know."

"They murdered them?" she said. "They lied to us? All these years?"

He raised his hands. "I'm saying it's possible. I just can't believe that a whole clan of Delphians just decided to go and join the Arawaj in the Badlands."

She shrugged, jutting her chin in stubborn denial of what she was hearing. "Maybe they had a reason."

"You said there were seven children?"

"Yes. Us four on Velen Phar's ships and three more girls working with Hariah's outfit. That crew just got back from a long tour so they're spending a summer on Tadonna." She scowled at him. "At least they were there when we left a few weeks ago. Unless Hariah gets them off-planet, too, they'll be captured by your Air Command friends."

Seth came around the galley counter and gestured to her to join him in the cockpit. "Sit over there."

She complied after a moment, sitting down by the com console. Seth prepared a long-range message packet while she watched. "That's going to Magra? Who are you sending that to?"

"A friend. He's going to help us get more information about you."

Her eyes narrowed. "There is nothing your Union pals can say to convince me."

"He's not Union," Seth said and activated an overhead camera. "He's Delphian."

"I thought Delphians didn't like offworlders."

"You just have to know how to talk to them politely." He sat down beside her when the message began to record. "Hello, Caelyn. Yes, I know, I haven't been around and only come knocking when I need something. I need something. Meet Ciela." Seth looked at her expectantly.

She frowned briefly but then faced the camera. "Um, hello."

"She's having a bad day," Seth explained. "She's had a bit of a make-over but I'm sure by now you can tell she's one of yours. I'm sending her profile. Take a look, will you, maybe ask some questions. There are six more like her but their names were probably changed. They are about to get traded to the Shri-Lan in exchange for fame and riches. I don't know where or how, but at least I have this one. Air Command is tracking down the others. I'll be in the area in a few weeks. Let me know if you're around and I'll drop by." He completed the message packet by adding the *Dutchman*'s interpretation of Ciela's DNA and then sent it on its journey through the jumpsite and then to Magra.

Ciela watched him for a while. "What's this supposed to accomplish? What difference does it make how I got here? When your Air Command gets their hands on me I'll end up having to work for them or rot in some jail until I agree."

"That is likely."

"Well, thanks for not lying to me." She looked up at the inactive screens. Her skin seemed almost translucent and he saw dark shadows below her eyes.

"You're exhausted. We'll shove off and then you should

get some sleep. This whole day has been terrible for you."

She appeared not to have heard his advice. "What are you doing now?"

"Setting a course." Seth signaled the station's control tower and was given clearance to move into the flight lane above the moon. Although he directed the ship mostly through his neural interface, the displays before them charted their progress.

"That's not the jumpsite."

He nodded. "We're not going that way." The *Dutchman* separated with a shudder and drifted away from the docks.

"What do you mean?"

"You're Delphian. That changes everything. In a very big way, in fact. We're going to the keyhole. You will jump us to Delphi. I'm taking you home."

She blinked, speechless for a few moments before replying. "Delphi's not my home. They'll want nothing to do with me."

"Would you rather rot in some jail?" Seth leaned toward her and took both of her hands in his. She resisted only briefly. "Look, I haven't known you very long but I have the feeling that not even Air Command can make you do anything you don't want to do. You belong on Delphi or you should at least have a chance to see it. And to find out how you ended up on Tadonna. That won't happen if I give you to Air Command. You'll just disappear and your people, your real people, will never know I found you."

She looked down at his hands. "So if being Delphian makes me so special, your Union people would still keep me? That'd be no better than rebels doing that."

"Perhaps not keep you, but they'd want to, ah, deprogram you. Rehabilitation, they'd call it. Decompression. They're very efficient and by the time they're done you're on someone's crew on the other side of Trans-Targon. But they don't understand Delphians. Nobody really does. Give your people a chance to meet you, first."

She smiled sadly. "Not many choices before me, are

there?"

"Not really. We have hours before we reach the keyhole. We'll both try to get some sleep and you'll spend some time learning about Delphi. I have lots of material in my database. You might actually like to… to visit Delphi. Air Command has no influence there. They have a small air field that they aren't even allowed to leave it without Council's permission. I can't think of a safer place for you than Delphi."

"Even though I'm Arawaj."

"That has no meaning for them. You will find that out. All I'm asking is that you at least give it a look. I can send you to jail later if you don't like it."

She pulled her hands out of his grasp. "You're right. I need some sleep. You can lock me up now or tie me up in the cargo bay or whatever you had in mind." She stood up and wearily slouched into the main cabin. "I'll read your stuff. Then we'll see."

* * *

Seth slept far longer than he meant to and when he finally crawled out of his bunk and checked their bearings he found the *Dutchman* already slowing its approach to the keyhole. A small convoy of freighters also headed this way but they were hours behind them. He yawned hugely and scrubbed his fingers through his hair on his way to Ciela's cabin.

"You awake?" he said softly as he unlocked the door.

"Yes," she replied from within, sounding not at all sleepy.

She sprawled comfortably on the bunk, holding a reading tablet in her hands. He noticed that she had made some attempt at cleaning the room by folding a chair out from the wall and piling things onto it.

He leaned against the door frame. "Find out anything good about those Delphians?"

She waved the data sheet in the air. "This is interesting stuff. Peculiar people. Why do they hate outsiders so much? And what's with the hair?"

"A source of pride for them. They only have hair on their

heads and down the spine, so they grow it as long as possible. At least the men do. And they don't hate outsiders. They just don't consider them worth interacting with."

"Sounds kinda snooty."

"Yep. But they have ways of training their minds that you really need to expose yourself to. Some of that takes years to learn and a lot of that you won't find in that database. They don't advertise their abilities."

"Hmm, yeah. Some sort of telepathy. I know that. We came across that when we were little. Miko and I can do it a bit. But it's hard."

"Not if you learn how to do it properly. It's called a *khamal*. A state of mind. Actually they have quite a few very distinct states of mind. Amazing brains. Delphians aren't hugely smarter than anyone else, but they have a gift for logical thinking. Incredible memories, too. There is a reason why you're so good at hacking into places you shouldn't. Don't think I didn't notice you playing with that lock."

She stuck her tongue out at him.

"Imagine what you could do with that head of yours if you had a proper teacher. So have you decided to return to Delphi or are we jumping to Targon? You still have that option."

"Not much of a choice! Either I end up enslaved by the damn Union or I get stuck in some backwater that doesn't even need more navigators."

He shrugged. "Maybe a long break to learn something new will do you some good."

"Oh, you think they'll cure me of my rebel ways?"

"Yes." He turned to leave the room. "We're almost at the keyhole. Time to get jumping."

She joined him in the cockpit not long later, looking rested and, he realized not for the first time, quite pretty in that not-blue Delphian way. She had replaced that stubborn demeanor of yesterday with an expression of quiet confidence that he found much more appealing. It was also a little worrisome. Was she up to something?

He studied her curiously. "How'd they change your coloring? Can't be permanent."

She tapped a spot just below her ribs. "Got a patch that controls our pigmentation. I left everything I own on the *Othani*. I guess once this one wears out I'll start sprouting blue hair again."

"You'll like it," he said. "The hair on Delphian women is almost silvery. Very fetching."

She shrugged. "I'm not here to be fetching."

"Just making conversation, Ciela. So, are we going to Delphi?"

She nodded. "Yes. You are right. It's stupid not to want to know more about my people. And it looks like Delphi is very beautiful. I'd like to see it."

"It is. You may never want to set foot on another freighter again." He gestured for her to attach a headset to her interface node. "Time to meet the *Dutchman*." He entered the code to allow her access to the ship's system, engaging only the navigational controls to let her reach for the keyhole. All command functions, com, and security systems remained locked to her and he grinned when she rolled her eyes at him.

"You don't trust me?"

"Of course not."

"But you'll let me jump?"

"You don't seem the suicidal sort."

She grinned and turned her attention to the controls. He kept his eyes on the indicators, watching as she engaged the processors and outlined her intentions to reach the Ud Mrak sub-sector, the first leg of their journey to Delphi. "Easy jump," she said. "This is a fine machine. It feels like it's anticipating me. Impressive." She closed her eyes. "Let's go."

He accelerated toward the keyhole coordinates and sent the ship's energy stream to the aperture. It opened before them, soon large enough to allow entry.

"There it is," she said after only a brief search. The *Dutchman* confirmed an exit not far from Mrak Four. From there a three day real-space journey would take them to the next keyhole to Magra and from there to Delphi.

Seth steeled himself, taking a deep breath for no particular reason as she guided the *Dutchman* into the breach, her mind now the only thing connecting this point in space with her chosen exit. The processors churned through their calculations, relying on her in the absence of pre-programmed charts. A fleeting sense of panic threatened to overwhelm him as their physical reality disappeared, leaving only their thoughts untethered in the vast nothing of subspace.

He gasped when only seconds later they emerged again, struggling to clear his mind to take over flight controls and steady the ship. He scanned the diagnostics panel for any alarms needing his attention and saw none. Once sure that the *Dutchman* was firmly back in his control, he reached across to the other bench to tap Ciela's arm. "Hey, we're here."

She lay limply in her couch, slow to regain her senses. Even the most talented spanners paid the price of taking uncharted jumps and she would need rest to recover from this one. She waved a hand in a weak gesture to show that she heard him.

Seth turned back to the displays to set their course to the next keyhole. "What the...?" None of what he saw looked correct. He rubbed his eyes, thinking the jump had left him a little befuddled. He conferred with the navigator and then checked their bearings again. "Ciela, we're not anywhere near Mrak!"

She did not open her eyes but her lips curled in a smile. "Oops," she said.

EIGHT

"What the hell did you do?" Seth checked the *Dutchman*'s charts again, knowing perfectly well that the Mrak system wasn't about to materialize anywhere within range.

"Jumped us to Tadonna."

"Tadonna? How? This keyhole doesn't have an exit to Tadonna."

"None you know of."

Indeed, his sensors reported Tadonna a few hours ahead of them now, part of a binary star system in a far-flung region of the Badlands. A remote, sparsely populated planet without even a jumpsite to make it accessible. "Why? What are we doing here?"

"This is my home. I've already lost three of my friends. I need to know what happened to the others. I don't care about Delphi. *These* are my people and I can't leave them. I won't."

"So you decide to just kidnap me?"

She smiled tiredly. "That's what you did, isn't it?"

Seth stared at his displays in disbelief. The *Dutchman* had absolutely reported a heading for Ud Mrak. Somehow she had reworked the entire set of calculations at the very last minute, when he was no longer able to monitor the change. He had flown with a good number of Delphians and none had ever displayed this talent. "You're unbelievable."

She pointed at herself. "Arawaj, remember? You don't have any place to be right now, anyway. With any luck we'll find Hariah's crew and you'll have three more spanners to arrest."

He looked from her to the console and back again. As outrageous as this was, the whole things struck him as oddly amusing. She had neatly tricked him once again and, he had to admit, she was right. He had decided to trust a rebel and she took full advantage of it. He smiled ruefully. Without a stable jumpsite in this sub-sector he had no way back without her help, leaving him no choice but to head for Tadonna. "You've planned this all along?"

"Since you said you'll let me jump, yeah." She finally opened her eyes and sat up on her bench with some effort. "I need to lie down for a bit." She came to her feet but did not immediately leave the cockpit. "I had to do this, Seth. These people are all I have. Miko is a brother to me. And he's gone now. Maybe the others are also sold to the Shri-Lan by now but I have to know. I think you're probably a decent man. I think you understand this."

He watched her leave. "Ciela?"

"Hmm?" She peered back into the cockpit.

"You could have just asked."

A long, peculiar moment seemed to spin out between them as she held his gaze until a small smile lit her face. She nodded and left to find sleep.

* * *

The silent hours drifted past Seth as unnoticed as the empty space between them and their destination. Time like this always meant either raucous music and hard exercise for him or a deep immersion in whatever studies currently held his interest. Today was a day for learning something about Tadonna and this peculiar band of rebels.

Seth loaded all available files about the sub-sector onto his screens and the holo display and dug through more recent updates about the planet's politics. He had volumes of fairly new stuff that he hadn't perused yet – he was sure he had seen something about Tadonna on the index. The only thing he knew until now was that it was habitable and not easily accessible.

The Union news archives held the most interesting bits. Indeed, the small local population, begun by settlers over three hundred years ago and since invaded by explorers, speculators and rebels, sought to make a deal with the Commonwealth in exchange for trade agreements and protection. Eventually, it would mean turning the keyhole he just travelled through into a stable and charted jumpsite to ease traffic in the area. Inclusion in the Commonwealth meant giving up complete control to Air Command in all matters concerning rebels or other enemies of the Union.

Seth stared at the slowly rotating hologram of the planet, lost in thought. Fleeing Tadonna ahead of Air Command's arrival made sense. A small rebel hideout would be routed like a rat's nest in a ballroom on this remote world. Rebels thrived far more easily on crowded, high-traffic planets, often right under the garrisons' radar. But Velen Phar's attempt to keep his spanners out of Shri-Lan hands seemed to have little to do with the imminent annexation of Tadonna into the Union.

Seth dug into his archives for Velen Phar and found little that he didn't already know. Smuggler, wanted by Air Command for gunrunning, operating a crew that seemed to come and go very quickly to do their work. Working for his dinner, like so many Arawaj rebels, without any direct ties to terrorism or major calamities. And when faced with seeing his navigators go to the Shri-Lan, he had preferred to give them up to the Union. The Great Enemy.

Why not just set up shop elsewhere? Trans-Targon had a thousand corners where a good shipping company stood to make profit, legally or not. But someone had taken notice. Someone, Ivor Sebasta specifically, deemed these four a worthwhile trade for an alliance with the Shri-Lan rebel faction. But how could this possibly be worthwhile? Any allegiance was bound to splinter the Arawaj along bitter lines of ideology. Four, now three, spanners, even talented ones like Ciela, seemed a poor trade for more strife and confusion among the Union's opposition.

Perhaps it was time for Ciela to hand over a few facts and figures. There had to be a way to get through her distrust for all things having to do with the Commonwealth which, of course, included him. He spent enough of his time among rebels, especially the Arawaj, to understand their views and to know that many objected to the inevitable violence carried out in the name of their cause. Velen Phar and his crew seemed to be among those or he would have shifted them to one of the Arawaj's few battleships long ago.

He smiled, recalling her brief but fierce skirmish on Tayako. No pampered navigator on Phar's ship. He'd seen to it that they received proper training and dealt with hardship when necessary. Had he perhaps foreseen a day when they would have to fend for themselves? Or was it just Ciela who seemed born for more interesting things than lounging on the pilot's bench? He imagined her life within the safe, privileged shelter of Delphian society and could not quite reconcile it with what he knew of her so far. He suspected that her kinsmen would have no easy undertaking in reintegrating her into the fold. He had to admit that she'd make a far better rebel than a Delphian.

Ciela crawled out of her bunk a few hours later. He heard her hum to herself as she experimented with some of his equipment in the galley.

"You want some of this... *baze*... uh, *bazz'che*... whatever-it-is rice pasty stuff?" she called.

"No," he replied. "Make sure you put something sweet on that. You won't like it otherwise."

"Are we there yet?" she said when she joined him in the cockpit with her bowl. She had nearly drowned the nutritious but bitter grain mash in syrup.

"Yes. Got a couple of Union ships in the vicinity." He

took his feet off the co-pilot bench and turned toward the console.

She dropped into the seat. "Air Command?"

"One of them. Looks like there may be another on the surface, judging by the traffic."

She grimaced into her breakfast and stirred it in some futile attempt to make it taste better. "Think they'll bother us?"

"They might take a look. Maybe say hello in their usual tactful way. They don't have any jurisdiction here."

"Yet."

"Don't start."

She ate silently but he felt her watching him over the rim of her bowl.

"What?" he said finally.

"Are you purely Centauri?"

"Huh? Of course I am. Why?"

"You don't feel like a Centauri."

He gripped his forearm and gave it a squeeze. "How's a Centauri supposed to feel?"

"I don't mean that. Something was different when we made the jump."

"Different how?"

She made a vague gesture with her spoon. "We were both in the processors when we jumped. Usually I can tell the pilot is there, but that's all. Just another presence in the system. But you were different." She put the bowl aside and touched both of her neural implants. "I don't really know how to describe it, but you were part of the jump in a way that I haven't felt before. Like you were already out there. A part of it."

He shifted in his bench, fascinated. "It? What it?"

"Subspace. Or what we call subspace. Of course it's not really space at all."

He nodded. "I know."

She cocked her head. "You told me you're interested in subspace. What draws you there?"

Seth pondered her question. After a moment he smiled. "I guess the part you saw there. I've had some… experiences. Let's leave it there."

"Because I'm Arawaj and you don't trust me with your secrets."

"That's about it." He turned back to his console in preparation for entry into Tadonna's atmosphere. "We're about to land. No nonsense down there. If I see even one weapons signature I take off again and leave you with Air Command."

She seemed unwilling to let the subject of subspace drop but then just shrugged. "I just want to make sure they're all right. Hariah probably got the girls out, but I have friends there who won't get along well with your people."

He approached the northern hemisphere, following Ciela's coordinates. A sprawling harbor town occupied a broad delta basin and he followed the river up into a system of canyons that seemed barely negotiable on the ground.

"You grew up here?" He studied the terrain on real-vid and charts, seeing the rugged beauty of the planet's surface but no roads, towns or signs of agriculture. Soon there was only bare, red rock towering over the river, relieved only occasionally by scattered growth clinging to the scree. A few other aircraft shared the space above the canyons but there was no indication of regulated air lanes. But most importantly, Tadonna had water, the air was rich and crisp, and the gravity within suitable range for species like theirs. All of this made it a prime candidate for colonization and of great interest to the Commonwealth, no matter how remote the location.

"Yes, you'll see. It's quite pretty on the other side of these mountains. I lived here when we were children. We still rest here between runs. Some of those take years. But we always return."

Seth watched her smile, for probably the first time with pure joy. It lit her eyes and it was not hard to see a very striking Delphian woman behind the artificial coloring.

Perhaps Delphians, in general, ought to smile more, he thought.

"What?" She had caught him staring.

He returned his eyes to his screens. "Nothing. You love this place."

"It's home. It's got space. I like to walk. Sometime we ride in the hills. It's so utterly wonderful after being cooped up on the *Othani* for months at a time." She bit her lip. "I guess I won't have to worry about that anymore."

"You don't have to stop being a navigator. It's a gift and yours seems to be better than most. No one is taking that away."

"As long as I use it for your side."

"Obviously." He let the *Dutchman* swoop down into some foothills. Terraces of cultivated fields clung to the slopes, sharing a clever system of irrigation. He zoomed the cameras a little closer. It seemed that the same streams that fed the terraces also served to transport produce in round tubs into the valley. He saw a young boy use a pole to push a wayward vessel back into the stream out of which it had bounced.

She pointed at a crest up ahead. "There! Behind there is my home. The next valley."

"I see you also navigate by sight." Her coordinates matched precisely. "Lot of traffic over there. Or something."

"Really? It's pretty quiet here usually."

"Getting a lot of buzz, anyway." He looked up when an alarm chirped overhead. "Talk to me," he said aloud to the *Dutchman* but it was his neural interface that swapped the display settings.

"What is it?"

He frowned, puzzled. "Radiation."

"What? What kind of radiation?"

"The bad kind." He switched the ship's shield configuration. "Thick, too. Looks like what you see after a razer drop."

"That's not possible. There isn't any—" She gasped when they cleared the last of the peaks and the valley opened before them. It, too, had slopes covered by terraces but the small settlement at the bottom was a landscape of charred outlines of what might have been buildings once. "No!" she cried. "What happened? Gods, no!"

He ignored her panic and scanned for weapons, vehicles, people moving among the ruins. His sensors balked at sifting through the conflicting emissions but a visual check didn't show any aircraft in the area. "What kind of power source do you use down there?"

"Hydro," she said. "Wind. We don't have anything that can do this!"

He came about and carefully settled the *Dutchman* on a plateau of bare rock ringed by landing beacons. No other craft parked here today and no one was about. "Stay where you are," he snapped when she leaped from her bench.

"I have to see what happened!"

He gripped her arm. "You're going to take a deep breath before you do anything else."

She glared at him but then sank back again, shaking off his hand. He returned his attention to the sensors. "There are some life signs but it's hard to tell how many, or if they're injured." He let the cameras create a panoramic view of the ship's surroundings. Smoke still rose from the ruins. The buildings, many made of stone blocks, lay in crumpled heaps although some, roofless, remained standing near the north end of the little town. He saw barns and a pond and even a few windmills in the distance. This didn't look like the rebel stronghold he had expected. Just another far-flung settlement of no consequence to anyone. A perfect place to raise a gaggle of stolen children. "I'm getting readings from those hills there. No power signatures. Maybe your people are hiding. Maybe they got away." He checked his data sleeve against the ship's systems and then turned to her. "Can you do this?"

She nodded, seeming a little less frantic now. "I have to see."

He rose and waved her along into the main cabin. There

he pulled two sets of weather gear from a bin; sturdy coveralls designed to withstand most planetary conditions and even short exposures to space. He made sure she geared up properly and that the gauges inside her hood displayed correctly. With only a brief moment's hesitation, he handed her a projectile weapon. "Don't try this at long range," he said, recalling her questionable marksmanship. "But it's solid at less than that."

She took it without comment.

"Stay with me, don't wander off, do not lose sight of the *Dutchman*, whatever you do. Not until we have a better idea about what's going on."

"Can we take that?" She pointed at a pack of medical supplies.

He hung its strap over her shoulder. "Drop it and run if you see anything odd."

"What? Odder than that?" She gestured at the still-active screens at the front of the ship. "I'm your Arawaj prisoner, not your baby." She turned away only to halt again by the door to the cargo hold. "Sorry," she said. "You're right. I'll be careful. But I can look after myself."

They passed through the sealed area of the ship and cautiously stepped outside, scanners held before them. Seth pointed to her left and they went that way, down into the settlement. Ciela walked slightly in front of him as they passed ruined buildings and charred vegetation. He was startled by a massive four-legged animal rounding a crumbled wall but Ciela just slapped it lightly to send it on its way.

"Scanners aren't helping much," he grumbled. "Didn't even see that coming."

"Something over there, though," she said. "Life signs."

"Probably more livestock. This happened just hours ago. If anyone was still here they would have come out to the ship."

"Not if they're scared. Or hurt." She switched on her suit's external speakers. "Hello? Is anyone there?"

Seth examined some scorch marks on a wall. "Lasers," he

said. "They didn't just drop ordnance on these people from above." He crouched to pick up a twisted piece of metal and rubbed some soot away to show markings. The camera on his sleeve sent it to the *Dutchman* for identification. "Union issue."

Her lips formed a thin line. "Your people did this?"

"I can't imagine why."

"You can't? How about the other three spanners? Why else would anyone come all the way out here if not for them?"

He peered through her visor to see her angry face. "You really believe that Air Command would do this? Destroy a whole town to get at three rebel spanners?"

"Yes! That's what you do."

He raised a gloved finger. "One, I am not Air Command. Two, this is not what they do. I know you've heard all sorts of terrible stories, but there is not a single reason why Air Command would take out a bunch of civilians, even if they are affiliated with rebels. Not if there is another way of getting what they want." He continued to walk, kicking a broken drainpipe out of the way. "You don't need a damn razer for this sort of thing, even if your people were armed to the teeth. This was done out of spite, or as a show of power."

"And Air Command doesn't show their muscle to keep the locals in line?"

"Not by scorching the earth they stand on. That doesn't make one bit of sense." He turned when a scrabbling noise from one of the buildings caught their attention.

"Hello? Is there someone there?" Ciela peered through a broken window. Light fell through tumbled ceiling beams to illuminate a young boy holding a gun levelled at the window.

Both Seth and Ciela ducked aside when a bullet whined along the sill. Then the small figure darted out of the open door and sprinted along the narrow street.

"Wait!" Ciela hurried after him.

"Stop," Seth called but she heard nothing. He set after

her and skidded to a halt when only moments later they reached an open square.

"No!" Ciela cried.

"Cazun!"

A light standard in the center of the open space, possibly a market square or some sort of gathering place, listed to one side under the weight of two people. They had been strung up by their feet but no life remained in the blackened, bloody faces.

"Gods, Seth, get them down." Ciela moved toward the macabre display when a bullet hit the dusty ground by her feet.

"Back!" Seth grasped her arm and they dodged more projectiles as they dashed into the cover of the alley. He looked back to see two men in an opposite alley carrying hunting rifles.

"Those are ours," Ciela said.

Seth grabbed her arm to stop her from running back, but she had made no move. "They don't recognize you in this suit. Try calling out their names."

She ducked when another bullet whined past them from another direction. They turned and fled back the way they had come, staying close to buildings that could well contain more snipers.

An alarm sounded at Seth's wrist when the *Dutchman* alerted him to incoming traffic. He consulted the screen and cursed. "Plane coming. Fast. Back to the ship."

But even as they neared his ship, well-placed laser fire stabbed to the ground, made visible by brightly colored tracers, obviously as warning. Seth shoved Ciela behind a ruin and dropped his visor to look up at the sky. The information displayed before his eyes now showed a small Trident class cruiser used by rebels of both factions. He hoped their scanners were no more effective than his own in trying to cut through the interference from the ground.

The ship dropped sharply and landed between the edge of the village and the *Dutchman*. The gunshots from behind ceased as everyone seemed to wait to see who had arrived this time. Seth wondered if the shooters thought themselves outgunned now and had retreated. He hoped so; perhaps they had no idea that their home had been contaminated.

Two men, also wearing protective gear, exited the cruiser and walked to Seth's ship. One of them tried the key plate and then shook his head. Others emerged now, also heavily armed, and headed toward their hiding place.

"Back," Seth pointed to the next likely hiding place along what used to be an alley between the farm homes, now strewn with broken masonry. "Watch for snipers."

"They're coming this way."

"It's these suits. Linked to the *Dutchman* and broadcasting like crazy."

Something impacted the stone wall and then ricocheted into the ground, flinging up a spray of dirt and gravel. Seth returned the fire and watched the rebels scatter for cover, as unorganized as he'd expected. "Not Air Command, if you were still wondering," he said. The rapport of automatic projectile weapons rattled over their heads.

"Why aren't you hitting them?"

He tapped the front of her hood. "Drop your visor and look over the wall by that gap. See if you recognize any of them."

"Are you trying to get me shot?" she hissed but squeezed between him and the wall to follow his instructions. The visor picked up some of the people scurrying between buildings looking for a better position. "Wait…" She squinted, hampered by the clear protective faceplate of her hood. "Yes, I know that one. That woman with the—" She yelped when Seth grabbed her collar and threw her to the ground. The wall above them disintegrated and showered debris onto them.

"Ruthala!" Ciela shouted. Seth, still bent over her, winced and pulled back when her voice transmitted over their sound system. "It's me, Ciela. Stop shooting!"

"Are these your people?" he said.

"If you mean Arawaj, yes. If you mean bloody traitors, then no." Ciela edged to the corner again. "Ruthala! It's me!"

They waited until they heard footfalls crunching on the loose debris but they still saw nothing of the rebels. "Which toe are you missing?" a woman called out, her voice muffled by her hood but likely Human.

Seth raised an eyebrow. "You're missing a toe?"

"The left little one," Ciela returned to the woman.

He slouched back against the wall and reached into the thigh pocked of his coveralls for a reload for his gun. "Your Arawaj security measures are stellar." He looked up when several of the armed rebels surrounded them, weapons aimed.

"He's with me," Ciela said quickly. "Put those away."

The Human woman gestured to the others. "Ciela is—" she started to say something and then caught herself. "Ciela lives here. You've been away a while, Sweetie. Not the homecoming you wanted. We came as soon as we got their message." She looked down along the destroyed street. "Not soon enough."

Seth came to his feet. "There are survivors over there. Shooting at anything that moves." Some of the others hurried away at once. "We found some bodies. Hung."

They heard voices shouting in a local dialect to reassure the people that help had arrived. Gradually, a few survivors emerged from the buildings, their suspicion clear on their faces. A Feydan woman was the first to join them. Her clothes were torn and dirty but once of good quality. Like most of her people, she had embellished her skin with elaborate tattoos describing the history of her ancestors. Her careworn face, too, showed small scripts that even Seth found difficult to interpret without his translator.

"What happened?" the woman named Ruthala said.

The Feydan shrugged, staring out over the devastation all around them. "Two cruisers landed. They wanted the girls. When we tried to hide them they punished all of us. Hariah is dead."

"Gods," Ciela moaned.

"Who did this?" Seth barely dared to breathe as he awaited the woman's reply. In spite of what he told Ciela, not all Air Command patrols cared about the difference between a rebel and a mere sympathizer. Their willingness to follow orders without question was probably the main reason he left the Air Command Academy the moment his flight training had concluded. Having witnessed the extremes with which some soldiers carried out those orders ensured that he never regretted his choice.

Her haunted eyes moved to him and he suddenly felt cowardly standing here with his coveralls and air filters and the gun that arrived too late to help them. He silenced the scanner persistently warning him about the hazards in the air.

"What difference does it make?" she said. "When Arawaj oppose Arawaj, what does anything matter? They came to find the spanners and just taking them wasn't enough. We now know what will happen to those of us who refuse to bow to the Shri-Lan. We can't hide, even out here."

"This was Sebasta and his goons. His ship left this system a couple of hours ago." Ruthala swore like someone used to swearing loudly and often. "We heard he took Velen Phar's crew." She shot Ciela a meaningful glance. "And his spanners. I guess he made them tell about this place."

"Where is he taking them?" Seth said.

"We have to get these people out," Ciela interrupted. "There are decon stations and a hospital at the delta. We can fit a bunch into the *Dutchman*."

Seth nodded. "Then we need to get you away, Ciela. They may come back for you. You're a danger to any of... of your people if you stay with them."

"Yes," she said through clenched teeth. "I guess I don't have much choice."

"Let's get these people out of here and to the hospital," Ruthala said. "We'll regroup in town. I have more bad news."

A shuttle arrived not long later and hours passed as they

combed the hills for survivors and marked off the contaminated area with warning signs. Besides the three missing spanners working for Hariah, the toll amounted to six dead and two dozen hurt. The shuttle began to move people to another village while Ruthala and Seth used their faster planes to move the injured to the hospital.

No one asked about Seth or how he came to be in Ciela's company, assuming him to be another Arawaj from some distant place. This wasn't his first time posing as a rebel and he was comfortable with their ways. The measure of distrust shown by Ruthala even for her own gang, however, was new to him. She did not mention the spanners in front of the others again and Ciela seemed to be just another villager, recently returned from abroad.

They cleared the village of survivors by nightfall and returned to the delta city where Seth found himself locked out of his own ship by the decon crew. When Ciela enthusiastically accepted the invitation, he had little choice but to also agree to stay overnight at Ruthala's home.

A ground vehicle took them into the hills and he wondered how things had turned so quickly. Friendly or not, he now found himself tightly wedged between two burly Arawaj rebels, both holding their guns as if expecting some imminent attack. Ruthala, sitting across from him, carried a laser in a shoulder holster although she seemed occupied with untangling her wiry black hair from the bonds that kept it in place. As if all that wasn't enough, even the driver sat with a rifle propped between his knees.

Ciela, slouching in the seat beside Ruthala, smirked when she guessed Seth's thoughts. Just a word from her would set her free and leave him, no doubt, with a bullet in his brain. He drew his brows together but she only grinned more broadly and quite meaningfully shifted her eyes to the capable-looking Human beside him.

The carriage brought them to a single-storied private home seemingly stuck to the side of the hill leading up into the mountains. The simple panels of which it was built made a serene counterpoint to the carefully designed garden that surrounded it. But it was the view of the distant coast that made both Ciela and Seth stare in wonder when they left the shuttle. Some sort of phosphorescence rode the waves along the shore, offering a stunning display of color and motion.

"Monopods in the water," Ruthala explained. "Their filaments glow at night near the shore to attract insects. In the autumn they turn red." She tipped her head toward the house behind them. "This is my father's home. We are quite safe here." She paused for a moment, perhaps remembering that, until recently, the people of Ciela's home had felt quite safe, too. "I suppose many of us will leave now that the Commonwealth has arrived. Some of us want to stay and fight the takeover. Make them build every wall three times before their damn base is finished." She pointed across the town to a cleared patch at the far side.

"They're putting a garrison on Tadonna?"

"Yes. They know we're here. But Father wants no trouble in this place. This has been a haven for us. These people are our friends. The governors' greed isn't their fault and many of them don't understand what goes on in other places. This only makes it clearer that we have work to do elsewhere. We've lost this one. Others can still see reason and those we need to convince." She gazed out over the sprawling town, one of only a few places where settlement was possible on Tadonna's thin soil. "Well, so it goes. Come in. We'll have some food. And we need to talk."

She ushered them and two of her companions into the house and then a tiled room strewn with thickly padded mats and pillows to be arranged in whatever way they pleased. A few low tables were soon stacked with plates and bowls and Seth was happy to see some favorite Magran dishes among them. Nothing here was reported by his scanner as objectionable and he ate with appreciation for whoever did the cooking in this place.

Their companions also enjoyed their meal and he saw no signs of weapons or guards nearby. Ruthala reclined comfortably on her mat, sharing a platter with another Human. In contrast to the woman's deep brown skin and generous curves, he seemed almost unhealthily pallid, like someone who spent more time in the air than on the ground. The third rebel, a Centauri woman, devoted herself to picking bones out of a plate of tiny sea creatures, cursing them even as she declared them to be her favorite.

Ciela picked listlessly at her bowl of fish and charred vegetables, only half-listening to the easy banter traded around the room. Seth came to sit beside her and offered a small dish of pink berries. "Try these," he suggested. "Good for you, I'm sure."

She peered into the bowl. "Those'll put me to sleep."

"Maybe that's what you need right now." He'd come to appreciate her tough, if not terribly thick-skinned, exterior but she was not a fighter like these people, nor had she gown up among the sort of barbarism her people were capable of, as he had. These past few days had brought more upheaval into her life than a dozen years of space travel.

She started to reply when Ruthala dropped into the pillows beside them. "Now then: business," she said. "I'm afraid the sky is getting darker over the Arawaj."

Seth looked up, wishing the woman and her bad news would go away and give Ciela a reprieve from all this. "How so?"

Ruthala weighed her words. "Tell me, how did Ciela end up with you?"

He stopped chewing the stalk of aromatic herb they had been served to finish their meal. "Uh, with me?"

"Yes." Ruthala pointed her own twig at him. "Last we heard, she was taken aboard Bastard Sebasta's ship. That's when Chonny decided to get out of Tayako and return here." She nodded to the Centauri sitting by the window.

Ciela leaned back into her pillow. "Yes, Seth, why don't you tell our story." That devilish grin was back on her face as she regarded him expectantly and wide-eyed.

He smiled back at her with more meaning than Ruthala

was likely to interpret. "Well, there's not much, really. Ciela and I are old friends. She's always on the go so I try to see her when I can. When she said they're stopping over on Tayako I thought, well, what's a little coolant to burn for a chance to see my girl. A night of love and wine is all I ask."

Ciela's eyebrows rose into the fringe of bangs across her forehead.

He reached out to flick her chin with the edge of his finger. "And she misses me terribly, so far away on that old barge. Don't you, Sweetness?"

Ciela rolled her eyes when Ruthala, perhaps a little embarrassed, turned to pick up a long-necked bottle.

"Anyway," Seth continued. "When I got to the *Othani*, Velen told me she'd been taken. I tracked her down and tried to get her off Sebasta's ship but we lost the others during all that."

"We got away on an escape pod," Ciela said. "That was interesting, I tell you."

"Hmm," Ruthala pondered. "It's true then. He's got them all. Except for you, Ciela." The rebel turned to Seth. "It's best not to discuss them around... others. These days it's hard to know whom to trust. Not only do we have to fear the damn Air Command, now we can't even trust our own."

Ciela's smile faded. "So what's this bad news you have on top of all this today?"

Ruthala looked up when someone came to take their plates away and, with a friendly gesture, asked them to return later. Once the doors closed, she sat up on her pillows, closer to Seth and Ciela.

"First, Velen Phar got away but he's got himself a price on his head now." She waved Ciela's response to that aside. "Serves him right. What was he thinking? We have a million places to hide you and instead he decides to give away the single biggest asset we own? To the Union? Idiot deserves whatever he gets. He's a traitor as much as Sebasta is and I'd shoot him myself if he were here. He sold you and betrayed you and because of him Hariah's girls are gone, too, remember that. We've lost a major advantage because of this. Now you're the only one left."

"Air Command is still better than the Shri-Lan getting them, don't you think?" Ciela ventured.

Ruthala scowled. "No, it isn't. At least the Shri-Lan will use them to do some good, even if their goals are ridiculous. But the big issue is Sebasta's trade. Practically begging the Shri-Lan to take over and bribing them with our spanners. It's an insult. For what? Wealth and power over some backwoods outposts!"

"You heard about the trade, too?"

"Lots of folks have. They're meeting the Brothers themselves for this."

Seth frowned. "Are you sure? Those two don't travel well or often."

"This is what I heard. Apparently, the Brothers are offering a full partnership of the Ud Mrak racket. And that'll mean Sebasta will get to run the operation out of Callas as well."

Seth whistled. "How many has Sebasta convinced to join Shri-Lan?"

Ruthala shrugged. "He's got a dozen other commanders following him now. Sebasta's own people are running at least thirty ships. Mostly just transports, but he's got a handful of Tridents that'll give your ship a good run. Plus he's already got everyone on Callas who's still Arawaj convinced that this is what needs to happen. Who knows how many others will turn over our assets, change their views in the fight against Commonwealth control and follow blindly."

"Or be forced to follow," Ciela said.

Seth regarded her thoughtfully. "High stakes, for a bunch of spanners." He did not miss the furtive glance exchanged by the women. "And bad news for what'll end up a weakened Arawaj base. It's likely that more commanders will follow."

"Exactly. But we still have a chance. A message I got just before we left here earlier said some others are going to try to sabotage the deal."

"Sabotage how?"

"No idea but whatever it is, it's not going to be good. I can only imagine the sort of security they'll have for the Brothers, so it'll be messy. I've sent a message packet to Magra to see what's going on." She held up her wrist band. "I'll hear the moment the packet gets back here."

"And the spanners will get caught in the middle," Ciela said. "Miko and Luanie and the girls... We can't let this happen!"

"Surely they'll be all right," Ruthala said. "They'll have tight security on those spanners. No one wants to lose them."

"If the only choice is between letting the Shri-Lan have the... the spanners and nobody having them, what do you think would happen? What would you do?"

Ruthala fell silent.

Seth came to his feet and pulled Ciela up along with him. "I think we could use some sleep," he said. "You'll wake us as soon as you get that message, Ruthala?"

"Of course," she said, a little bewildered by their abrupt departure. "Follow the terrace to the last room at the end. It's a comfortable space."

* * *

Only the sound of wind in the trees outside and the soft gurgling of some stream or fountain nearby intruded upon the silence of the house now. Three open windows allowed enough light from Tadonna's two moons to make lamps unnecessary. Seth sat on a bench in front of a window, his arms propped on his knees.

"Why didn't you tell them?" he said finally.

Ciela lay curled on her side, without a blanket on this warm night. "Who you are, you mean?"

"Yes."

"They'd kill you. You know that."

"And you don't want that?"

"No," she said after some thought. "I don't. You're not like *them*."

He chuckled humorlessly. "*They* are not like them, Ciela. Just like not all of you are the Arawaj whose tales of terror are told to frighten children. I learned that a long time ago."

"And the Shri-Lan?"

"Shri-Lan are bloody bastards."

She smiled tiredly but he saw tears reflect the light of the moons.

"You're not all right, are you?" he said.

"No. I need to cry. I lost family today. Everyone. And all I can do is run away and hide on Delphi so I don't get lost, too." She held her hand out to him. "Lie down here with me. Please. I guess after your tall tale you have to sleep with me, anyway."

"I didn't really think that through before she sorted out the sleeping arrangements." He removed his guns and jacket and walked over to her mats to stretch out behind her. She reached for his hand and pulled his arm to drape over her shoulder. He waited for her to start sobbing, to let her grief break through that Arawaj exterior that had, in some ways, left her as reserved as the Delphians she no longer resembled. But she lay quietly, letting tears run over her face and onto the pillows without a sound. He stroked her hair, too aware of the small space they shared. It had been a long while since he held a woman like this and he had to remind himself that he fell to their charms far too easily. He knew himself well enough to realize that she had slipped under his skin at some point during these past few restless days and that he welcomed the intrusion.

"Ciela," he said a long while later.

"Yes."

"Are you going to tell me why the Shri-Lan value you so much?"

"I want to."

"And will you?"

She turned halfway toward him to look into his eyes

reflecting some of the dim light in a mellow gleam of violet. Her hand reached out as if to touch his face but then she pulled it back with a small sigh. "Let's see what the morning brings," she said.

"Are you as valuable to the Arawaj as to everyone else?"

"Yes."

"So what makes you think Ruthala will let you leave here to run back to Delphi, no matter who I am in all this?"

"They wouldn't... I mean..."

"People died because of this. And it looks like a whole lot more will get drawn into this little rebel rebellion. They need you. You seem more like a piece of property than a member of the team."

She started to reply when raised voices in another part of the house reached them. A woman, probably Ruthala, called for someone and a man answered. Another voice joined them, now coming closer. Seth sat up quickly to pull his shirt over his head and then covered them both to the waist with a blanket. Ciela gasped when he drew her close but then relaxed against him.

A brief knock on the screen door to the terrace was immediately followed by Ruthala's entrance; apparently the woman wasn't worried about disturbing her guests. "The packet came back from Magra," she announced and touched the light strip above the door.

Ciela rubbed her face to hide the signs of her tears. "Already?"

"Yes! We've got a group on Magra Torley ready to go within days. They've been working their way into Sebasta's command over these past few months and he's sending them ahead to the meeting. Part of his show to the Brothers that he's got something to offer."

"What's the plan?" Seth said.

"They're going to disrupt the meeting to demonstrate what the Shri-Lan can expect from the rest of us if they try to absorb our group. Something big."

"How big?"

"Well, if I know anything about Pacoby's methods, they'll just blow the place."

"Pacoby?" Seth said. "I think you're right. He likes fireworks."

"You know of him?" Ciela said.

"Yes, he runs suicide missions. Strangely, he's never there when things happen. This doesn't look good for the spanners." He looked to Ruthala with that last sentence.

The Human nodded. "His ways are... extreme. But effective. Air Command has backed off from him in the past. The Shri-Lan may, too."

"Air Command is a bit more concerned about collateral damage," Seth said but then bit his lip. "Where is this happening?"

"They didn't say."

Ciela's expression had turned into one of utter despair. "Pacoby's bunch stops at nothing. They'll turn this into some senseless stunt and blow up whatever they can blow up. It won't accomplish anything except their name in the news. People will die and we will get blamed for yet another list of casualties." She turned to Seth. "We have to go, too. We have to help. Get them out, I mean."

He nodded, thinking how much easier it would be to sneak Ciela out of this place and head for Delphi. But Pacoby's willingness to sacrifice utterly unaware bystanders had galled him for years. The man was not just on Air Command's list of Most Wanted, but also on the one Seth kept very close to his heart. That aside, he wasn't sure Ciela would be in any way agreeable to jump to Delphi at this point. "Trouble is, Magra is two weeks out."

Ciela glanced at Ruthala. "No, it isn't."

Seth turned his head very slowly, not sure he had heard her words correctly. "What?"

"Doesn't matter," Ruthala interjected. "We can't have you go there, Ciela. What are you thinking? You're all we have left."

"I don't care!" Ciela said. "I had to leave them behind

and it's killing me. We now have the chance to find out where they are. If we can stop this from happening we have to try. We are going to Magra, and that's it."

"I'm sure Ter Dace will have something to—"

"Ter Dace is your boss, not mine. Last time I checked, Velen Phar was in charge of my crew. So Ter Dace can go and ask him where I'm working these days."

Seth grinned and reached for his discarded shirt. "So are you going to call up a shuttle or make us walk down the hill, Ruthala?"

The woman looked from one to the other, clearly at a loss.

"You can come with us," Ciela said.

After some consideration, Ruthala shook her head and went to the door. "Sebasta's people know me and what I stand for. It'll give the whole thing away if anyone saw me. My father can get you recommended for Pacoby's group. This is on your head, Ciela. I hope your boyfriend knows what he's doing."

Seth gave her a benign grin. "I have the feeling it's Ciela who knows what she's doing."

NINE

Four high-ranking Intelligence officers already faced the conference screen when Colonel Tal Carras arrived at the administrative wing of Air Command's main base on Targon. General Tanvin Dmitra was among them, as was Daphine Verick. The other two were specialists in matters dealing with rebel politics rather than military operations.

Carras saluted the general and took a chair beside Major Verick, a question on his face. She leaned forward to activate the conference displays. "Thanks for coming so quickly. It's not often that Delphi decides to just drop in on us."

"What's happened?"

"We're about to find out," General Dmitra said. Something in his densely tattooed, bronze-colored face called for caution among those seated here. Whatever the matter was, it had come unexpected and unwelcome. He nudged a recording onto the screen. "This is what we got earlier."

Carras nodded when he recognized Captain Anders Devaughn, a Human ambassador living and working on Delphi.

"General," the blond, fresh-faced officer began. A scientist by training and inclination, his rank was largely a formality. Having been raised on Delphi, the man was one of the few non-Delphians whom they did not consider an outsider and uninvited. He usually carried a pleasant grin and an arsenal of quips and jokes in direct contrast to the reserved natives with whom he worked. Perhaps it was because of his guileless, straightforward dealings that even the Clan Council of Delphi counted him as one of their own. Today, however, there was no smile on the sun-bronzed face and the tapestried wall behind him suggested that the recording was made in the council hall itself. "The Council wishes to meet at once and decided not to travel to Targon. Please prepare to receive a coded transmission. It is meant for Colonel Carras' team."

The recording ended without farewell.

Carras drummed his thick fingers on the table top. "I don't recall ever receiving a conference from Delphi."

The major nodded. "They do prefer to deal with us in person." She smiled. "Even if that means coming onto the base on Delphi."

"Captain Devaughn seems unusually reserved. Do we know what's got him rattled?"

"No hint at all."

"What projects do we have that involve Delphi?" the general said.

Carras pursed his lips. "None. That sub-sector is secure and silent."

A flicker across the screen announced a new recording received and decoded. Only about ten hours of real-space travel and a single jumpsite separated Targon from Delphi, but communication still required transmitting a message packet to the jumpsite where relays picked it up to send it through to the receiving side. Any two-way conversation made for a tedious and expensive exchange.

The officers looked up to see three Delphians facing a camera on their side, their expressions as non-committal as always. Anders Devaughn hovered in the background.

General Dmitra and the colonel exchanged a surprised glance. "Lord Phera," Carras breathed. "What the hell is going on over there?"

The elder sat with his hands folded around the conference control pad, apparently in no hurry to begin whatever he was prepared to say here. He served as the head of Delphi's most prominent clan and his leadership, although unofficial, was uncontested. Like the man on his left, his dark blue hair was braided and pulled back from his gaunt face. The deep color suggested an age rumored to be approaching two hundred. The woman on his right, younger, bore softer features and short blue curls. All three were garbed in the official robes of the Council, making this official business, indeed.

"He's not often seen by offworlders," Verick said. "In person or otherwise."

They noticed Anders Devaughn, behind them, lift a finger as if asking the observers for patience. No doubt the Delphians were still conferring among themselves although they rarely did so in the presence of those who were not part of their mental link. The slight breach of manners added to the peculiar atmosphere of this meeting.

"There are others in the room," one of the specialist working on analyzing the message said, measuring sound, light and the shift of Anders' eyes.

"General," Phera finally spoke. Verick turned off the translator when they realized that the elder used thickly-accented Union mainvoice rather than his native Delphian, perhaps to avoid any misunderstanding created by mechanical translators. His thin lips barely moved but the eyes under the profuse brows darkened, betraying a strong emotion that his face did not. "We have come to some information and must ask you to act upon it immediately."

"Here we go," Carras murmured.

"We have evidence that several of our people are living among your Arawaj rebels, possibly held against their will, almost certainly the children of expedition members that set out from Delphi long ago and did not return."

"What what?" Verick said. "They turned up?" Her aide immediately accessed the database to start searching.

"What evidence?" Carras said, leaning forward.

"A recent message sent to one of our people working on Magra is very conclusive," Phera continued as if he had heard the colonel's question. He slid a few symbols around on the pad in his blue-nailed fingers and his image was replaced by another recording. This one was of a couple sitting in some sort of cockpit or control room. Carras grunted when he recognized Sethran Kada. The woman beside the agent at first glance also appeared Centauri. They listened, astounded, as Seth's message played for them, hearing his suggestion that she was Delphian, trained as a navigator, and that others like her were about to be sold to the Shri-Lan. Most damningly, Air Command was mentioned in the recording.

The Delphian elder reappeared on the screen. "Your people seem to be aware of the situation. We have identified the woman by the DNA sent along with that message. She was part of the expedition—" the recording stopped abruptly when General Dmitra waved his hand over the sensor.

The others turned to him, startled.

"Colonel," he said. "I've been following your investigation into the rebel activity on Taancerum. You suspect some spanners are changing hands as part of a significant deal between some of the factions. Is Lord Phera about to inform us that those spanners are, in fact, Delphian?"

Carras looked back up at the screen where Phera's cold countenance was frozen in mid-sentence. "We have no intelligence about them being Delphian. We weren't sure that this was even happening. All we have is hearsay." He cleared his throat. "It is not impossible."

"The Centauri on that recording seems to think it is. Phera would not contact us with this if he wasn't damn sure those are his people."

"Time line checks out," the Intelligence officer said, his eyes still on his work. "Those kids would be roughly the age of that woman now."

Dmitra jerked his chin to the screen. "That was Kada, wasn't it?"

"Yes, sir."

"Where is he now? Where is that woman?"

"We… er, we have lost contact for now. It is of course not unusual for the operatives to stay silent."

Dmitra's face seemed lost in a cloud of smoldering rage when he resumed the recording.

"—that set out from Delphi for the Badlands forty-five years ago. They never returned. We have always understood the possibility that they were taken by your enemies and that seems to have been the case all along. It gives us hope that they may return to us some day."

The woman beside the elder leaned forward. "As you know, our children are mentored and taught through ancient mental disciplines to nurture their innate intellect. This message offers no news about the adults that were part of this mission but we are of course anxious to ensure that the children receive the care they undoubtedly need most urgently by now."

"Never seen an anxious Delphian," one of the agents mumbled and received an icy glance from Verick.

Phera placed his hands flat on the table in front of him, a Delphian gesture meaning that negotiations are complete. Perhaps he had done so without realizing it. "To see our people used in this despicable fashion is unacceptable to us. General, given the harmonious relationship between our people, I will assume that you simply meant to verify all details before informing the Council of this discovery. The families of these individuals are most anxious to see them returned to us without delay. I have assured them that you will of course leave no option unexplored to retrieve these captives." He paused a moment, perhaps in silent conversation with the others.

"Get ready," Verick murmured.

"We'll remain here until we receive your reply, General. I will remind you that your enemies are not ours. The harm that befalls us because of your wars is not of our making and yet we continue to offer our skills to your service. We trust that our losses will not keep Delphians from leaving our homeworld in the future."

Dmitra hissed and leaned back in his chair when the recording ended. Although never directly voiced, Delphi's single trump continued to be the simple fact that their people made it possible for the Commonwealth to keep its enormous fleet moving. Without potential spanners carefully recruited and taken off planet for training, the Union would have to rely on lesser talents to navigate the keyholes. Creating a new jumpsite from one of them could take years. Although most of the Clan Council despaired at seeing so many leave to find adventure away from Delphi, it was not in their mindset to forbid it. But they had learned from others and everyone knew that, should Council ask it of the people, the exodus of talented minds would end.

"Sir, I assure you—" Major Verick began.

The general held up his hand to silence her and looked to her specialist instead. "Write me up a reply to send back. Of course we're trying to extract them and thank you for their message and then add something polite." He turned to Carras and Verick. "What do we have."

"A problem," Carras said. "We're largely viewing the situation from a distance. Taancerum is off limits to us. We can't even get a satellite in orbit without it being taken down. We have agents on the ground, but no forces. Our influence in the matter is managed by infiltration."

"How."

"We're counting on the ongoing infighting within the Arawaj faction. The opposition to any cooperation with Shri-Lan is considerable. It's of course in everyone's best interest if the two groups remain separate and at odds. But they've seen successes when they do collaborate. The Arawaj are fearless and have some good thinkers among them. Shri-Lan have the capital. Our best option is to disrupt any formal merger."

"You're counting on the Arawaj core group to do that for you. Sabotage."

"Yes. We've given them, through our agents, the location of the meeting. It's going to be limited to a few groups and security will be tight. A sabotage attempt there would mean minimal collateral damage but deliver their message. Shri-Lan look for easy prey and quick victories. They don't have the appetite for seeing the remaining Arawaj turn against them."

"Very tidy," Dmitra said. "Except for this." He gestured at the blank screen before them. "Now we have not just our agents in there, we also have civilians that we don't particularly want to see thrown off a cliff when this goes down." The general rose from his chair. "Figure it out, Carras. Send backup if you have to. Get those Delphians off Taancerum."

Major Verick waited until the general moved away to join the technician at the camera to record his response for Delphi's council before leaning close to Colonel Carras. "That's your boy in action, Tal," she said under her breath.

"You caught that, eh?"

"Kada didn't inform us who the spanners are. He told Delphi. He knew it'd light a fire under our backsides if Air Command gets mentioned in that message to Delphi, didn't he?"

Carras sighed, once again reminded that Major Verick's ability to keep Kada's quirks to herself was another reason he valued her so highly. "He's not about to let us have the woman, or anyone else we might be able to recover."

"Well," she said. "At least he's on his way to Delphi with one of them. It may keep Council at bay for a while."

TEN

The reddish ball that was Tadonna slid slowly from the *Dutchman*'s uncaring view to be replaced by millions of points of unblinking lights, a few of them explored, others never to be reached. Ciela stared up at the unremarkable display until Seth reached over from his pilot's couch to poke her arm. She flinched.

"So talk."

She rose from her bench to go back into the main cabin. They had expected resistance from Ruthala and her people but other than more grumbling from the rebel, no one tried to stop them from returning to the freshly-decontaminated *Dutchman* and launching immediately toward the keyhole.

Seth followed her and leaned against the entrance to the cockpit to watch her move about the cabin, picking up discarded clothing and other items he hadn't organized yet and likely never would, and piling them where they probably didn't belong, either. She stopped this after a while when he simply stood his ground. "We've been up for twenty hours. I need to sleep if I'm going to jump."

"We've got hours till we get to that keyhole."

She sat on the edge of his sleeping bunk with an audible exhalation of air. He came to sit on the bucket chair fused the floor beside it. "Let's have it."

"It's a secret."

"Sounds to me like it *was* a secret."

"I mean, outsiders aren't supposed to know. Um…"

"I am not an outsider. I'm no one at all. I'm a sometime mercenary and I pick jobs that suit me. Sometimes I get paid, sometimes I get locked up. If that makes me a rebel, I'm a rebel. If that helps the Commonwealth, then so be it. I don't agree with either side on what is basically a pretty stupid conflict."

"Stupid? Is it stupid to fight for our freedom?"

"Freedom from what? Trade agreements? Exploration? New technologies for people who'd never even dreamed of leaving their solar system?"

"From exploitation. Those people should be left to figure things out for themselves."

"And you decide that?" Seth returned, amazed to find himself drawn into this argument yet again. Since when had he ever cared what these fanatics thought? Precisely since Tayako, wasn't it? Why did this girl refuse to stay in that mental space where he categorized rebels by affiliation and temperament? She had him teetering from absolute suspicion of every word she said to handing her a gun to fight at his side. Had he lost all judgment of the situation? She was an enemy specialist who had to be removed from the field like any other, be that through capture or elimination. And right now she was a not-so reluctant captive who might just be the key to finally hunting down Pacoby and his gang of radicals. Nothing more, he told himself. "It's not the Commonwealth that makes First Contact, in case you don't know. That happens long before they're even interested. You're looking in the wrong place to put your blame."

He got up to put some space between himself and this pointless debate. "Let's not do this," he said from the galley, prodding the tea press more firmly than he had to. "I should not call this stupid. Your ideals are not wrong. The results of all this are stupid. People dying is stupid. Now your own people are burning villages to make some point and that is stupid, too. I think we can agree on that."

She looked down at her hands. "Yes."

He returned to hand her a cup of warm berry juice, pleased when she smiled at him to let him know he remembered correctly. "Let's start over," he said, sitting down. "If we're going to try to help your friends, you have to trust me a little. So if you can get to Magra faster than every single chart ever made says you can, you've got my attention."

She sipped and thought a moment. "All right. I guess I—"

He leaned forward and put his hand on her knee to squeeze it gently. "No games now, Ciela. No more trickery, no lies. Let's pretend we're on the same side because if Pacoby decides to stop this deal he will find a way to make it spectacular. Taking out the Brothers is about as spectacular as it gets and he won't give a damn who gets in the way. So you and I pretty much have the same goal here. Agreed?"

Her eyes met his without wavering and he suddenly felt that it might be possible to simply fall into those dark pools, perhaps to drown. His breath stopped when her teeth caught a trembling lower lip as if to stop some unspoken words. "You're right," she said then, startling him out of his trance. "You've been right all along. And honest with me. I owe you nothing less."

He pulled back, amazed by the moment that just passed. She seemed not to have noticed. *Delphians*, he thought with grim amusement.

"Something happened a while back," she said. "We were out, taking some troops from Feron to Callas. Something happened during a jump. I was working with Miko. We... we sort of came across something. At first it was kind of scary but we made it through. We didn't tell Velen Phar right away because of the way he is with his ship. But it happened again during the next jump we made together."

"What was it?"

"I still don't really know. Once we opened the keyhole, it

was like the parallax changed even after the processors were already set. Talk about vertigo." She tapped her temple to indicate her neural node. "It was like we could just touch it and make it shift. Without moving, I mean. I don't know if that means anything to a chartjumper. At a regular gate, you're standing on one side of a chasm holding a thread tied to a very small pebble on the other side. You can follow that line only there."

Seth nodded. "That's what the charts are for."

"Yes. Of course, *we* don't need the charts. We just see the pebble and can head straight for it without anyone tying a string to it. Sometimes we can choose from more than one pebble, depending on the keyhole, but they're always in the same place. We just have to *see* it."

"And this was different?"

"Oh, Seth, you have no idea! It was amazing and terrifying. We found a way to look past all that, maybe even into another layer of subspace. And there we can just shift to another terminus. We can emerge at any keyhole."

"You mean they all open into this… this new space?"

"No, but they're connected in there. Like a web, or a net. There are sort of nodes where you can just change directions instead of following a single path." She waved her hands beside her head as if to shake out words to give meaning to what she was trying to explain. "It's like you get to a point and the truth of the formula changes. We can make it change. The math changes."

Seth reached past her to take a display screen from the bed and called up the *Dutchman*'s archive. "Can you enter this web from anywhere?"

"No, we still need a fixed keyhole to start and to exit. The processors act as a sort of anchor. We can even change our destination after we've already opened the keyhole."

"Inside subspace?"

"As long as we grab it before we go in, yeah." She leaned forward to look at his screen. "What are you looking for?"

"Is this something any Level Three spanner could do?"

"No, I don't think so. Just the seven spanners working for Velen Phar and Hariah. We tried to teach it to two spanners on Ryne L'va's crew. They thought we were crazy or trying to have a giggle at their expense so we haven't mentioned it since."

"They're not Delphian."

"No. Caspians, both. Using jumper shots." She tried to pull the tablet from his hands. "Have you heard of this?"

He moved to sit beside her and pointed at some data. "Daziel Killian. Astrophysicist. Used to work out of Targon. Dead now. He theorized something like what you're describing."

"Really? That's terrific."

"Sort of. What you said about another layer of subspace reminded me of this. We pretty much assume that there are some, but of course we've been able to only breach one. But he came up with some models where the subspace strings are connected, like the net you mentioned, acting like intersections." Seth called up a massive set of extremely tiresome-looking calculations. "It was named Killian's Maze and shelved as improbable."

Ciela pointed at the screen. "That part looks about right. Why improbable?"

"Because, just like breaching a keyhole in the first place and going anywhere that doesn't leave you dead, you need a certain type of mental ability to find an exit. Killian suggested that we don't have that. It would take even Delphians more time to evolve to that stage. Or another species we haven't discovered yet. So because that idea is very scary, he was not taken seriously."

"Scary?"

"The reason Velen Phar kept you secret. The reason the Shri-Lan want you so badly. Keyholes dictate which leaps we can take to get anywhere. Which worlds we can visit. Our territories are defined by how we get there. But you seven can get from any keyhole or jumpsite to any other of your choosing. This could change this war in ways even your captain didn't want to see happening. Who all knows about this?"

"Hariah, of course." Ciela paused for a deep breath. "Well, she did, I guess. Her fleet managed the other three spanners. Ruthala and her Father know. Our crew. One or two others. But I guess Sebasta found out and now the Shri-Lan know, too." She shuffled some of the data on his screen but her thoughts were elsewhere. "Velen thought it best to keep us out of people's notice. But he said it was because it was just a matter of time before someone wanted us to do more important work. We keep losing more and more spanners as they get caught by Air Command. Maybe some people started demanding that Velen gave up some of us to the frontline groups." She looked up at Seth. "I know this'll sound silly to you, but I think all of us just wanted to do our bit by supplying our people with what they need and smuggling to raise funds. Nothing more. I don't know if I could, you know, go into a battle against Air Command."

He smiled. "Not silly at all. I'm pretty much against you going into battle, too." He fought an urge to brush the long strands of hair from her eyes. "We just have to make sure you don't fall into the wrong hands."

She pursed her lips. "So whose hands are the right ones?"

Seth considered the question, one for which there likely was no answer. What place existed that would not take advantage of what these spanners had to offer? He looked into her pale, expectant face, realizing that, once again, Delphi was the most likely solution. They would grasp the danger presented by Ciela's peculiar talent to the stability of the entire sector and they would step up to ensure that she and the others remained out of sight. Especially since all of them were, in fact, Delphian.

"What?" Ciela said when he sat up straight in his chair as if struck by some sudden revelation.

"Cazun!" he exclaimed. "The Delphians!"

"Huh?"

He stared at her, almost feeling the gears grind in his

head. "I said before that you are not in any way a GenMod. That might not be... entirely true."

"What do you mean?"

He ran his hands through his hair, staring at nothing as things fell into place. "A long time ago, almost back when the Commonwealth was first formed about three hundred years ago, the Delphians started to tinker around with their genes. Mostly selective breeding, but also some mental manipulations. Neurogenesis, even. They're very good at that. Especially an old sect of experts called Shantirs. Delphians don't fight wars but they felt threatened by the Union. They tried to breed someone to look after them."

"What, like some sort of warrior?"

"Sort of, but with mental capabilities. There were some successes and a lot of failures. The whole experiment was not just abandoned; it was outlawed at some point. But I'm guessing a few of the old guard kept tinkering. Eventually things went very wrong, just a few years ago, actually. I'm not supposed to know about that, of course. It's all classified but I try not to let that stop me."

She grinned. "I didn't think so."

"They ended up with someone who did things they didn't exactly plan for. Horrible death toll. Soldiers, rebels, too many civilians. They've had to live with that since. They've tried to make reparations. The Shantirs involved were censured, which, as Delphi goes, is a very big deal."

"What does all this have to do with us? You think we were caught up in this?"

"Yes, I do. Maybe you weren't driven out of Delphi. And probably your parents weren't rebels. That just doesn't fit the way Delphians do things. But what if they were actually fleeing Delphi?"

"Fleeing? Such paradise?" she said with no small edge of sarcasm in her voice.

"The Shantirs back then tried different ways of influencing a new born mind through one of their khamal mind links. It's really no different than the way our neural nodes communicate with our machines, except they access much more complex processes. Well, and they don't need machines. Nobody really knows what they can do, but it frightens a lot of people. It's another reason they keep to themselves. Anyway, their experiments didn't always work out."

"What happened?"

"I'm only guessing. It's not something they'd publish anywhere, but I assume some of those kids just disappeared. Inside the Shantirs' enclave or maybe they even died."

She stared at him wide-eyed, caught up in his speculation. "So you think we are part of that and our parents took us away? Ran away so those Shantirs wouldn't take us?"

"It certainly fits. As does this other-space theory. Let me guess: you seven are all pretty much the same age."

"We assume so. We don't really know."

"It's my guess, if I'm right with this, that you were part of a certain generation that achieved some result that the Shantirs didn't want. Maybe your ability to see beyond subspace. Maybe they foresaw the trouble that can cause. And for some reason, your parents decided to remove you from the Shantirs' oversight. And got caught by rebels."

"So what about that super warrior, then?"

"The Tughan Wai. Their greatest success. He was able to do things that I don't think anyone was able to explain, short of magic. But after what you told me, I think it's possible he simply accessed Killian's Maze to reach another point in space. Mentally."

"He destroyed things?"

"To say the least, yeah."

"And you think we're like him?"

"I hope not. But you are different. You are, like Killian proposed, a different breed of Delphian. It's not in your DNA, but it's in your head. A physical change of your neural net."

"Is that possible?"

"You have no idea..." Seth took the tablet and scrolled

around Killian's work, wishing he had the capacity to understand half of what the man described. Was it possible? He stood up and held out his hand. "Come."

"What?" She let him pull her up, smiling at something in his expression. "You find this exciting, don't you?"

"Don't you?" He ushered her ahead of him into the little cargo bay. "Stand over there. We're going to run another med-scan."

She sighed dramatically as if indulging a child in some play and stood where he pointed. He programmed the scanners that analyzed and, when necessary, treated for contaminants but also looked for disease and injury. This time, he specified Delphian anatomy and physiology.

"Smile big."

She made a face.

The scan completed in moments and they returned to the cabin to await the results. Seth actually found himself pacing a little until the screen fixed above the galley delivered the report. Ciela sat on the lounge as if expecting great entertainment.

"Hey, I look naked!"

"That's just a representation."

"I hope so. She's got shoulders like a Feydan."

Seth ran some comparisons. Xenobiology was not one of his strengths but his library made up for that lack quite well. The display soon enough shifted to a view of a Delphian brain as a point of interest, as he had suspected. "There it is," he said.

"What?"

He reached up to spin the image and pointed at the center of the brain. "The Delphian hippocampus is larger than most Prime species' in general. That explains your memory and why so many of your people end up as pilots and engineers. You, however, seem to have an extra lobe."

"That thing? Looks like a worm."

He nodded. "My equipment here can't look any closer than this, but I'll bet your neurons are generating just nicely in there. This could explain your ability to find your way through that maze. That other space." He reached up to shift to another part of his archive. A quick search found no further reference to Delphians in Killian's notes. Nothing here hinted at their involvement in his theories. "The problem is, we can't really ask anyone about this."

"Doesn't matter," she said. "Clearly I'm not going back to Delphi. Those people are insane."

He returned his gaze to the slowly rotating view of her brain. The Shantirs of Delphi would not dream of banishing someone like Ciela from their oversight. Likely, they would have been aware of this peculiar anomaly since before she was born. "Things have changed. I don't think you'll have to worry. There is so much they can teach you. But the main thing is that they're the only people who will make sure you're not exploited by rebels or Air Command. No other place can guarantee that."

She sighed. "Tadonna sure didn't."

"What about the other six in your group? If they can't be extracted. I mean, if we can't find them, how will they deal with being turned over to the Shri-Lan?"

She stared at nothing for a while. "Miko won't work for them. They'll have to find a way to force him. I'm so scared about that." She bit her lip. "It'll kill Luanie. She gets very depressed. We have to watch her. Velen promised he'll find someone to help her but you'd need a Delphian for that, I guess. Deely hates the Shri-Lan but he hates the Commonwealth more. They may... get to him. The girls won't even notice who they work for. They don't pay much attention to what happens, ever. We don't even know what they're thinking half the time." She drew her knees up onto the lounger and wrapped her arms around them. "So, yeah, as long as we're out there somewhere, we're a danger to everyone. I guess I finally realized that when I saw what Sebasta did to my village."

He studied her expression for a moment, seeing nothing but genuine grief there. "Which is why you didn't tell them who I am. You're a catastrophe no matter who you work for. You know, you're not just a terrible shot, you're a terrible rebel."

* * *

"So are you nervous?"

"What?" Seth chuckled and realized that he sounded precisely as nervous as she assumed him to be. Now that they were about to enter the keyhole apparently leading to Magra despite all mathematical evidence pointing elsewhere, he wasn't so sure he wanted to try it. "Not a bit. Once I waxed two Rhuwacs with nothing but a pistol in each hand set to stupendous level. I fear nothing."

"My hero." Ciela reclined in the co-pilot's bench and engaged her neural interface. Seth did the same, prepared to let her show him what she had found beyond subspace. She insisted that whatever it was that set him apart from the pilots she had known would let him see what she did. "I've already taken you through that maze once, you know. You just didn't know it. And anyway, it's not moving us in space at all."

"I'm not nervous!"

"Not in subspace, anyway. You know, I wonder sometimes what'd happen if I got lost at one of the nodes, like taking a wrong turn or something. That'd be scary. Who knows where you'd end up. Or maybe you'd just zip around forever. I guess that's why this Killian guy called it a maze. I can see—"

"Stop it, Ciela!"

"Want me to hold your hand?"

"Let's do this."

He aligned the *Dutchman* with the keyhole, invisible before them, and fed the minute aperture with the ship's energy to create a sufficient opening. The processors ramped up, ready to provide the navigator with the calculations she needed to determine their destination.

Ciela closed her eyes, feeling her way into subspace, and

he did the same. At this point, once she had found the terminus, all that remained was to shove the ship forward and into the breach and trust that it would come out where intended. For all their reliance on mathematics, astrophysics and the simplest laws of nature, this part was likely not something he'd ever truly understand.

But she held off. "All right. I'm going to reset the processors. You'll see sort of a weird, uh, parallax shift. You'll feel it more than anything. Don't worry; it's always like that."

Seth tried to breathe evenly. He had made a thousand leaps; the simple chart hops that any pilot could manage through a jumpsite, and he had ridden along when a Level Three spanner cracked the most complex of keyholes that felt like they'd never emerge again. This was just another leap, he told himself.

He knew quite well that the Big Nothing was not at all a Big Nothing. He had seen it. Touched it. He had interacted with it and it had changed him. Not even Delphi's Shantirs had been able to determine exactly what had altered, however subtly, his neural net after that strange encounter not that long ago. But something had and, so far, it had not affected his life in any noticeable way. Not in real-space, anyway.

And so when she had offered to show him her glimpse of subspace he had accepted with great enthusiasm. That enthusiasm was slightly compromised now by a growing realization that perhaps minds like his were better left oblivious to the mysteries of subspace.

He swallowed. "Tell me something…"

"Hmm?" She frowned, already focused on her task.

"When you're in there, do you ever, uh, do you ever feel that there's something, well, *alive* in there?"

"Do you really want to know that now?"

"Gods, no!"

She reached for him and gripped his hand. "Go!"

He punched the *Dutchman* forward, grinding his teeth as

they passed the threshold into the breach. At this point, sentient beings lost all five senses; no time, no gravity, no light, nothing existed except a certainty in the most primitive regions of the brain that knew only that death was imminent.

But he caught a glimmer of something. For an instant or two, she delayed the jump and he saw what she did; what she glimpsed when entering this space, this *other* space. Instead of the single, charted, prescribed terminus, the possibilities before him exploded into an endless, ever-expanding network of paths, each accessible through the power of his ship's processors. He perceived it as a network of glowing lines, as chaotic as a tangled net while as logical as zero and one. He tried to look for her but then the darkness took over, as always, and nothingness replaced the vision his mind had witnessed.

"Cazun," he gasped when the *Dutchman* tumbled out of the terminus Ciela had targeted and back into real-space. He sat up clutching his chest as if that would ease the deep gulps of air he drew into his lungs. He barely managed to reach for the ship's control system to bring it back on course and check for bearings and damage. "What the…"

She reclined on her bench as serene and still as she had been those few seconds ago. "Quite the ride, huh?"

He still breathed heavily, shaken by the experience. "You didn't say there were a billion exits!"

She smiled and opened her eyes. "You would have just worried." She waggled her eyebrows. "You look kinda sexy panting like that."

"You are something, you know that?"

"Yeah. Did you like it?"

He looked over the cockpit displays, seeing nothing to indicate that the *Dutchman* was at all put out about this trip through whatever that was. "Gods, yes." He fell back into his couch. "How did you know where to go? They all looked the same to me."

She tapped her forehead. "Special Delphian, remember? I wouldn't pick any of those exits if I didn't know where they end up. That'd be foolish. I've made friends with your ship. It's so much smarter than the *Othani*. I could do this all day." She sat up with a groan. "Well, that's a lie. I'm going to pass out for a while." She paused. "Why did you ask me about something being alive in there?"

"Is there?"

She pondered this for a moment. "Sometimes I'm not sure. It can't be possible, of course, but we don't really understand what 'alive' means, do we? Sometimes I do feel... watched during a traverse. Like someone is noticing me pass by. Strange, isn't it?"

He shook his head. "Maybe not. There's a lot we don't know about subspace."

She squinted at him. "You've felt something in there."

He grinned. "Yeah. Like I told you before, poking around subspace is a bit of a hobby for me. You just made it a whole lot more interesting."

She raised herself up and gripped his arm when he offered it. "You'll have to show me your hobby, Headhunter. I thought you mercs just hang around and drink heavily in your time between shooting people."

"That just gives me a headache," he said, catching her when she stumbled. "The drinking part, I mean. Are you all right?"

She nodded, apparently content to let him keep an arm around her to walk her to the sleeping cabin. "Was a long jump. That takes a toll."

He waited until she dropped onto her bunk before returning to the cockpit. Only then did he realize that he no longer bothered to lock her door when not supervising his prisoner. Prisoner? "Some merc you are," he said, grinning at his reflection in an inactive screen.

* * *

Equatorial Magra Torley rarely made the list of favorite vacation destinations when those living on other parts of the continent or, indeed, other planets, looked for a place to get away. Temperatures here rivalled those of Feyd but the humidity and endless rains made them seem even more unbearable. Seth landed the *Dutchman* amid a collection of other cruisers on a metal platform raised above the mud, wincing when something seemed to give beneath the ship as it settled.

Ciela studied the screens above the cockpit. There was little to see beyond the air field other than massive vegetation whipped by ferocious winds. Seth had had to compensate for the shear upon landing and she had covered her eyes when the *Dutchman* had more than once threatened to career into the massive trunks. She watched them bend impossibly far against the wind's ferocity. "Do we have to go out there? It's pouring. Make them come here."

"They're waiting for us over there. I guess they're making some sort of point before letting us tag along."

She followed him into the main cabin. "Hot outside, too."

"And buggy." He picked up his medical scanner and compared Delphian physiology to the conditions of this environment. The northern sectors of both main continents were safe for most Prime species but this area teemed with hazards. "You're going to need a little patching up."

She watched him sort through a collection of vials and other medication in his kit. "I don't want a shot. I don't like needles."

He found the patches he needed. "You and me are two of a kind, lady. Don't worry. This should do." She wore only a sleeveless shirt and loose trousers and now held her arm out while he applied two of the thin slips to her skin. "Sort of bloodsucking moths out there. They can leave nasties in your blood. Tuck your pants into your boots to keep leeches out."

"Leeches?"

"A bit smaller than the ones on Tayako. But they hurt. Don't drink the water here. Actually, don't eat anything, either. Take this anyway." He handed her a gel capsule.

"Don't you need a patch?"

"Just the one for the arsenic in the rain. I grew up on Torley. Not around here, though."

"But you didn't grow up to be a rebel."

Seth shrugged. "I was on my way. Seemed more exciting than what my parents had in mind for me." He stuck another patch on her arm just for good measure.

Those had been thrilling times, he recalled. Magra Torley's government, perpetually at war with the vast continent on the other side of the planet, tolerated rebels for no other reason than the steady supply of stolen technology, stolen planes, and masterless mercenaries willing to use them. In response, Magra Alaric had opened its doors to the Union, installing extensive military bases and allowing fully armed orbiting stations above its dominion. A conflict like that held much excitement for a young Centauri with few restrictions put upon him by his long-suffering Human foster parents.

"So what changed your mind?"

He sat to pull his boots on, following his own advice to tie off the hems of his ancient combat trousers. "Dead bodies, mostly. Scared people. Ruined towns, like yours. It gets old. Spent a season in a very small jail cell before my parents shipped me off to teach me manners at the Air Command academy."

"Ugh," she said.

"I will be forever grateful to them." He pointed toward the *Dutchman*'s cockpit. "Turned me into a damn fine pilot, if I can boast without shame for a moment, even if they couldn't turn me into a soldier. I'd still be blowing up bridges if not for them."

"Some bridges need to be blown up."

He came to his feet and gestured to the exit. "That's Arawaj talking, Ciela. Start seeing things for yourself."

She frowned and took a breath as if to launch into another fierce bit of rhetoric. He raised his hand to ward that off. "Just try. I used to think there was just one exit on the other side of that keyhole. Maybe you'll find a few out here in real-space, too."

"Sounds kinda preachy," she mumbled and walked ahead of him to the ramp. She raised an eyebrow when he handed her a knife, a thin blade inside a quick-draw holster, but made no comment as she belted it around her hips.

There was no hood or poncho that would serve to keep the rain away and it took just moments for both of them to get drenched to the skin. The steady downpour shifted occasionally to blast them from the side as they walked down from the platform. Beyond the wall of whipping treetops lay the town of Riva but they would not see that today. The Arawaj gang they were to meet waited for them in the huddle of outbuildings near the air field. Broad overhangs reached nearly to the ground to channel rain water into a stream running through the middle of the narrow lane between them.

Seth and Ciela ducked under the awning of a building whose signage seemed to suggest some sort of outfitter. Seth was glad to have resupplied his coolant supply on Tadonna; his data sleeve warned of leaking radiation from the stores next to this building.

Two Feydan men sharing a meal of dumplings on the raised porch watched the new arrivals hurry into the shelter. Their unwavering leer was focused on Ciela. Seth glanced over at her and saw that, although her shirt was black, it was soaked through and left very little to be imagined about the shape beneath. She frowned at him when he took a step forward and in front of her.

"Looking for Pacoby," he said.

The man whose ear was pierced by what appeared to be a Caspian's toe claw shifted his gaze to Seth. "Not here. Not fond of rain. You'd be Kada, then?"

"Right."

"Tadonna's vouching for you. Pacoby's not so sure. Says to check you and send you topside if we like you. You'll jump with him."

"Just tell us where he's going. We can find our way

there."

"Not going to happen."

Seth muttered a silent oath. Finding Pacoby still down here would have made things a whole lot easier for them. He had envisioned a quick bullet to the brain and a quicker exit on the *Dutchman*.

The Feydan rebel held up a scanner. "Would ye oblige us, kind sir," he said, grinning when his partner guffawed around a mouthful of mash over the wit he displayed.

Seth leaned forward to allow a scan of his retina. The rebel sent it to wherever it was going to be scrutinized and then raised his scanner to Ciela. She also leaned toward him and it took a moment before she realized that he had lowered it for a better view of her soggy neckline. Seth felt anger rise, a rare sensation for him.

Ciela turned to him. "Can you shoot that man, please? He's rude."

Seth blinked but recovered before the others did. He drew his gun and poked it into the rebel's ear before the man had time to reach for his own.

"No need for that," the rebel said, holding his hands up to placate the madman with the gun. "Just having some fun here."

The other rebel had stopped chewing in surprise. He drew back when Ciela pulled her knife and moved closer to him. She raised it slowly and then stabbed down to skewer the food in their bowl.

"Remember what I said about the food here," Seth said when she turned up the knife with the dumpling. She flipped the morsel out into the rain where two lizards darted from under the porch to devour it. He returned his attention to the rebel at the end of his gun. "Going to send that?"

The man nodded and fumbled with his transmitter.

Seth lowered his gun and they all waited in uncomfortable silence until the rebel received his response.

"That's Kada," a voice without video spoke from his wrist unit. "Not one of ours but he's worked with Pe Khoja so that's good enough for us. The other one doesn't show up."

"She's my spanner," Seth said loud enough for transmission. "Part of Velen Phar's crew."

Another silence followed while someone weighed the value of Seth's word against the lack of Ciela on their database.

"Tadonna confirms," a woman cut into the conversation. "You're cleared, Kada. We can always use another spanner on the trip. Cie Pacoby wishes to meet her."

"Are we done here now?" Seth said genially when the transmission ended.

"You're damn lucky," the rebel snarled, having recovered his wits if not his pride. "You'd not get twenty steps if you hadn't checked out." He allowed Seth's data sleeve to copy the coordinates for Pacoby's ship in orbit.

Seth turned his back on them and slung his arm around Ciela's waist. "Enjoy your dinner."

They hurried back to the *Dutchman*, both aware that the disgruntled rebels would surely complain to Pacoby about their treatment.

"You did that well," Seth said when they waited for a full decon cycle to complete before entering the ship. "By the time we get up there they'll have told Pacoby we're homicidal hooligans intent on skinning them alive. Pacoby appreciates those qualities in his people."

"So I hear," she said, shivering. "You should have zapped that guy a little for his bad manners. It's freezing in here!"

He unlatched the pressure door when the Dutchman announced them safe to enter. "Get into some dry clothes," he said, unable to divert a glance at her damp shirt. "Please."

ELEVEN

As Arawaj rebel accommodations went, this was the most peculiar one Seth had seen up until now.

They had found Pacoby's convoy and obeyed his request to lock onto his ship, a powerful little Fleetfoot flanked by two others. Arawaj shunned the small luxuries Seth allowed himself on his own cruiser, either by inclination or simply shortage of funds, but this ship suffered no lack. They were met by two well-dressed Centauri, near perfect gravity and excellent air quality when they stepped aboard. Like on all Fleetfoots, the walls were unclad, showing their complex network of conduits, supports and service grids, but the structure looked well-maintained and spotless. Seth and Ciela exchanged a surprised glance when they heard music piped softly through overhead speakers.

They were searched thoroughly and not especially gently, making them feel a little more at home.

"This way," was the only thing the Centauri woman said before walking ahead of them through the main corridor. They passed several doors and junctions to other passages and Ciela busied herself, out of habit, with memorizing any variances from the standard Fleetfoot design. They walked past the bridge, located in the heart of the ship, and into an adjoining cabin.

Left alone in there, Seth turned to Ciela with raised eyebrows. She shrugged and looked around what seemed to be some sort of lounge, oddly furnished in carved Feydan designs. Beautiful in their primitive way, but heavy and not something found on ships capable of entering planetary atmospheres. Whatever way the thickly cushioned seats and tray tables had been fastened to the floor was invisible. The walls contained a more practical display system with multiple screens. One of them, made to look like a window, showed a real-vid view of the ship's surroundings.

A door to their left slid aside and Sco Cie Pacoby entered from the adjoining bridge. He carried a data sheet in his hand and said nothing when he held it up, apparently comparing the information on it to the two people in front of him.

"Thank you for allowing—" Seth began but Pacoby raised a finger to silence him.

"Let the music play," he said softly.

Once again, Seth and Ciela exchanged a bewildered look. The music piped into the hall outside did not enter this room.

The rebel's eyes remained on his data sheet. Human, this small, neatly dressed man came as a bit of a surprise. Seth had seen headshots of him but had not expected someone as delicately formed as him, reaching barely to Seth's elbow. Centauri and their Delphian cousins were the tallest of the Prime species but Pacoby seemed petite even for a Human. As one of the more feared Arawaj commanders, his carefully groomed appearance seemed oddly out of place.

His guests had dressed in preparation of several days aboard their ship in loose, comfortable clothing while he wore a tailored set of trousers and jacket, matched carefully with a spotless, creaseless shirt. Seth rubbed his chin, suddenly feeling a little rumpled.

But Pacoby seemed entirely disinterested in the Centauri before him. He smiled at Ciela as if moving his lips that way required some calculation on his part. "You worked for Phar?"

"Yes. Five years on his flagship."

He glanced briefly at Seth and then back to her. "So you're here to liberate your companions? Is that what I'm gleaning from Ruthala Cedre's message?"

"Uh, yes. I guess…"

"Sebasta must be stopped," Seth said quickly. "This alliance can't happen. I have a ship, she's got a talent. We're here to join your mission. To serve."

Pacoby's pallid eyes travelled to Seth as if finally and actually seeing him. "Are you? Nothing personal, then?"

Seth returned his gaze firmly, wanting nothing so much as use his bare hands, in the absence of his weapons, to put this man out of everyone's misery. The horrific acts he committed in the name of the Arawaj cause would soon earn him the sort of command he undoubtedly craved. Even the fairly unorganized Arawaj leadership was known to harbor doubts about his influence on their methods. But unlike many of Pacoby's followers, Seth was not quite ready to give up his life for the Commonwealth on a ship full of armed rebels. "Of course it's personal," he said instead of strangling the man. "She's lost friends. As have I. All the more reason to join you."

Pacoby nodded. Although his eyes had returned to Ciela, his words were for Seth. "Your name is not unknown to us, Kada. But so far your allegiance seems a little… uncommitted. Are you joining this mission, or are you joining the Arawaj?"

"My service on this mission will show my commitment," Seth said.

"Will my friends be hurt?" Ciela said, unable to keep her fears to herself any longer. "If you plan to sabotage the meeting, what about them?"

Another lifeless smile played over Pacoby's lips. "We plan sabotage, not annihilation," he said. "The meeting place is a fortress and we stand little chance of breaching it." He turned away to place his data sheet on a nearby table, thoughtfully fussing over its alignment with the edge. "There are two flight decks. One houses a hangar for the Shri-Lan fighter planes. The Shrills. So we'll be told to dock onto the west deck where they can keep an eye on us. Or so they think. Our plan is to destroy the north air field. It'll cost them their Shrills and whatever cruisers they have there. Simple, expensive for them, and making our statement sufficiently. The Shri-Lan may want to buy our people, but they don't want to buy our troubles. They will know what an alliance with Sebasta's camp will cost them and they'll send him and his defectors on their way. So have no fear for your people."

"But then how will you free them?"

He turned back to her. "That is not our mission. However, we will attempt to pursue Sebasta after our work is complete. I will welcome four additional spanners under my command."

"What? But…"

"Your smuggling days are done, dear. There is greater work for all of us." He gestured at the door to the hall. "Return to your ship. When we get to the keyhole you will demonstrate your abilities and take us through."

Seth nudged Ciela toward the exit, hoping she'd keep any further protest to herself.

"Mister Kada," Pacoby called as the door opened.

Seth turned back.

"You will observe com silence from here on. There will be no communication of any kind from your ship other than to this one." His bland, expressionless face revealed nothing of his suspicion for his newest recruits but Seth felt it coming from the man in waves. He doubted that someone like Pacoby could ever fully trust anyone.

* * *

"Come look at this."

Seth rolled off the lounger and padded into the cockpit when Ciela's call roused him from his study of Killian's musings about subspace. It was putting him to sleep anyway. He propped his hands on the top frame of the doorway and stretched his body. "Are we there?"

"Yes, look." She gestured at the screens.

As he watched she honed the *Dutchman*'s external sensors onto a small spot on the planet now not far ahead of them. Seth glanced over the other monitors to see Pacoby's small fleet still in loose formation around them. So enticingly in weapons range and utterly out of reach. There had been no chance to send a message to Air Command when Pacoby finally revealed their destination as Taancerum. By Commonwealth rules of conduct the planet was off limits to the military now but both Pacoby and Sebasta were fair game outside the planet's air space. It didn't matter. Pacoby's people still monitored them closely and he had no doubt that any message packet sent to Air Command would simply end up with the mission aborted and the *Dutchman* in a lot of tiny pieces.

Likely, Seth thought, Air Command was already well aware of something brewing on Taancerum. That it involved a new breed of Delphian was probably not common knowledge.

He had not been surprised by Pacoby's demand that Ciela led the way through the keyhole. She proved herself easily, taking the jump ahead of the others to allow them to follow in her wake without using their own resources. Now, six hours later, Taancerum had come into visual range.

"Any sign of the *Hajsa* yet?"

"Yes, he's on approach."

"Is that Daos?"

The main screen now showed a broad valley surrounded by bare-faced mountains, some identified as having volcanic activity. Streams and rivers flowed from those ranges into the plain where ragged patches of green seemed to have attracted settlement. A scattering of windowless stone blocks typical of the planet's building traditions followed the rivers without any definite order to shape them into towns.

Above it all rose the Union-built pyramid. As if it tried to compete with the mountains around them, the solar-paneled colossus loomed out of all proportion to its surroundings. And yet, its five blank and featureless slopes resembled the bare rock of the cliffs guarding the valley, seeming to belong there. A sprawl of outbuildings and aircraft hangars reached out from its base, all of it covered and protected against Taancerum's poisonous air.

"It's a fortress."

Seth gripped the back of the pilot benches and vaulted into his seat. "From what I've read, it was never designed to be a fortress," he said, broadening the scope of his sensors. "Looks like the festivities are about to start."

Besides Pacoby's detail, two Arawaj delegations loyal to Sebasta cruised the sector and now approached the planet. Several ships belonging to Shri-Lan already patrolled the air space above the Daos valley, rudely questioning each new arrival. Seth and Ciela listened silently to conversations no doubt designed to impress upon the visitors who was in charge here. Like the core group of the Arawaj, there were those among the Shri-Lan opposed to the alliance, preferring to use Arawaj only when it suited them.

"There are so many of them!" Ciela said when they had locked into a synchronous orbit to await orders, sounding a lot less confident than she had back on Tadonna. "What can we possibly do here?"

Seth propped his bare foot onto the edge of the com console. "The situation at the air field is going to cause a lot of confusion. It'll help us get to your friends."

"You're joking with me. If that air field blows my friends are either blowing with it or Sebasta will turn tail if it happens before he gets there. We don't stand a chance against the *Hajsa*."

"He's going to leave the *Hajsa* in orbit." Seth beckoned her to take a closer look at the image of the pyramid. "Look up there, the level below the apex. Those are docking ports on that terrace. Small craft. I'm betting that everyone that counts in this little party will be meeting up there, not on the air field. Pacoby can light all the fireworks he wants, it won't do much to the people up there."

"So you think the trade will happen anyway?"

"I don't know. Pacoby was right when he said that the Shri-Lan won't be interested in dealing with Arawaj internal problems. They could send Sebasta on his way if things get ugly. They might even just take the spanners and let him leave with his life if he's lucky."

"If they feel attacked, the Shri-Lan are going to murder every Arawaj they can get their hands on. Pacoby must know that."

"He does." Seth pointed to the foot of the pyramid. "He's counting on everyone's attention on the north hangar or on the Shri-Lan commanders at the top, giving him a chance to get away."

"A small chance."

"That's his way." Seth shrugged. "He'll be ready to launch the moment this goes down, whatever the outcome. I hope to get to him before he does."

She frowned. "What do you mean?"

"I've been chasing him for years. This is my chance." He grinned. "Oh, sorry. I keep forgetting you're one of them."

"What are you thinking, Kada!"

He shrugged. "Pacoby needs to be eliminated. If you forget for a moment who you were told to be and think about what he does, you can see that, too." He watched the stubborn expression on her face for a few moments. "Ah, there," he teased. "You know I'm right. You just won't admit it."

She narrowed her eyes at him. "Fine. He's a monster. But he's our monster."

"Monsters are best kept on leashes if you want to use them as a weapon. He has none." On the way out here, Seth debated with himself the wisdom of showing Ciela examples of the recent works of Pacoby's group, likely a far nastier collection than anything she would have been told about him. In the end he decided against it. She had lost her adopted family, her friends, her home. Only the Arawaj remained as any sort of base for her. He'd leave it to the Delphians to restore her sense of family. They would even let her keep her distrust of the Commonwealth as she adapted and found her own purpose.

And yet, he wanted to convince her, shake some sense into her as she clung to her Arawaj upbringing. Seth himself had no illusions about the Commonwealth or the means employed by Air Command to achieve their objectives. He had witnessed their shortcuts and compromises and had done his part to frustrate their efforts when he could get away with it. He supposed that, in a way, made him a rebel, too. He sympathized with the smaller factions and their fear of Commonwealth expansion. But nothing would ever justify, to him, the means by which Shri-Lan and Arawaj operated.

"I'm not turning on my own people," she said. "Don't ask me that."

"They are not your people. Certainly not Pacoby."

"What do you know?" she said angrily and jumped out of her seat.

He followed her into the main cabin where she whipped around to face him. "Is it not enough that I agreed to go to Delphi?" She pointed at her head. "I understand perfectly that we need to be removed from... from all of this. I got that completely when I saw what's left of my home. I will go freely and I will ask the others to if we find them. What does that tell you?"

"Tells me that you don't really want to do this. Any of this. You've spent your life in some fantasy, pretending what you do doesn't harm anyone. It does. Every gun you deliver harms somebody. Every fighter you smuggle past Air Command harms somebody. You damn well know it but it's not you with the finger on the trigger."

"It's the only way to stop the Commonwealth."

"Stop living your damn life worrying about the Commonwealth! What have they drummed into your head on Tadonna? This is your life, Ciela. Your life and an immeasurable talent and you're using it to blow up bridges. Wake up!" Seth stopped himself, suddenly aware that he had never shouted at anyone like this. He had many passions but he rarely lost his temper. This was new. Even in the worst despair, he usually managed to keep his composure, something he had learned long ago from his Delphian friends.

Ciela only glared back at him, apparently not daunted by a little shouting. "Maybe it's you who's wasting his life chasing after rebels. For every one you hunt down, three more get recruited."

"Into Shri-Lan."

"Doesn't make your calling any nobler than mine."

"Calling? Is that what you call this? People are going to die down there. Shri-Lan, Arawaj, civilians. Not in some battle. Just going about their business. That is your calling?"

"It's what..." She halted, searching for words. "You have no..." She stopped again and raised her hands in some unfinished gesture. "I don't know, Seth. I don't know who I am anymore. Or even what I am. I just want to find Miko and Luanie and Deely. I want to go home and there is no home for me. There never has been." Her eyes shone with the depth of her emotions and unspilled tears. "I don't know what to do, Seth!"

Seth felt that familiar punch in the weak spot that invariably led him to capitulate when seeing a woman in despair. Those tears were his fault at a time when he needed her to keep her spine straight. He ground his teeth, telling himself that she would not get to him, knowing she already had. And then he watched himself reach out to touch her arms. "Ciela..."

She let him draw her closer.

"I'm sorry. I shouldn't have said all that. You will have a home, I've promised you. And if we find Miko and the others, they will, too. But I need to be able to trust you. I need you to hold together. Pacoby is a fox and he'll know if you're not on your game. Forget what I said. It doesn't matter."

She shook her head. "It does matter." She looked up. "You matter."

His eyes travelled to her lips and no force in this universe could stop him from bending to touch them with his own. He kissed her softly, feeling whatever distance there was between him and this rebel vanish into nothing.

Her eyes were still on his when he pulled back. "Don't stop," she said.

He drew her close to kiss her again, holding nothing back when he felt her body press against his own. The minutes drifted away and there was nothing here now except the woman in his arms and the hands touching him as if they had always done so.

"Ciela…" he whispered finally, nearly swaying on his feet. He cradled her head in his hands and leaned his forehead against hers. "This isn't—"

She pulled his hand from her face until it rested on her breast. "Don't. Stop."

He succumbed, utterly and completely. The lounger waited only a few steps away. A frantic tussle to shed unwanted clothing and then her skin touched his in a way that seemed meant to be. He drew whimpers from her that soon grew into moans of pleasure in answer to his touch. Her cries urged him on and he gave himself up to her embrace, certain now that the craving that had hounded him for days now had not been one-sided.

Ages passed before time resumed and he became aware of their surroundings. He smiled when she moved to sprawl over him, not in any hurry to leave their tangled blankets.

"You gave that up far too easily," she said, touching her lips to his chest.

"Yeah. I'm weak."

"Not that I've noticed." She gave him a lewd grin, but then closed her eyes and arched her back when he ran his fingers along the thin line of hair growing along her spine.

"You know," he said, watching her face. "On Delphi the

young people choose a teacher, a mentor, to learn all about things going on in the bedroom."

"Uh huh," she said, only half-listening.

"That's because they can join their minds and things get complicated. I imagine that can get pretty… interesting."

She opened her eyes. "You think I need a teacher?"

"Gods, no. But you've missed out on some amazing Delphian tricks growing up on your own."

"Maybe." She watched her finger trace the faint scar on his chest, suddenly very somber. "I'm sorry I got so blubbery, earlier. I'm tougher than that. I just…"

He tilted her face to kiss her softly. "Don't. I understand. You've got to deal with this and I won't keep pushing you. I've had my chance to do my job and turn you over to Air Command. I have no right now to tell you what to do. You'll figure out where and what you want to be. In your own time."

She just nodded.

He sat up and put his feet on the floor. "And in case you haven't noticed I'm stuck out here, anyway. The only way back to civilization is through a keyhole I can't open. Sometimes I think I must be crazy to get myself into things like this."

She draped herself over his shoulders to nuzzle his ear, feeling so good against the skin of his back that he decided that perhaps getting out of bed was not entirely necessary right now.

A squawk from the com console put an end to that notion. "Damn…" Seth mumbled and leaned back to slap at the com panel above the bed. "What?" he snapped.

"Time to head down. The *Hajsa* is in orbit. Fall in behind us and wait for co-ords."

"Now?" Seth swatted at Ciela's hand when it wandered a little too close to where it probably shouldn't be right now.

"Are you too busy for this?" came the peevish reply.

Seth winked at Ciela. "Never too busy for you."

* * *

The Daos pyramid was even more impressive upon approach than from a distance. Seth, like some of the other cruisers forming part of the tribute payable to the Shri-Lan, circled the valley to get a closer look. He tiled the overhead screens to give them a panoramic view of the entire valley. Next to the edifice, the attendant outbuildings and nearby settlements seemed like scattered toys in the bleak landscape. The massive solar collectors on all five faces of the pyramid gave the impression that it was made entirely of glass, currently reflecting an orange sky in its facets. One of the upper levels featured a broad terrace from which several umbilicals extended toward two small landing platforms on each side of the pyramid. Two cruisers were already locked on, one of them impressive enough to belong to the Brothers. If so, the only thing still missing was Sebasta and his cargo.

"How did they ever build this thing out here?" Ciela wondered.

"Modules. The whole pyramid is a stack of interchangeable pieces, all transported fully assembled. Like a three-dimensional puzzle. All shipped in from Magra, I suppose. Maybe Pelion."

"And those? Don't they have windows here?" She indicated the buildings used by the local population. Unlike the homes in the valley, these lined up in precise rows, many of them near the flight decks on two sides of the pyramid. They, too, had flat roofs and sloped walls but showed only solid, unadorned surfaces on the outside.

"Those walls are translucent," Seth said, recalling his earlier study of the planet and its history. "Made from a type of sediment here. Clever, but far too expensive to export. Light enters but you can't see through the walls. I don't suppose there is much to look at outside, so they don't bother with windows."

"Yeah, looks kinda dreary here," she said. "A little sad."

"I'm sure the Taancers are quite happy here. You don't see them off-planet very much." He pulled up an image of a small bi-ped resembling Prime species in principle but covered in miniscule scales ranging from green to pink along their double-ridge backs. Instead of a nose, two short tubes drooped from either side of their faces. "Used to be amphibian but things dried up here quite a bit after some disaster with the volcanoes a million or so turns around the sun ago. Now they're land-based. They breathe mainly nitrogen, like us, but the air has very little oxygen and just enough chlorine to drop you in about ten minutes."

"No wonder they have scales still. We're going to need to carry tanks?"

"No, the whole installation is enclosed. At least the places where we're supposed to be."

"The Shri-Lan may not want us to debark at all," she pointed out. "Not much trust between them and Arawaj."

"That is true." Seth changed the display to show an overlay of control tower instructions highlighting the docks and required flight paths. "*Dutchman* Pacoby Three," he transmitted. "Requesting permit."

"And these people don't mind the Shri-Lan here? Seems odd."

Seth nodded. "I don't think anyone really knows what goes on here. Guess we'll find out." He shifted his attention to the landing maneuvers. "Damn! Son of a Rhuwac was wrong."

"Huh? Who? How?"

"Pacoby. They're making us land on both air fields, among their own ships. To make sure we don't cause trouble, I guess." He hovered over the northern deck, seeing three of the Arawaj visitors settle among the Shri-Lan. Like the smaller terminal on the west side, a short tunnel connected it to the bottom level of the pyramid.

"So how is he going to destroy it?"

"He'll destroy whichever one he's not docked to. And that means us. You know how you hacked into the *Dutchman* to look around the other day?"

She blushed. "You weren't supposed to notice that."

"The *Dutchman* did. So you know your way around. Quick. Disable the Eill class clamps on the locks. Corrupt the program."

She linked her neural node to the ship without further question.

"Tower," Seth said, continuing to hover over his assigned deck. "Hey, you know you're not actually a tower? I can see you there on top of the pyramid."

"What's your query, Pilot?"

"Tower, *Dutchman* Pacoby Three here. Got trouble with the Eill pogs. Request other instructions." Ciela nodded when a warning light appeared on the console. He held his breath while someone scanned his ship for some sort of subterfuge.

"*Dutchman* cleared for west deck," the controller said. "T-3 pogs enabled there. Follow guides to new designation."

Seth sighed and moved to the space next to Pacoby's cruiser. "You're quick, lady."

"Must be that extra piece of brain matter in my head." She scanned both landing platforms. "Busy place. The port I mean. Four of Pacoby's ships, counting us, and another six Arawaj cruisers on the ground. Looks like at least six Shri-Lan cruisers down here. That class carries at most a crew of six but who knows how many Shri-Lan were already here? Three transports in orbit, not counting Sebasta."

"You're right. Busy place."

"Hmm, I can't tell how many Shrills they're keeping in that north hangar. But that'll mean additional armed fighters."

"Those Shrills will cause trouble for Pacoby when the time comes to get out of here. If he doesn't blow them all to bits, first."

"Then you've got yourself a nice little diversion, don't you?" she said with a grin.

He switched the com channel to accept a signal from Pacoby's cruiser. It was addressed to all four of his ships. "Our Shri-Lan hosts have offered hospitality," Cie Pacoby said in a voice so cheerful that it was nearly unrecognizable. "You may all debark and join them in the main hanger for some entertainment while our leaders see to business. No weapons. Please be courteous."

"Isn't that interesting," Seth mumbled. The *Dutchman* settled smoothly into its berth and they felt the clamps lock. He kept the pressure door to the cargo space sealed while the gas mix equalized. After a moment the ship reported acceptable conditions.

Ciela went ahead of him into the main cabin to step into her boots. She wore a long tunic and vest pieced together from his haphazard, multi-planetary wardrobe. "Please tell me they have clothing shops on Delphi," she mumbled.

"They don't have shops at all. But they have clothes, don't worry." Seth handed her a small projectile weapon and the knife she had used earlier.

"He said no weapons."

"That only applies to Arawaj." He went to the com console and withdrew translating devices. After loading a fairly rudimentary program able to exchange basic language with the locals here, he held his data sleeve over her own to transfer it to her as well. "I've never met a Taancer before," he said. "Should be interesting. Can't wait to meet them."

"Do you think we'll find the others? This place is so crowded with Shri-Lan…"

He brushed a strand of hair from her face. "I'll do everything I can to get to your friends. You know it may not be possible but we'll try, I promise. But I need to be able to trust you. I can't have you second-guessing me or suddenly decide you want to be Arawaj down there. That'll just get us both killed. Are we clear on that?" He cocked his head with a grin. "Or do I have to lock you up while I do this?"

"You can count on me." She looked up to study his face as he tucked the receiver behind her ear. "Seth…"

"Hmm?"

"What happened before…" She pointed a finger at the lounger behind them. "I mean… That was just because, right? I guess it was bound to happen. You… well, you're so… Uh, I guess you have lots of girls."

He took in her intense expression as she waited for reply. Intense, but devoid of any clue to the right response. His place in her life right now should be the last thing on her already troubled mind. Why was he still making things more confusing and stressful for this woman? Willing or not, now he had helped himself to someone who was, technically anyway, a Union prisoner. Since when was that acceptable? Once again, he was allowing a quick mind and enticing body to compromise his objectivity. The thing to do was to accept the escape she offered and treat this like nothing more than an inevitable outcome of their close confinement aboard his ship.

Instead, he tipped her chin up to kiss her softly. "Right now I have one girl," he said. "Let's not worry about anything but why we're here."

TWELVE

The concourse to which all umbilicals from the west deck connected greeted them with a confusing mingle of Centauri, Human, Feydan, Magran and a variety of others, including the white-haired Bellacs and a smattering of Mraki. All in civilian dress ranging from simple kilts on the Caspians to complete battle gear worn by the tank-like Mrakis. A black bandanna tied around their necks ensured that everyone recognized the Shri-Lan among them. Of course, the Shri-Lan walked about fully armed while the Arawaj, like Seth and Ciela, had discreetly concealed their own weapons.

The deck, covered and sealed against the outside air, seemed to be a sort of forecourt to the pyramid, serving as repair station and cargo transfer point as well as meeting space for the crews. It may have been a pleasant space once, but now the grease-covered floor was cracked in places and the battered walls sagged. A hint of chlorine in the air made Seth question the quality of the seals.

"Look for a spot where you can access the schematics for this place," he murmured as they strolled toward two Centauri he remembered from Pacoby's ship. Indeed, the diminutive leader stood nearby.

"Lovely party," Seth said, looking across the vast space where a bearded Human was regaling a crowd with some tale involving much hand-waving and shouting. Smaller huddles of rebels, mostly segregated by faction, wandered the hall, not looking very certain about what they were to do here. Seth suspected that all of them had been made hostage while the Brothers and Sebasta worked out their deal.

Pacoby turned from his conversation with his men to look up at Seth. "Take a position by those portals," he instructed, glancing toward a series of large doors at the end of the hall. "Report any changes in security activity. Nothing more. We'll take care of this. When we succeed, you can leave."

"So what's the escape plan?"

Pacoby glanced at Ciela. "Stay by my wing. Don't worry about anything else."

"Got it, boss," Seth said and waved casually at Pacoby's guards.

"That piece of dirt!" Ciela hissed as they walked to their post. She ducked around a couple of Feydans who were already taking advantage of Shri-Lan hospitality and alcohol. "He wants us around to make sure he gets through the keyhole later. What about the others?"

Seth looked over the concourse. Nearly a hundred men and women gathered here now and he supposed the same thing was going on at the north deck. A few Shri-Lan paced the crowd, scanners in hand and looking not at all interested in this gathering. Seth guessed their duty was to survey what sort of army Sebasta was offering in exchange for a place among Shri-Lan upper echelons. Not a bad trade, he thought. Ten battle-class cruisers, the hardware still in orbit, a few dozen fully trained fighters and pilots, six spanners. And not just any spanners, he reminded himself. As part of this tribute, they likely outweighed anything else Sebasta brought to the table.

They passed the triple set of doors which were probably as heavily secured as they looked. Armed guards loitered nearby, glaring at passersby. One of the doors opened for a group of Taancers pulling carts loaded with offerings of food and drinks for their Arawaj guests. Seth strolled closer, raising a hand in greeting as he activated his translator.

"Hello," he said, offering a smile which he hoped would be interpreted correctly. The Taancers were smaller than he expected, likely in answer to the meager oxygen level outside. "We are pleased to visit your beautiful planet."

The Taancer stopped and regarded him curiously, making no sound but a heavy rasping through its short trunks. Its chest heaved as if each breath was an effort.

"Perhaps we can see more of it," Seth tried.

"You want food?" grated though his earpiece when the Taancer made some sounds.

"No, thank you. I'd like to know more about this place."

"We have food."

"Seth, look," Ciela nudged his arm. "That's a ticker."

He looked more closely at the Taancer's head. Nestled between two raised ridges of scales behind its ear holes a small metal device glowed pale green to show its activity. "Damn," Seth whispered, astonished. Shri-Lan employed the mechanism to control their army of Rhuwac foot soldiers during training. By delivering pain signals directly into a victim's brain it allowed them to turn the ferocious, brutal, but nevertheless sentient beings into an army of killing machines used to bring local populations under control. Union soldiers called them cannon-fodder.

"We didn't show any Rhuwacs on the scanners," she said.

"Because they don't need them here. If Air Command thought these people were being forced to comply by Shri-Lan, they'd have cleared this place ages ago." Seth kept his eyes on the slave to ensure that it understood him. "Without evidence or a call for help, they have no reason to interfere."

Ciela scowled at a Shri-Lan walking past them. "And we want to join these bastards?"

Seth gave her his best told-you-so look. He turned back to the Taancer when a Mraki rebel came up behind them and shoved his elbow into the slave's back. "Get on with it. People want their dinner." He laughed when the Taancer stumbled away, after its companion. "Damn lizards. Don't let them bother you. They're harmless."

"No kitchen duty for you, eh?" Seth said.

"Not a bit. They do good cleaning, too. Of course most of 'em work with the ore. They've got nimble fingers. Best part is they can breathe proper air, not just that shit outside. For a while anyway."

Ciela stared after the man as he strode away to shout at the Taancers over the din in the hall. "Seth, this is terrible!"

"It is. Come on. I have the feeling we don't have much time." He looked past her and his brow furrowed. "What the…" He stopped her when she started to turn to see what had caught his attention.

"What?" she whispered when he also turned away.

"Air Command agents."

"Here? Now?"

He hurried her to one of the shelves along the wall where unappetizing bowls of food stuffs had been placed. "The tall redhead by the door and the Human beside her. Vanguard agents. There are probably more here, then, that I don't recognize."

She peered past his shoulder. "Big rifles on them. Shri-Lan cover?"

"I guess so. What are they doing?"

"Talking to the guards at the door to the pyramid. Do they know you?"

"She does."

"They're going through the door now."

"Can you see what's behind there?"

"A tunnel, looks like. More guards on the other side. We'll never get through there with all this going on."

He searched the end of the hall, careful to not even present his profile to the Union agents. If Air Command had infiltrated the Shri-Lan side, chances were that they were here for the Brothers or the spanners, possibly both. For now, his instincts told him to stay well out of their way.

"Over here." He hustled Ciela away from the crowd and

into a hygiene station along the far wall. The damp room was rife with the smell of stale steam, unwashed towels, harsh soaps. Unlike many such places on orbiters or planetary air fields, plentiful water on Taancerum allowed them to use that instead of the usual decon systems for cleaning.

Seth glanced at his sleeve to check for security cameras and then moved past a row of shower cubicles to the toilet system. Here, too, puddles of water splashed under his boots. The blue light strips designed to provide disinfection worked only sporadically, casting a sick pall over everything.

"Come up here." He stood on a commode and waited for her to also climb up. "You should be able to get over the partition and drop down on the other side."

"And then?" She grimaced when her sleeve brushed against the damp wall. "How do you know what's behind there?"

He pointed to a door without a handle near the rear of the chamber. "That goes somewhere. It should have a lock on the outside. You'll be able to crack it. This place wasn't designed for high security. So far, it looks like everything is being guarded by manpower, not electronics."

The door behind them opened and Seth quickly stepped down to lift Ciela from her perch. He pushed her against the wall, for good measure slipping his hand under her vest as he kissed her. She grinned against his lips and raised a knee up along his thigh. When a shadow moved past the door she moaned loudly and grasped Seth's hips to pull him closer.

"No place to get away, huh?" a rough voice spoke, sounding amused. They heard the sound of a gun being set aside before the man went about his business. Eventually, he strolled out of the room, whistling.

Seth released her and took a trembling breath. Despite the unsavory surroundings, touching her like this was just a little too stimulating. "I always wanted to do that."

"In a toilet?" She twisted to look what sort of filth had rubbed off on her clothes.

"I'm an opportunist. Hurry. People will keep coming in."

He lifted her up and watched her wriggle under a ceiling tile and into the plenum. She paused up there, listening for movement in the space beyond, possibly more of the Taancer slaves. Finally, she slid down and disappeared.

Breathless moments passed before he heard some soft clicks near the service entrance and then the door moved aside to let him enter the dim passage beyond.

As he assumed, this bypass led around the main concourse to deal with supplies, garbage, air conduits and other maintenance systems. They crept silently around a corner where another passage led to an unmarked door. His scanner showed no one beyond this and she got busy with the keyplate.

"Yes!" Seth whispered when they stepped into a work room. Racks of tools, chemicals and portable oxygen tanks stood on one side. The other was taken up by a small communications console and work station. "See what you can do with that."

She dropped into the chair while he waited near the door. "It's got an interface." She rubbed her hands together. "I'm as good as in."

"Be careful."

"I'm glad you said that. I wasn't planning on being careful till you reminded me."

"How about careful and quick?" He shifted his eyes from his scanners to her as she linked her neural node to the station and began to probe its system, looking for security triggers as she dug deeper.

"Got it," she said. Above her a map of the pyramid came into view, showing a wireframe of all levels along with the systems that supported them. Clearly meant for housekeeping, this display highlighted service areas along with engineering system and supply lines for water, power and air.

"Can you download that?"

"Not without launching an alert. Give me a moment." She placed her hands flat on the console and stared intently up at the monitor. The wireframe shifted, zoomed in and away, rotated as she directed it, barely blinking as she concentrated. Several levels of the building extended below ground where they met a subsurface water source, more river than aquifer. He saw the outline of some sort of underground machinery but its purpose was less clear. "All right," she said. "I think I got it."

"You can remember the whole layout?"

"Yes." She still seemed a little distant. "There are a few ways to get to the upper levels. But there is no way into the pyramid that doesn't involve a lot of guards. There are only a few entrances."

"And no doubt the guards are twice as alert as usual." He watched her shut the display down. "How do the Taancers get in?"

"The main doors, I'm assuming. Outside. They work in the bottom two levels of the building."

He went to the supply shelves to survey the oxygen bottles stacked there. "Then we'll go that way, too. The east side might be less guarded. You'd think they'd keep a few suits in here. Doesn't anybody go outside?" A mild vibration on his wrist alerted him to the proximity scanner. "Someone coming. Just one."

They stood aside, on either side of the door, weapons drawn. He noticed that she had chosen her knife instead of the gun, likely the better choice in this small space. When the door opened and a stooped figure entered, he lunged forward to grasp the intruder.

A high-pitched wail drove into their translators, making both of them wince. Their quarry dropped to the floor and scrambled into a corner of the room, arms flailing wildly as if to keep a swarm of insects away.

"Stop, stop," Seth said, raising his hands. "No harm. All is well. Silence, please."

When they made no further move, the Taancer ceased its keening and flailing and just sat with its arms around its knees, squinting up at them. Like the other they met earlier, it labored to draw air into its lungs. One of the trunk-like proboscises on its face was half the length of the other and scarred.

Ciela crouched and approached slowly. She reached out and stroked the Taancer's arm. "No harm, see? Gods, Seth, it's shaking all over."

Seth, aware of his size in this small room, kept his distance. "What do they do to these people to get them into this state?"

"Do you understand us?" she said, keeping her voice low and even. "We won't hurt you."

The Taancer looked at her hand still moving over its scales. "I understand."

She pulled her hand away, unsure of what her touch might mean, if anything, to them. "We will try to help. Can you help us?"

"Help."

"Yes. To make the bad people go away."

Seth sighed. "And how do you propose we do that?"

She looked up at him. "By telling your Air Command what's going on here. If they're such awesome guardians of Trans-Targon, they better be prepared to put a stop to this outrage."

He grinned at the Taancer. "Well, you heard her."

She turned back to her conversation. "We are looking for friends. In the pyramid. The big house. But we don't know how to get inside. Do you?"

"Door."

"Yes, but we need a door without the bad people."

"Shri-Lan."

"Yes, Shri-Lan."

The Taancer sat quietly for a moment before coming to its feet. It regarded her curiously, then looked to Seth. Finally, it pointed at the door. "Go below. Where the water is. Other doors underneath."

"Show us."

"Wait." Seth indicated the emergency oxygen bottles.

"Do we need those?"

"No. Your air all over." The Taancer went to the exit, apparently expecting them to follow. It moved quickly along the passage without looking to see if they kept up. They took a corner and then ducked into a low crawlspace lined with pipes and cables before emerging into a larger space. It finally stopped to point at a hatch on the floor.

"Door," it said. "Down to water, follow path to generator. Up from there. Pyramid."

"The Taancer's talking about the oxygen generators," Ciela said, recalling the building schematics. "Where they separate the oxygen from the water to supply the building. There are a few access shafts to the upper floors from there." She bent to help the Taancer lift the hatch. "This entry isn't on the maps."

The Taancer looked down into the narrow shaft leading into darkness. "We erased. When Shri-Lan start hurting the people. Sometimes people need hide." It raised a clawed hand to touch the small ticker affixed to its head and then looked to a door behind them, likely leading outside.

Seth adjusted his pistol to serve as a torch. "Let's take a look." He sat on the lip of the hatch and felt for a set of rungs lining the shaft. He already felt moisture rising from below. "Are there people down there?"

"Sometimes. My people. Some Shri-Lan. Not many."

Seth stepped down a few of the rungs and waited for Ciela to also lower herself into the shaft. She looked up. "Thank you," she said to the Taancer. "If we can, we will help you. Tell no one you saw us."

It tilted its head. "Counter-productive obviously," their systems translated.

Ciela snorted and quickly covered her mouth. "All right, let's go." She slid lower, between Seth's hands gripping the ladder. "Are you worried I'll fall or are you trying to cop a feel?"

"Bit of both," he said to her backside and began to descend, giving her a bit more room to make her own way down.

They took their time to navigate the slippery metal rungs and to stop for a look around when space allowed. The shaft broadened into a cave system and the sound of rushing water seemed to vibrate the air. Some light source now reached them and they quickened their pace until they finally stood on a narrow catwalk. Rusted bolts fixed it to the cave wall above the underground river. Perhaps ten paces across, the river's depth was hidden beneath the churning foam.

"Someone's down here," Seth said, working with his scanner. "Multiple life signs."

Ciela looked along the deserted catwalk. It eventually disappeared into the mist rising from the water but nothing moved within sight.

Seth held his arm over the low railing that would probably do little to keep a body from tumbling into the river. "In the water."

"Look!" She pointed to the shapes of some water creatures move beneath the surface. Pale and flat, each of these was as long as she was tall with fins that looked like slow-moving wings. As they watched, two of them leaped out of the water, spun once and dove back to join their shoal. "Did you see that? I think it looked right at us. How beautiful!"

"Must be what the Taancers have for dinner." He smiled, touched by her enthusiasm. "Keep moving. Where's the access shaft?"

"This way." She moved ahead of him. "The generators are fairly close to this side of the pyramid."

A movement at his peripheral alerted Seth before he was even aware of moving. He pushed Ciela against the rock wall just as another of the enormous fish sailed out of the water. Its maw gaped to show backward-slanting teeth. Ciela shrieked when the massive jaws clamped onto the railing with a hair-raising crunch. Finding nothing edible there, the creature flopped back into the river.

"Beautiful indeed," Seth said. "Are you all right?"

She pushed his arm aside, a little embarrassed. "Yeah, just surprised."

He bent to pick up a broken tooth. "Swimming is probably not recommended on this planet. Remind me to add that to my database."

She started to walk again. "There are monitors all through the generator station. Probably manned."

The roar of the water as the channel narrowed soon made it unnecessary to guard their footfalls on the metal walk. A sluice gate diverted water and the occasional winged fish into a broad basin from which massive tanks rose toward the roof of the cave. Grates at the intakes of the tanks kept the fish from slipping into the generators, evidenced by a tangle of decayed parts caught there.

"Electrolysis," Ciela said. "Hydrogen just gets vented outside."

They ducked out of sight when, among the jumble of pipes and support structures above the tanks, something moved on an open platform.

"Engineers, probably," Seth said. "Stay close to the wall. They don't process the hydrogen?"

"Not that I saw. Just some for cooling the generators."

"Does Pacoby know this?"

"Huh?"

"Hydrogen is flammable. If he's planning an explosion outside we've got a bigger problem than we thought. He'll be counting on the oxygen pipes going everywhere here for his fireworks, not the hydrogen outside when the roof blows off. Where are the vents?"

"At the top of the pyramid."

He nodded. "That'll help matters some."

She pointed to a door set into a metal wall and they sidled toward it, staying out of view of those above. "How do you know he'll blow the place? He might just try to cut the air supply and be done with it."

"Because it's not as spectacular. He won't want this to look like an accident." Seth scanned the space behind the door. "Clear."

They stepped through the door to find a circular staircase flanking one of the cylinders. The sound of the water still covered their steps and whatever creaks the not-quite steady treads made but they moved cautiously, hoping that the workers down here had no interest in scanning for intruders.

"Is it necessary for the stations to be monitored?" Seth asked when they neared the next floor. "Two people up there." He changed the setting on his gun. "If these are Taancers I'm going to drop them anyway. They won't be harmed. We just don't have time to keep explaining what we're doing here."

She smiled. "Thanks."

"For what?"

"Worrying about me. Do what's necessary, Mr. Union Agent."

He grinned back. "I keep forgetting you're one of those murderous, evil, bloodthirsty Arawaj."

They crept to the top of the staircase to reach a platform overlooking the generators. Control stations kept the system functioning to separate hydrogen from oxygen and deliver each to its destination. A man and a woman, both Caspian, stood near one of the consoles, sharing some conversation.

Seth aimed and shot first one, then the other. They dropped without a sound.

"Now where?"

"There's a lift over there."

"An elevator? A box with just one exit? Are there no stairs?"

"There are. One set per level, leading around the pyramid. We'd be exposed on each landing."

"Go. Lead the way. Stop when I say if my scanner picks something up."

She headed for another open staircase beside the lift. The indicator on his wrist would soon be useless. Above them now and all around dozens, perhaps hundreds of life signs moved and merged, making it impossible to discern numbers. The electromagnetic interference from the power conduits leading down to the generators didn't help, either. He poked at the sensor's settings, hoping for more precision when he noticed that she had come to a halt on the next landing.

"I told you—"

"Look," she said.

They had reached the pyramid's ground level. Much of it was one open space supported by massive pillars. Equipment and construction parts littered this level along with drifts of dust and debris. Among this, they saw groups of Taancers huddled on the floor, busy with piles of ore spread out around them. Smaller slaves pushed carts of finished pieces or carried sacks of raw stone.

Not one of them bothered to look up when they entered although surely some must have seen them. No one spoke but they could hear their rasping breath even from here.

"Gods, Seth, can't they even open this space to give these people better air? What would that take?"

He tugged her along. "Not much. If they cared enough. Come on."

She followed, not without another look back at the misery behind them. They found the same conditions on the next floor and hastily moved along. Perhaps the Taancers thought them to be part of their Shri-Lan overseers. Perhaps they didn't care who passed by here.

"Next level are living spaces," she reported. "Dorms, suites, kitchens, common areas. Kinda built like base station modules. The next five floors aren't really used for anything. Storage, mostly."

"I'm guessing everyone is downstairs at the meet-and-greet. Try to look like you belong here in case we run into anyone. We need to find a com station with more access to the other systems."

They made it past the residentials to the level above, finding storage, indeed. Seth whistled appreciatively when they walked among crates of weaponry, ammunition, stolen goods of all description, and small machinery. He ran his hand over a stack of Air Command flight jackets, half tempted to take one for himself.

"Why do they need diamonds?" Ciela ran her hand through a bin of the sparkling gem.

"Worth a small fortune on Shaddallam. Oh, look, drugs, too." He moved on to a row of wheeled bins and lifted a lid. "Whoa! Know what this is?" He raised another cover.

"No. What?"

He reached in to retrieve a small, shielded cube to show her the inscription. "Fuel tabs. Pure thorium, stolen from a transport going to the Magra Alaric base a couple of months ago." He surveyed the number of bins here. "Could run the entire Shri-Lan operation for the next five years with this."

"And they just store it here in buckets? That's crazy."

"They've been called worse." He returned the cube. "I could use some of this."

"No time for looting! Stairs are over there. There should be a sub-station there that controls the air exchange for these levels. Might have more access."

Seth crept up the metal stairs, testing each riser for creaks. Someone less concerned about making noise walked around up there, not far from the stairwell. Ciela peeked past Seth's shoulder to get a look at the equipment.

She shook her head and indicated her neural node, then her hand. The model used for this station required a live handprint as well as a neural interface to operate. Seth nodded and cautioned her to stay behind. He shifted his weight and waited until the technician moved to the control console before he launched himself soundlessly at the Human. With just a few quick moves he had him firmly in his grip and his gun at the man's throat. "Not a sound," he said.

Ciela came up and surveyed the control console. "Ancient," she whispered. "Look at those levels."

"You're an expert in air conditioning now?"

"No. It says 'warning' on them. I'm guessing that's a

warning. You know, that something's wrong somewhere."

Seth shuffled the Human to the interface panel. "Let's see your hand."

The Human struggled weakly in some token effort at resistance but like most rebel encounters like this, Seth expected him to look after his own life before serving his cause. He appreciated that about rebels. It was Air Command personnel that didn't give up so easily.

Ciela pulled the man's hand away from his body and held it to the console while she linked her interface. "Got it."

Seth discharged his weapon and let the man sink to the floor. Once Ciela had absorbed herself in the pyramid's com system, looking for any sign or conversation about the captive spanners, he looked around the control room. A door nearby led into a hall, nicely appointed and likely reserved for more important residents. At the far end he saw a broad, paneled staircase, far less utilitarian than the one they were using. "See if you can find out where that goes," he said to Ciela, who just nodded.

Seth checked his scanner and stepped into the hallway, then peered into an adjoining room. An empty lounge. There was music playing somewhere up here. Perhaps not everyone had been sent below to keep an eye on the Arawaj visitors. The entire pyramid seemed strangely deserted.

He moved a little further when a boot caught him in midriff to slam him into the wall and a fist met his jaw when he doubled over. Another shot to the side of the head dropped him. He groaned and looked up into the barrel of a gun. Someone stepped on his arm until he released his gun.

Then someone else came into view. He squinted at the woman now bending over him and dropped back with something halfway between a moan and a laugh. "Whiteside." He rubbed his jaw. "Should have known."

The tall, red-haired Human seemed less amused. "What the hell are you doing here?"

"Leave him!" a new voice ran out behind them.

The woman turned to face Ciela standing in the hall, gun

in hand. She grasped it inexpertly but the look on her face showed clear determination.

"Drop that!" Seth and the Human said at the same time.

"Step away from him!" Ciela said, looking confused.

The woman nodded to the Centauri that had brought Seth down and both backed away. "What's going on, Seth?" she asked.

Ciela blinked. "You know her?"

Seth sat up, wincing. "Meet Captain Nova Whiteside. Vanguard." He waved at the Human. "Nova, meet Ciela. Ciela, please put that down. They're not Shri-Lan."

"Air Command, then?" Ciela said with obvious distaste but lowered her pistol.

The captain glanced from Ciela to Seth. "Another of your Arawaj pals, Kada? It's going to end badly with you some day." She offered her hand to help him to his feet.

"She's my navigator," he said.

"Uh huh. So why are you here?"

"Probably the same reason you are. How many on your team?"

"Five." Three more Union agents stepped into the hall behind her, weapons poised. "He's one of Carras' people," she said to them and then turned back to Seth. "Two more in the west hangar. We couldn't get more agents in here. Took us two months to get this far. Our initial mission was to take out the Brothers but then someone decided they want the spanners real bad."

"Well, that's something we all have in common, then," Seth said.

"Mission priority's shifted, in fact. I'm guessing someone on Targon is making noise. So here we are, sifting Shri-Lan for damn Delphians."

Ciela glared at the captain.

"She doesn't mean it," Seth said. "She's married to a Delphian officer."

Nova Whiteside smiled. "Who had the good sense not to try to disguise himself as a Centauri on a mission crawling with Centauri rebels. Navigator, huh?" She raised an eyebrow at Seth. "Something tells me this is the missing spanner. Who, for reasons utterly inconceivable to me, you decided to bring right into the lion's den instead of straight to Targon."

"That's a big cat," Seth explained.

"I know what a lion is," Ciela snapped. "I'm here to find my friends. To you they might be just some prize but not to me."

"And she kinda brought me," Seth added. "She's not a prisoner. The others don't really look like Delphians, either. So careful where you shoot." He tapped his data sleeve. "So how'd you get past my scanner?"

"Top secret."

"Don't hold out on me, Red."

She exhaled a dramatic sigh. "New scatter pattern. We're field testing. I'm sure Carras will let you work for your own copy soon enough."

"You people have all the fun toys," Seth said. "Shall we team up?"

"Seems wise, since you're lit up like a Qivafest pole on the sensors." Whiteside smirked. "Although you seem to have lost your touch. What happened to those cobra reflexes, Kada? You went down awfully easy."

Seth frowned at the massive Centauri beside her. She was right; he had been careless, convinced that the place stood empty. He turned to Ciela. "Did you find them?"

Ciela still glowered suspiciously at the Human. "Yes. Did you people know the Taancers are being used like slaves?"

"We do now. Air Command is launching a clean-up operation. Some ships should be here in less than ten hours. The Brothers will be long gone by then. So if you know where the... your friends are, this is the time to share the information." She tilted her head in the direction of the main staircase. "We're assuming they're on the upper decks somewhere. But anything from two floors up is heavily guarded. We won't be allowed through there, Shri-Lan or not. We were trying to find another way when you started stomping around here." She tipped a wink to her silent companion. "Unfortunately, I didn't see you before Retan did."

"Apology accepted." Seth led the way back to the control room near the service stairs. "Ciela was able to hack into their database. She knows the layout, what with having a big Delphian brain."

"They're on the same level where the planes are," Ciela reported. She reactivated her open link to the console and quickly retrieved the schematics of the pyramid while all but one outlook crowded around. The space seemed to be some sort of lounge overlooking the valley. Three of the five sides were made of panoramic windows with a door at each corner leading onto the transparent terrace. From there, steps led down into the umbilicals to the parked ships. "My people are locked in this room there, on the side of this big open space. From what I heard, there are guards there, keyed up. Waiting for something to happen. The meeting, if that's what is, is on the level above, beside the control tower. I didn't find any recording of what's going on in there but someone complained that they're drinking a lot up there."

"What sort of planes?"

"Sebasta came on a Fleetfoot, same as one of the others. The Brothers are using a loaded Trident."

Captain Whiteside nodded. "If we can get the captives out and onto one of those ships we should be able to get away without backtracking through the pyramid."

"They've got a lot of ships in orbit," Ciela said. "And Sebasta has more armament than I've seen on any transport. You'll have a fight on your hands."

"I'm counting on it. Don't worry; between Seth and me we'll have them shooting each other."

"You have a lot of confidence," Ciela muttered while the captain conferred with her team about a course of action.

"They breed 'em for that," Seth said with a wink. He tapped the pistol holster hidden beneath her vest. "Don't use that unless you have to. You're too dangerous. To us."

She pinched his arm, out of sight of the others.

"Lasers only," Whiteside said. "Who knows what those windows are made of. Try not to break any. Clear out the uglies to get across to the target. Retan and Jessana cover the stairs to the upper level. Two weeks furlough for each Brother you wax. Seth, you and your friend will cover the captives while we bully through to the ships."

"Ciela," Ciela corrected her.

"Right. Ciela. You're to get to the umbilicals leading to the nearest ship, no matter what goes on. We may need you to hack into the egress ports. Are your people able to use weapons?"

"Deely, the bald one, is a good shot. Luanie, too, but she gets nervous." Ciela shrugged. "You're basically dealing with civilians. We've been trained but we haven't really seen a lot of combat."

"Wonderful." Whiteside adjusted her weapon. "Free fire on sight. No one gets up."

A low buzz alerted them to the captain's com band. She lowered the volume and held it to her ear. Her eyebrows rose. "Fighting on both flight decks. Sounds bad." She listened to more talk on the com bands.

Seth snapped his fingers. "Oh, did I mention Cie Pacoby is pretending to be friends with Sebasta these days and got himself invited?"

Captain Whiteside gave him a look that suggested a response better not articulated.

"Yes," Ciela said. "But he was going to blow something up, not start shooting."

The officer continued to listen to the com band. "Sounds like the Shri-Lan started this. They've got Arawaj outnumbered."

"Why do I think my earlier hunch was right?" Seth said. "The Brothers are going to grab the spanners and call off this whole alliance thing. They don't need Sebasta or his band of traitors."

"All this for a bunch of navigators?" Whiteside said. "No

offense," she added for Ciela. She gestured to her team. "Let's use the diversion. Expect response from upstairs coming down this way. It'll thin the herd. Go."

THIRTEEN

The agents moved soundlessly up along the stairs, instinctively shaping their formation to the layout of the building. Seth blended easily into the unit, holding back to keep an eye on Ciela. The troop stopped as one and ducked behind the central support when footsteps thundered toward them; a detail dispatched to the skirmish taking place below. They opened silent fire at the last possible moment, blasting indiscriminately into the knot of rebels coming their way until a dozen bodies lay scattered over the stairs.

A moment's silence followed, waiting for more. Whiteside signaled for them to continue moving up and they soon reached the landing. With more hand signals, they spread out, making their way to the open, windowed area Ciela had pointed out. Two more rebels met them and were dispatched.

At the end of a corridor, the big Centauri agent bent to place a crawler onto the floor. The tiny camera-carrying robot scurried along a wall and fed its data back to his wrist unit. He signaled to the others: fifteen rebels, much activity, no order. As expected.

Whiteside signaled and the agents poured into the room to fan out and open fire on the surprised rebels. The schematics they had studied only showed the room's shape and the pillars that supported the topmost level and control tower. Furniture, once quite elegant for this remote location, cluttered the lounge to offer cover for both sides.

Their fire was silent and they moved in a way that suggested a greater attack force, but the rebels outnumbered them three to one and followed no organized strategy in their defense. Confused shouts rang out, no doubt alerting more of the rebels upstairs. The Vanguard agents seemed to be everywhere, yet their line moved systematically forward until two darted to the staircase leading up while the others shifted to the room holding the spanners.

Seth fired at a rebel running past the windows. The Feydan tried to jump aside and slammed into the sloping window before he fell to the floor. Whatever the window was made of held up against the assault.

Ciela reached the door to pick the lock but Captain Whiteside simply raised a heavy boot and slammed it below the door handle. "This isn't a dungeon," she said when the door sprang open. She stepped inside, weapon raised to look for more rebels. "Everyone back!" she shouted, unsure which of these people was actually a rebel.

Ciela moved in behind her when a Human dropped onto the captain from the rafters above. She went down face-first. The rebel's fist gripped the knot of red hair at her nape and slammed her head onto the metal floor as he set his pistol to her neck.

"Hey!" Ciela lunged forward, knife in hand. She threw all of her weight at the rebel and buried the blade into his side, avoiding the muscles of his chest which could too easily tighten around her knife. She withdrew it and slashed again before he, in a panic, threw her off. He lurched backward when she went after him, feinting and stabbing. Then his surprise wore off and he raised his gun only to find her ducking under his massive arm to deliver another deep wound into his gut. He howled in pain and fury and dropped to his knees, clutching his stomach. She groped for her gun and ended it.

The captain came to her feet. "Thanks. Civilian, huh? Not bad." She touched her forehead and then cursed when her fingers came away bloody. She turned to the others crowded against the far wall. "Let's go. Move!"

They entered the lounge, now cleared of rebels, and joined Seth in a race to the door leading to the docking ports. Across the expanse of the lounge another door also led outside, located at the foot of a staircase leading upward. Whiteside muttered another oath when she saw one of her men on the floor. She gestured to the others. "Outside!"

A tracer strafed past her to sear a line into the floor and she lunged forward to roll behind a food station. The spanners huddled behind two of the pyramid's support pillars.

More rebels than expected now came down the stairway, firing but making no move into the open space as they covered the hulking shapes of the Brothers among them. The two men were of K'lar origin, densely-built and walking with a pronounced stoop as was common among their desert-dwelling people. Their guards, better trained than the average Shri-Lan, fired at the Vanguard officers to keep them down as the two leaders slipped through the door and onto the glassed-in passage to the ships.

"What the..." Seth heard Ciela gasp behind him. Two cruisers soared past the windows, firing at something below them, perhaps clearing the way for the Brothers to escape.

"Looks like they're taken the fight outside," Seth said.

Astounded, all those still inside flinched when a metal partition suddenly crashed down from above to seal the docks from the rest of the building, plunging the lounge into darkness before the overhead lights realized they had work to do.

"Whoa," Ciela said. "Didn't see that on the maps."

"Back!" Whiteside yelled, waving at them from her cover when the remaining rebels fired in their direction. "Seth, get them the hell out of here."

"Go!" Seth turned to the frightened spanners behind him.

"That way! Ciela, the elevator."

The Vanguard held back the abandoned rebels as Seth and the spanners raced across the lounge and back to the corridor. Seth snatched a gun from the floor near a fallen rebel and handed it to Deely.

"Go go go," he yelled when the others hesitated at the door of the lift. He shoved them forward, into the car, and fired back outside while the doors closed. Ciela hit the button for the lowest floor before turning to throw herself into Miko's arms. "We found you!" she cried. "Gods, I was so worried." She hugged Luanie and then kissed Deely on his bald pate.

Seth looked around. "We're not out yet." He found his thoughts wandering back to the Vanguard officers they had left behind and reminded himself to keep his focus on these captives. He scrutinized the three blonde women who looked strangely identical. "Triplets? Delphian triplets? That's unheard of. They're lucky to make one kid at a time. No wonder you keep calling them 'the girls'."

"What's going on?" Deely said to Ciela. "How did you find us?"

"We're here with Pacoby's crew," Ciela said with a quick glance at Seth. "I'll explain later."

The elevator came to a halt and both Seth and Ciela aimed their guns as the door opened.

"Where the hell are we now?"

"The Taancer factory," Ciela said, looking out over the dusty hall. "Guess this elevator doesn't go all the way down."

"All right. Staircase. Quick now."

An unnerving squeal rose into the air. They turned to see one of the Taancers race toward them, even dropping to all fours to use its powerful legs to leap over obstacles. The others shrank back when it jumped up onto the elevator platform but Seth put his hand on Ciela's barrel.

"Our friend," he said, recognizing the damaged nose.

The Taancer wheezed with the exertion of its dash to reach them. "People fight," it said. "Why. Dead many. Planes in the air. Shooting."

"We know. We need to get back to my ship."

"No. Other people down below making bad." The Taancer waved its arms in an unclear gesture. "Breaking generator. Will be hot light."

"Hot light?" Ciela said.

"Fire? Explosion?" Seth guessed.

"Fire yes. With the bad air."

"Pacoby," Seth said. "He's going to sabotage the generators."

"If he is thinking about blowing the pyramid this whole valley is in trouble. Gods, Seth, this could get hot enough to get at the thorium upstairs. The radiation will kill everything."

"Told you he was going for spectacle."

"Pacoby wouldn't do that," Deely said. "Not with all these… these people in here."

Seth looked to Ciela.

"Yes," she said firmly. "He would. And he will if we don't stop him."

Seth gripped the Taancer's arm. "Get your people out. Everybody. Try to get people out of town, into the hills. Everybody, understand? Go."

The Taancer loped away without another word.

"Let's get out of here before they open a door somewhere," Seth said. "Stairway, now."

Ciela led them to the metal staircase that had brought them up this way. "What are we going to do?"

"I have no idea. Let's see how many Arawaj he's got with him."

"Bastard never meant to just blow the air field, did he?"

"No, I don't think so. The eyes of Shri-Lan are on this place as long as the Brothers are out here. He wants to make his point." He turned to the others. "Maybe you should wait here."

"No," Luanie, the white-haired member of the group, spoke up. "We stay together. Give me a gun."

The others nodded. With a look to Ciela, Seth pulled a pistol from his belt. "Are you all as stubborn as this one?"

"More so," Miko said. He gestured to one of the triplets. "Take your shoes off. They're too noisy on the stairs. Hurry."

She bent to follow his advice. Miko stepped out of his cloth shoes to remove his socks, short slips of exuberant purple. "This'll help with the metal grating."

Seth activated his scanner, hoping Pacoby was too busy to keep an eye on his. With the Taancers clearing out of the floors above, life signs were more easily detected here now, even with the interference.

He led the way to the next level and soon the sound of water and generators reached them from below. The vibrations moving through the metal plates under their feet were the same as before. No alarms sounded, suggesting that, whatever was going on, the system had not yet detected a problem. He recalled Ciela's comment about the ancient gauges on some of these machines and decided not to count on alarms.

Wishing for one of Air Command's crawlers, some of which were doing absolutely nothing aboard the *Dutchman* while he wished for them, he crept down to peer around the corner. His eyes confirmed the unstable readings on his scanner. "Pacoby and two others," he whispered to Ciela. "Do you think you can work your way through the generator controls?"

She lifted her shoulders. "I could probably get in, but I wouldn't know what to do. We can't just shut them down. We'd suffocate."

He shook his head. "We'll have time. I'm more worried about the hydrogen." He pointed up. Among the other conduits, power lines, and pipes rising upward along the staircase and elevator shaft, the one bearing an oxygen symbol branched into many directions above them. A larger pipe not far from this one seemed to lead straight up to the vent atop the pyramid.

She shook her head. "If he closes the vent the reduction will stop. It'll have fail safes."

"He only needs to cause a leak somewhere. There are air pipes everywhere, including the flight decks, and they'll have emergency oxygen tanks everywhere. He'll incinerate the pyramid, all the loot stored here, anyone still upright and I'm guessing most of the town outside. And we may end up with radiation as well."

"So what do we do?" Miko said. The others waited silently to be told what to do, as always, perhaps not even realizing that their Arawaj days were numbered. Like the Taancers, like the Shaddallamites and Naiyads and so many others, they were just hapless victims caught up in someone else's disagreement. Brainwashed, corrupted, maybe delayed too far to ever take their place in Delphi's highly organized society.

"Arawaj," Seth said when an idea struck him. "He doesn't know. Pacoby doesn't know who I am." He looked to Ciela. "Who you are."

A smirk formed on her lips when she understood his plan. "No, he doesn't."

"Make noise." Seth waved them along and continued down the stairs, letting his boots land heavily on each riser.

The others followed, a little less enthusiastically, until they came to the control floor landing where Pacoby's gun greeted them. One of his guards also stood by with a poised weapon. The third Arawaj carried only some tools.

"Whoa! Wait," Seth said, sounding surprised. He raised his hands. "Take it slow, boss. What are you doing here?"

Pacoby studied the group for a few uncomfortable moments before lowering his gun and beckoning his men to stand down. For some reason it was no surprise that he had covered his impeccable clothing with a lab coat for his task here. The two Caspians that Seth had disabled earlier now lay at the other end of the platform, blood caked on their hides and dripping through the grate. "You were told to stay near the ships," he said while his narrowed eyes studied the people who had come down with Seth and Ciela. "But I see you found your people."

"Yes, this is the lot."

"Get back to the docks, quickly," Pacoby said, almost absently, as he turned back to the generator control board.

"They're fighting on the flight decks," Seth said. "I'm guessing our people aren't getting along very well."

"That isn't unusual." Pacoby shrugged. "I had the presence of mind to leave a pilot on each of my ships. You should be able to reach them if you hurry. A little distraction will keep the Shri-Lan busy for a while longer. These controls are... stubborn."

"What are you doing?" Ciela said. "You said you were going to destroy the air field."

"That's hardly worth anyone's notice." Pacoby raised a hand to caress the bank of indicators on the wall above the console. "This weapon is what I've dreamed of."

"Weapon?"

He walked to the edge of the platform and leaned over a railing to look up where support structures spanned several of the pyramid's floors. "That worked. We're ready here now," he said to the com band on his wrist. "You can evacuate as soon as the shunt springs." Apparently someone far above them gave some sort of signal and so he nodded and returned to Seth and the spanners.

He traced a manicured finger around a plain, black input panel. A single bar scrolled evenly across it. A gentle smile lit his pinched face. "Alarms are down, backup vents are perforated and now I'll just shut down the main exhaust. From here the hydrogen will rise through all floors. After that, a single, random spark will incinerate this entire building inside out. The entire Shri-Lan treasure hoard, up in flames." He turned his gaze to the spanners. "We'll have enough time to get out. Return to the ships now. I will trust Mr. Kada to keep you out of sight of whatever is going on out there."

The triplets exchanged confused glances and moved toward the stairs leading down.

"Stop!" Ciela said, likely confusing them even more. She turned to Pacoby. "Don't do this. It's too much."

"This is just a bunch of Shri-Lan," Deely said. "Who cares? Let's get out of this place already."

"No, it isn't. What about them out there? The Taancers. They didn't ask for this. If this pyramid goes, so will the whole settlement. We found thorium upstairs. Stored in nothing more than their cubes. You'll poison the whole valley, Pacoby."

"What?" Luanie said. "Is that true?"

"What's a thousand or so lizards living in a toxic desert?" Pacoby said. "Nothing. Air Command can't spin up sympathies for creatures few people have even heard of."

"The Taancers are sentient!"

"Living in misery under Shri-Lan rule. We're doing them a favor by ending all this. The survivors will rebuild and they'll be free." Pacoby scowled at Ciela for daring to disrupt this moment for him. "You've been marooned in the Badlands too long. We do not shy from doing what needs to be done." He looked to Seth. "Do they know nothing about our mission?"

"Like you said," Seth said with a smile. "Marooned. Sheltered. They probably haven't even heard about the skyranch you took out over Jupion. I think they're still looking for floaters over there."

Pacoby smiled. "I hear there are frozen farmers circling the planet now."

"That was good work," Seth said, crossing his arms to hide his clenched fists. "So was taking that immigrant ship out to Tilliera and stranding them there."

"I suppose there wasn't much left of them by the time Air Command got there." Pacoby's smile faded when Luanie slumped on the bottom of the stairs with a sob. The others stared, wide-eyed, at hearing these words from the Arawaj leader. "Infants!" he snapped. "It's time for all of you to grow up. Our work takes its toll and will continue to do so until the Commonwealth yields. And now it's time you did your part, Spanners. Real work."

Ciela looked from Luanie to Miko and then to Pacoby. "This cannot work," she said. "How can anyone think this can work?" She stalked toward him. "Arawaj is nothing more than a drain on Air Command's resources. How can that be worth taking all those lives?"

"Ciela..." Seth warned. Pacoby's hand was only a tic away from the shutdown he had installed.

She looked over to him. "You were right, Seth. Velen Phar was right, too. I've been living in some fantasy if this is the best my people can come up with." She uttered a small, humorless chuckle. "My people. Mass-murderers, no better than Shri-Lan. Fanatics." She shook her head and her jaw tightened with resolve. "These are not my people. Not any more."

Before Seth could react, she drew her knife, its blade still stained with blood, and launched herself at Pacoby. He raised his arms to ward off the attack and managed to grasp her wrist. Both of them careened across the platform and collided with the railing overlooking the generators.

Seth drew and shot one of Pacoby's men but the other leaped at him and grappled for this gun. There was little training behind his attempt and he wielded only a metal tool, no match for Seth whose only thought was for Ciela's rash attack on Pacoby.

Behind him, one of the spanners shrieked when the badly-maintained barrier bent outward. Ciela wrestled desperately with the Human, feeling his sharp-nailed thumb dig into her wrist. Although he was smaller than she, his strength spoke of a well-maintained body and considerable training. Both of them lost their balance when the barrier gave way and they tumbled out onto the sloped roof of one of the generators.

Seth leaped after them and reached for Pacoby. The rebel swung Ciela aside, forcing Seth to jump over her. The slippery surface of the sheeting seemed to slide him sideways and he stumbled back, grasping for a handhold and, at last, tumbled off the generator and into the water far below.

Ciela found a sudden, renewed burst of strength and shoved forward to ram her knee into Pacoby, pushing him backward. A snap of her arm finally loosened his grip and she swung back to slash her knife across his throat.

He recoiled and grasped his neck with both hands, eyes bulging in terror as he felt blood ooze between his fingers. Ciela grasped one of the power conduits and used her boot to shove him back to tumble after Seth into the basin.

She whipped around and scrambled back to the platform where Deely and one of the girls heaved her up. She went to the control console and linked into the system. "Aagh, what a mess! Deely!" She pointed to the other interface. "You're good with this stuff. Shut the whole thing down."

He started to link up. "The power grid?"

"No, just the cathode in the generator. Disconnect it from the grid, if you can't find the shut-off." She turned to the others. "Luanie, stay with him in case anyone comes down from up there. If it moves, shoot it. The rest of you get downstairs."

They raced down the creaking staircase leading to the catwalk over the water. Ciela nearly went over the insufficient railing when she bent over it to look for Seth.

"Over there!" Miko pointed across the holding basin. They saw Seth flailing in the water, making his way to the sloping edge. "What are you doing?" he added when she started to climb over the railing.

"There are creatures in the water," she said.

Nothing could stop her from stepping out onto the dam to cross to the opposite side. She did not hear the shouts that followed her when she balanced across the stone wall, hesitating only an instant before leaping across the sluice gate that funneled water from the river into the pool. Then she was across and dropped to the ground to reach down to where Seth clung to the wall. He had drawn his feet out of the water where several of the flat river creatures circled.

"Hey, nice to see you," he wheezed and reached up to

take her hand. His shirt hung in tatters and blood flowed freely from his shoulder. She looked back and kicked a pipe jutting up from the ground. It held firm and so she stretched out to grasp it.

Slowly, painfully, he pulled himself up, slipping a few times on the sloping wall of the basin. At last, he lay on level ground, panting. "That's one hell of an undertow out there," he gasped.

"You're hurt!"

He sat up and let her tear what remained of his shirt to stem the bleeding. "Believe it or not, I landed on one of those fish things. It took offense." He looked out onto the water. "Guess he wasn't so lucky. Did you do that?"

She did not look to see Pacoby floating on the surface. Her earlier peek at that showed something tugging on his legs. It wasn't something she wanted to see again.

They both looked around, startled, when something in the air changed. It took a moment to realize that the steady hum of the electrolizers had ceased, leaving only the sound of the power generator somewhere in the distance. The door at the foot of the stacks opened and then Deely and Luanie joined the others on the catwalk.

"Come on," she said. "Let's get out of here before someone comes down to find out why everyone's suffocating."

The stone wall separating river from basin suddenly seemed awfully narrow. The others watched in sheer terror as Seth and Ciela balanced across the dam like two drunken tightrope walkers. She nearly lost her nerve when they approached the open sluice. But, lacking other options, she took the leap and scuttled the rest of the way across where Miko waited to help her over the railing.

"Keep going," Seth said. "Single file along the river."

A sudden shriek startled them all. "I'm hit," Luanie cried. A long gash had seared along her shin. "My leg." A projectile ricocheted off the wall beside Miko's head.

"Up there!" Ciela pointed to the top of the generator.

Two women stood there with rifles, aiming at the fugitives.

"Run," Seth said. "We'll be out of view. Go!"

They obeyed, racing ahead of him to the ladder leading to the surface. Had the way in been as long as the way out now seemed? Two of the triplets seemed unused to running at all and their headlong dash was soon little more than a jog, further slowed by Luanie's limp.

"Up!" he ordered. "Quick!"

Miko took the lead, climbing quickly hand over hand toward the hatch far above them.

"I can't…" Luanie whimpered. "It's so high."

"You can stay down here, if you like," Seth said, forcing an edge into his tone. "Move out of the way."

The woman swallowed her reply along with, he hoped, her fear and began to climb.

"Faster up there. Ciela, hold up." He drew his gun from its waterlogged holster. "Time to practice."

Ciela had already ascended a few steps. She turned back to see the two rebels emerging from the door in the distance. They fired, their aim hampered by the mist in the air, but did not stop until both women fell, one into the river.

"You're getting better," he said, wincing when he gripped the rungs and felt his lacerated shoulder protest.

They climbed after the others. Miko was already at the top, wrestling with the heavy latch. With a loud grunt, he heaved it aside.

They found themselves in the hidden room where their Taancer ally had led them. Seth stumbled and dropped onto a crate, exhausted. "Ciela. The air tanks in that room. Remember?"

"We're going outside?"

"Unless you have a better idea. Doesn't matter who won the battle, we're the prize here today. Well, you are."

She waved to Miko and Deely. "Come with me."

Seth lowered his head, wondering how much blood he had lost while treading water out there. Luanie approached him and raised her hands as if asking permission to look at his wound. She hissed softly.

"Not good?"

"Not really." She bent to rip her skirt. "I'm sorry. It's not clean."

He pushed the hair out of his face. "I don't think a few Taancerum germs are going to make much difference right now."

She applied a bandage as best as she could. Her own wound, although painful-looking, was cleanly cauterized by the laser that had strafed her. The triplets watched, silently, from a distance.

Seth smiled at them. "So what are your names?"

They looked at each other.

"They don't talk much," Luanie said. "At least not out loud. We really don't know what they say to each other."

Seth sighed. Another bizarre side effect of the Delphian experiments. As objectionable as all that was, removing the children from Delphi likely hadn't helped any of them.

They looked up when the others returned, carrying a supply of oxygen tanks. "Tested and good to go," Miko reported. "Sorry, no goggles."

Seth nodded. "The air out there is going to burn your eyes. Not good for your skin, either. Cover yourselves as best as you can. You'll be fine if you keep those masks on. Ciela will lead us around the building to the cruisers..." he paused to address her directly. "Keeping as close to it as possible. Who knows what's going on out there." He pulled his data sleeve off. "You're Miko? Stay behind me and keep your eye on the scanner. I'm down to one useful arm and I need that for my gun. Everyone move quickly and try to stay out of sight."

Ciela and Deely experimented with the door. "There'll be some wind while the gases mix. Shouldn't be too much, but stay to the side just in case."

Seth checked everyone's equipment as they fastened their masks but they seemed to know what they were doing. He had to remind himself that, sheltered or not, these were not just civilians. He was grimly amused when Ciela had to help him with his respirator when it became clear that his arm would not cooperate.

They pried the door open against a rush of air and slipped outside. Seth signaled them to wait behind a shed of some sort. Sporadic gun fire from inside the hangars told them that whoever had won the battle – Shri-Lan presumably – was looking for surviving enemies. With luck, he thought, they'd start hunting their own people.

"Some dogfight going on over that way," Miko reported, his voice muffled by his mask. His eyes were already streaming with tears as the chlorine in the air took effect. Seth looked over Miko's shoulder to see the signatures for several cruisers and a handful of fighters in the distance.

"Good, they're busy."

"Seth, what if they destroyed your ship?" Ciela said.

"It'll take more than..." he paused. "Well, shields do help. Come on."

They skirted the side of the flight deck and scurried around to the docks. Seth nearly sobbed with relief when he saw the *Dutchman* still snuggled up to Pacoby's cruiser, apparently unharmed. "Hatch underneath, by the left landing gear," he directed.

The *Dutchman* recognized his touch on a hidden keyplate and allowed them inside where they crawled through its inner workings and into the small engine room. From there, a short ladder brought them up to the main cabin. They started to drop what clothes they could do without, well used to contamination protocols.

Seth flipped open a cabinet and pulled out bags of emergency decon sheets and saline. "Use this. On your eyes. We'll decon later. Hang on to something when we lift off. Those two chairs have restraints. Ciela, you're with me."

She followed him into the cockpit, wiping her face with the wet towel. "I'm not a pilot," she reminded him.

"I know," he said, trying to think of some joke to explain his request. He sat down and activated the ship's launch sequence. "I just want you here," he said finally.

The ship launched into an emergency take-off sequence which meant thrusters against this dusty surface, no gravity balance, no systems check. If someone had decided to sabotage the *Dutchman* in some way, this was the moment to find out.

The ship rose smoothly.

"They're on to us," Ciela said, pointing up at the sensor display. "Something coming from the valley."

"Shrills." He pulled a headset over his interface and shouted to the others. "Hold tight!"

The *Dutchman* swung around the docks, ready to launch into space, when the swarm of single-seat fighter planes descended from above, opening fire at once.

Seth returned their fire, barreling through the more agile attackers, looking for the correct angle to get out of the valley. A shudder went through the ship when the shields took a full hit. Someone in the back cried out when he veered. Something crashed to the ground.

A scatter of projectiles impacted the shield with little damage. "Not happy with this." Seth unleashed a full barrage and Ciela cheered when two of the Shrills spiraled into the ground. He dove under the others who seemed to have no clear formation that his systems could interpret. "I hate these things."

"Four left. Over there! Heading for the pyramid."

"Need a hand, pilot?" a female voice broke into the open com system.

Seth grinned. "Is that you, Red?" He felt a weight lifted from him that he had not even been aware of carrying. "Made a getaway, eh? How's the head?"

Captain Whiteside entered the field, guns blazing. "Party got boring," she said tersely and turned her attention to the enemy planes. Seth matched her flight path toward the pyramid.

"Watch this," he said to Ciela. He switched to solid projectiles and unloaded at the ship on the north flank of the pyramid. Most of his fire went wild and shattered a vast swatch of the solar panels covering that side. Shards sprayed out over the hangars below and pieces of the support structure for them gave way when the Shrill slammed into it.

They heard the captain whoop as she did the same on the other side, also taking down an enemy plane. Both raced after the other two Shrills, blasting until they hit the ground. A scan of the vicinity showed no more enemy planes in the air.

"The Brothers got away," Whiteside said and added a curse that made Ciela blush. "Sebasta didn't. Most of the Shri-Lan fleet's bugged out. Seems some awfully big Air Command battle cruisers are about to drop into this sector to do a little house cleaning. Do you have our newest acquisition?"

"All seven accounted for. And Pacoby has gone swimming. He won't need that fine ship of his anymore." Seth finally engaged the stabilizers to create a steady gravity inside the ship.

"Excellent," she replied. "This boat here is utter junk. Had to leave my Eagle at home."

"All yours," he said. "If you can get into it. I'm taking these folks out of here."

"No need. The Delphians sent an escort to take them back. You can turn them over to the *Scole* when you meet up with Colonel Celois at the keyhole. They'll make sure they're looked after."

"Will do," Seth replied, winking at Ciela. "See you around, Red."

"Try to keep your guard up next time."

EPILOGUE

"You're sure about this?" Ciela said when, hours later, the *Scole* came into view near the sector's only keyhole.

Seth glanced over his shoulder to check for anyone near the entrance to the cockpit where he and Ciela had withdrawn. The others were resting, sharing the bunks in the crew cabin and Seth's bed. "No. Not really."

Air Command's orders made it clear that Seth was to deliver the spanners directly to the science vessel filled with Delphians and, he was pleased to hear, navigated by his friend Caelyn. He had considered making a run for the keyhole and heading directly for Delphi to ensure Air Command had no chance to take a closer look at his precious cargo. But perhaps that was pushing his tenuous relationship with Colonel Carras just a bit too far.

He had taken a wide berth around the flight path of the Shri-Lan rebels who had no choice but to meet the arriving Air Command force in combat to reach the keyhole. Others, he assumed, were now hiding in other parts of Taancerum, as inhospitable and unsustaining as the Daos valley they no longer owned.

In the hours since leaving Taancerum, Seth and Ciela had talked with the others, squeezed into the small space of Seth's central cabin, in an effort to ease their fears. There were no promises to make and Seth had steered clear of talk about rebel politics, a subject too vast for now. But they had all seen the extent to which Pacoby had been willing to take his ambitions. Miko and Luanie seemed ready to accept that things were not what they had been taught to believe. Deely reserved judgment. The triplets didn't seem to care one way or the other.

Ciela, like the others, was eager to learn more about Delphi and to meet whatever family there may be for her, finally looking forward to discovering something other than war and rebellion. He was glad for that while at the same time wishing some passing black hole would suck Delphi out of existence.

"I have faith in your Shantirs," he said. "You'll be fine."

She sniffed. "Holy men. Wizards."

He grinned. "A lot of them are women, actually."

"Who'll treat us like some sort of lab specimen to see how we turned out."

"For a while, I suppose. You've been gone a long time. You've missed out on what it's like to be Delphian. You've seen things and learned things they'll never experience." He concentrated on his approach to the *Scole*, which took him past two Air Command Eagles whose sensors tried their best to probe into the *Dutchman*.

He ignored them but could not ignore Ciela's eyes fixed on him. "What is it?"

"Nothing," she said quickly and turned to the display screens. "I'm just scared."

"You're going home," he said. "Think of it that way. You're not a stranger."

They followed the *Scole*'s instructions to lock onto one of several ports. The science vessel dwarfed the Air Command ships hovering protectively close, majestic not only in size but in its elegant design, graceful crossdrive supports, banks of brightly lit windows and of course intricate arrays of sensors on all levels. Had he assumed Delphians to travel in anything less than that?

He placed his hand on Ciela's back when they went into the main cabin, a little surprised when she flinched away from his touch. The others were waiting for them, having done their best to clean up and present themselves as best as they could in preparation of meeting their kinsmen. Like Ciela, their apprehension was clear on their faces.

"Here we go," Seth said when they moved through the cargo bay and into the umbilical. "Now keep in mind that they're going to look a little stern. They do that when they're around strangers. No one's going to arrest you. In fact, their politeness is probably going to seem a little creepy until you figure out what they're really thinking. Hopefully they'll have some dinner for us."

Luanie smiled at that. She straightened her white hair for the tenth time. "They won't approve of the way we look, will they?"

"Nope," Seth said. "They don't approve of most things that aren't Delphian. But they'll never say so. Keep your hair any way you like." He opened the gate. "Deep breath, everyone."

But when they stepped out into the *Scolé*'s landing bay, only three people waited there to meet them, all of them Delphian. They wore the sort of clothing found on any planet frequented by offworlders and two of them were women. Seth recognized one of them as a Shantir by the two rings on her fingers joined by a delicate chain. There was no surprise or judgment on their faces over the disheveled, oddly-colored visitors. Seth could feel the collective sigh of relief at this carefully thought-out meeting, a first contact of sorts for all of them.

"Welcome," the Shantir said. "I am Korynn. We're so glad you've decided to visit with us." She smiled at Seth, to his surprise. "We are grateful to you, Shan Sethran."

"Thank you for meeting us," he said. "Our journey to Delphi would have been very rough in my small ship."

"Indeed. We have comfortable accommodations for all you."

"We want to stay together," Miko said at once.

"Of course," Korynn said. "We have anticipated that. We have a meal for you, too. Everything else will wait for as long as you like."

"No soldiers here?" Deely said.

"There is no Air Command aboard the *Scole*," she said. "Nor will they come aboard. We are going to Delphi; they are merely here to safeguard the journey."

"Guess we're taking the long way home," Miko said under his breath.

Seth grinned at him. "It'll be a vacation compared to the rust buckets you're used to."

"Come, we're going to jump toward Aikhor-Magra within the hour. Then we'll have some time before moving on." Korynn gestured to the entrance to the ship's interior. Her eyes moved to the makeshift sling supporting Seth's arm. "Our med station will see to any immediate needs. I see you can use some care, Shan Sethran."

Ciela turned back to him as she headed for the doors with the others. He nodded reassuringly. "I'll join you in a while."

A crewman arrived to take him to another part of the *Scole*. They walked past some of the services, all as neat and quiet as he would expect to find them on a ship operated by Delphians. And like all Delphian medical centers, the *Scole*'s did not resemble a clinic at all. No doubt, other parts of the ship were outfitted with the sort of equipment required for exo- and astro-biology, but when it came to simpler matters, Delphians required little to heal themselves.

A Shantir awaited them in a graciously appointed cabin where he was made to recline on a lounger after removing his shirt and bandages. It took only a light touch of her hand on Seth's neural node to remove any vestige of pain and to persuade Seth's own brain to begin to heal his body. If she encountered the unusual artifact that still remained within Seth's neural structures she gave no sign. He supposed that most exobiologists would by now be familiar with the subspace encounter that had caused it.

After what seemed like nothing more than an interval of shared meditation, she withdrew from his thoughts and busied herself with more conventional remedies. She applied a decon wand to the still-ragged wound and used a fine instrument to repair what she could. "You'll be able to remove the scar if you have it treated soon enough." She placed her cool hand over his forehead. "For now, just sleep."

"No, I want to go—"

* * *

It felt like hours had passed before time resumed. Seth looked around the dimly-lit room, unsure of where he was but feeling more refreshed and awake than he had in a long while. An enterprising individual, he thought, could make a fortune by convincing the Delphians to hire out their Shantirs. Of course, several of them made their healing abilities available at the exobiology center on Targon, but these little naps could be lucrative.

The cabin door opened and the Shantir returned as if she had sensed him waking. She looked at his wound and seemed satisfied by what she saw. He needed no help in putting his shirt back on and returning his data sleeve to his forearm.

"Shan Caelyn is waiting outside," she informed him.

He grinned. "Delphi! Come in!"

The door opened again and the navigator entered with a pleased smile for his friend. "Good to see you still in one piece, Centauri."

Seth tested his shoulder. "Got bitten by a fish."

"You would. We've made the jump out of Taancerum and you're back where your tiny brain can find its own way through the jumpsites."

Seth thanked the Shantir healer and followed Caelyn into the corridor. "How are things going for my passengers?"

"Let's go take a look. I hope I did what you expected by going to the council with your message?"

"There is a future for you in the spy business yet," Seth

assured him. "These people belong nowhere but Delphi right now. Lord Phera will make sure of it."

"He already has, from what I gather. Unless your friends wish it, none but Delphians have access to them."

Caelyn led him into the entrance of a crescent-shaped room. A curved window took up most of the far wall, looking out into space. Low, polygonal pieces of furniture were scattered about the room where the spanners lounged with a number of Delphians. In their midst, two girls bent over stringed instruments, apparently providing some sort of entertainment.

Seth stopped at the door to watch. There was something very peaceful about the scene and he shook his head when Caelyn looked at him with a raised eyebrow. "It's their party now," he said quietly, his eyes on Ciela reclining near the window in conversation with a woman. They each had a data screen in their hands and seemed to be comparing something. Ciela did not look up and he heard her gentle laugh from here.

After a moment, he backed out of the room and into the corridor.

Caelyn followed and so did a blue-robed Delphian whom Seth recognized as Shan Moghen, one of the leaders of Delphi's Shantir enclave. "A word, Shan Sethran?"

Seth gestured a respectful greeting. "Of course."

"I'll get back to the bridge," Caelyn said. "I'll see you before you shove off, Centauri."

Seth watched him go and then matched his steps to the Shantir's to stroll down the curving corridor.

"I understand we have much to thank you for, Shan Sethran," Moghen said, using his native Delphian language. "Our gratitude for returning our children will not fade with time."

"They have healing to do," Seth said. "Have you reached them?"

The elder nodded. "They are unaware, but our therapies have already begun, as you saw. We are a long lived species;

there is no hurry for any of us. Some fare better than others."

"How so?"

"They are unfamiliar with the khamal but they've allowed us some brief contacts. Ciela and Miko are untroubled by their… unique natures. Deely's pain will be healed by time and education. Luanie is suffering from a depression that should have been cured in infancy. The triplets will require the most care. Their isolation is not something we understand but, in time, we may. They will remain with us at the enclave, as will Luanie, for now."

"Do you know who they are?"

"In part," Moghen said. "Deely and Luanie have kin in the valley. We are still looking for a clan that can claim the sisters. No one's been found for Ciela and Miko just yet. I'm sure that, in time, we will. As you know, our families are not extensive."

Seth nodded. "They know nothing of family. They'll adjust, I'm sure, with your help."

"They have a secret," Moghen said. It was neither question nor statement.

"They do. And you need to know." Seth glanced around the deserted hallway. "They have a gift that goes beyond that of most navigators. A way to divide subspace, perhaps. Discern exits that none of us, nor our machines, can even see, never mind contact. It will allow them to emerge from subspace at any stable keyhole or jumpsite."

Shan Moghen pursed his lips. "And your enemies are aware of this?"

"Some are."

"And Air Command?"

"Not so far." Seth halted and grasped the Shantir's arm, which he allowed. "They can't leave Delphi. It's only luck that those who've fostered them haven't already used them against us."

"We cannot imprison them again," Moghen said. "We won't."

"They are a danger to us all."

The elder resumed his walk down the corridor. "So are you, my gun-wielding friend. But we all use our gifts for the common good, do we not? In time, your friends will come to love their lives as they should and they will learn to use their skills with care, if they wish to leave Delphi. That shall be our goal. But we won't choose theirs." His jaw tightened under his nearly translucent skin. "Not again."

Seth sighed. "Fair enough. Delphi has much to offer."

Shan Moghen gestured back the way they had come. "Won't you join them?"

Seth hesitated. "Maybe it's best if I just got on my way. I'm sure Colonel Carras has something for me to do. I'll head to Magra to get the *Dutchman* its overdue check-up."

"If you think that's best."

"Let them forget what happened. I'm just a reminder of it. They look very happy there with your people."

"*Their* people," Moghen reminded him. He twitched a smile, barely noticed before vanishing again. "Even if they currently look rather peculiar."

"Tell them I'll visit. Delphi is not so far." Seth waved and turned down another corridor to find his way back to the docks.

But each step farther away from where he had left the others - where he had left *her*, he corrected himself - felt like there was some long string holding him back, tightening more and more until it would surely snap in some painful way.

"Bloody nonsense," he grumbled. The *Dutchman* beckoned, as did his incurable desire to escape whatever gravity held him in one place, to walk among the endlessly fascinating bits that made up the worlds of Trans-Targon. He was blessed with talents, connections and funds to go where he pleased and, usually, do as he pleased. Could anyone ask for more?

"Yes, you're an idiot, Kada," he said to himself as he entered his ship. "Falling for the wrong girl once again. Go and shoot yourself some more rebels. Get laid somewhere, maybe. That'll be fun, too."

Still, he found himself procrastinating as he prepared for departure, fussing needlessly with the *Dutchman*'s navigation system, going back to ask for a tube of coolant from the *Scole*'s crew, wondering if a full systems check was in order.

A gentle alarm startled him when he had run out of things to do and actually begun to tidy the cabin. A broad grin brightened his face when the external camera showed Ciela in the umbilical. She wore new trousers, a pretty shirt, and an utterly unreadable expression.

"Leaving without goodbye?" she said when he opened the gate.

"What's going on? Are you all right?" Seth asked, alarmed. He stepped aside to let her enter the ship. Once he had secured the gate and pressure doors he found her waiting for him in the cabin.

"I am not staying here," she said, sounding a little defiant.

"What happened? What did they do?"

"Nothing. They're all right. They keep giving us food and making us listen to music. No one's asked us anything about... about before."

He smiled. "Too nice for you?"

"Yeah. You were right about us. About why we were taken away. They haven't come right out with it, but they made sure we knew our parents were not rebels. One of them, one of the Shantirs, touched me and we were able to talk in our heads. He seemed to be looking for something but he said that can all wait. He said no one would take us away again."

Seth nodded. "They will keep their word."

"Luanie is so happy, Seth! They found her family. Same with Deely. And Miko is going to stay at the Shantir enclave with the girls." She smiled. "I think he's cast his eye on one of the musicians."

Seth furrowed his brow. "But you don't want to stay with these evil evil people?"

"No."

"So," he said, wondering if she could see the heart pounding under his shirt. "Where do you want to go, if not Delphi? Back to the Arawaj? A return to your smuggling days? I can—"

"Here," she said. "With you. I don't care where the *Dutchman* goes."

He felt some sort of bubble rise deep in his chest until it seemed to want to explode through his throat. "With me?"

"I can tell these are good people. And they'll keep us safe from... from others. But..."

"But?" he said, suddenly breathless.

"I can help you. You can use a navigator. We can go anywhere."

"Oh," he said, exhaling sharply. "You want to join our team of operatives?"

"Well, yes." She put her hand on his arm when he folded them. "I can't be Arawaj. I won't. I'm done with that."

"Does Shan Moghen know you're here?"

"He does. They'll arrange for some credit for me on Magra. They want me to return later, to study with them, when I can. He said I should learn more about my people. Our language. I told him you can teach me."

Seth looked around, feeling a little helpless. "This is dangerous work. And sometimes pretty miserable. You'd be much safer on Delphi. More comfortable."

"Dammit, Seth! I don't want to be comfortable. I don't care about being safe. I just want to be with you."

Seth suddenly felt as he had as a boy, the time when Sikiki had offered to show him what she kept hidden under her blouse. A mounting hopefulness while at the same time wondering if maybe he was misunderstanding what she was actually saying. "Me?"

She tugged on his arms until he uncrossed them. "Yes. I've thought about nothing else since we got here. They talked to us and showed us pretty things about Delphi and gave us clothes and such good food. And all I could think about is you." Her voice trembled when she continued. "All I want is you."

He stepped forward and his arms wrapped around her as if by their own accord. He buried his face in her hair, smelling her sweet scent, wanting only to hold her until maybe forever. "Are you sure?"

She pulled back to smile at him. "Never been surer."

He took her face in his hands to kiss her and everything about that felt like nothing else mattered, perhaps not ever. "We'll leave right now. Before you change your mind."

She nipped his lip with her teeth. "Seth, if you don't take me over there into your bed I am going to scream."

He picked her up to carry her to the lounger, completely unaware of the pain in his shoulder. She pulled him down with her. "We can go anywhere together. I want you to show me everything."

He grinned, somewhat lewdly, as he unfastened her pretty blouse.

"And we can both explore subspace. I can show you—"

He looked up. "Subspace?"

"I saw your notes. Something draws you there. I want to help you find it. And you got that subspace scanner now. We could do much with that."

"It's just a... just an interest, that's all. But you're right. With your gifts we could find—" She placed her hand on him and whatever he meant to say no longer mattered.

* * *
*
*

ABOUT THE AUTHOR

Chris Reher is a first generation Canadian currently and out of necessity residing on planet Earth (which, in the general and interplanetary scheme of things, could *really* use a catchier name. Imagine heading past Proxima Centauri and someone asks you whence you came and you tell them "dirt". All theological implications aside, that just won't do.)

When not finding ways to defy the laws of physics or torture her subjects or entice them with inter-species hanky-panky, she designs web sites or writes about designing web sites. She enjoys long walks on the beach or, given the local beach shortage, writes about beaches far beyond Proxima Centauri.

www.chrisreher.com

Also by Chris Reher

Quantum Tangle

Entropy's End

Sky Hunter

The Catalyst

Only Human

Rebel Alliances

Delphi Promised